ABSOLUTE
SOUTHERN JUSTICE BOOK II
CORRUPTION

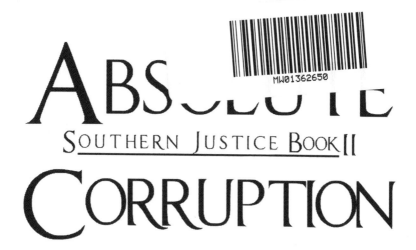

BESTSELLING AUTHOR
Cayce Poponea

Absolute Corruption
Southern Justice Book 2
Copyright © 2016 Cayce Poponea

ISBN-13: 978-1530662715
ISBN-10: 1530662710

All rights reserved. Without limiting the rights under copyright reserved above, no part of this publication may be reproduced, stored in or introduced into retrieval system, or transmitted, in any form, or by any means (electronic, mechanical, photocopying, recording, or otherwise) without the prior written permission of both the copyright owner and the above publisher of this book.

This is a work of fiction. Names, characters, places, brands, media, and incidents are either the products of the author's imagination or are used fictitiously. The author acknowledges the trademarked status and trademark owners of various products referenced in this work of fiction, which have been used without permission. The publication/use of these trademarks is not authorized, associated with, or sponsored by the trademark owners.

Cover Design by Jada D'Lee Designs
Editing by Elizabeth Simonton
Proofread by TCB Editing
Interior Design and Formatting by Champagne Formats

www.caycepoponea.com

Chapter One

Austin

"It's a funny thing coming home. Nothing changes. Everything looks the same, feels the same, even smells the same. You realize what's changed is you."
- F. Scott Fitzgerald

The sounds of the city echoed around me, as I walked down Broadway. Car horns blaring, and the squealing of taxicab brakes were all sweet lullabies that played on the streets of New York City. My hands were stuffed in my pockets, and my eyes were on the sidewalk before me, a sure sign I was a local. Well, as local as I could possibly be.

Pulling the steel handle of the storefront, the glass doors opened, casting the reflection of the street around me. The white vinyl letters affixed to the glass reminded me of where I was; a place I should have visited weeks ago.

"Austin Morgan!" Katarina Swiss, or Kiki, as she liked to be called, stood at her station with her comb in one hand, and a pair of sheers in the other, both resting on her poor excuse for hips. She was dressed head to toe in black; even her hair lacked any trace of another color. In all the years I've been coming to see her, I've never seen her wear any other color.

"Good mornin', Miss Kiki. "When I first moved to Manhattan, I learned my southern accent either really turned people on, or completely pissed them off. Fortunately for me, Miss Kiki melted when I walked into the room. My dad said it was a curse, the way we affected women. But he was an old married man, lost to the love of his life, no longer searching for his other half. To him, the attention we received would be a curse.

"Don't you 'good mornin' me, Austin Morgan." Having good manners would only go so far with Miss Kiki. But I had her pegged, I knew what she loved. Crossing the space between us, I gave her my pouty lip, and lowered my thick eyelashes. Pulling the hand without the scissors toward me, I placed a kiss on the pale skin of her knuckles.

"Oh my, tell me there are more where you came from." She winked, as she pulled, not too firmly, her hand from my grip. As many times as I have sat in her chair, she knows just about everything there is to know about my brothers and me.

"Yes, Ma'am." I tossed one more ounce of southern charm in her direction, laying it a little thicker on the accent she melts for. It worked, as she pointed to the empty chair, shaking out the black cape to keep the clippings off my clothes.

Miss Kiki takes her time, as she pulls her polished fingernails through the strands of my hair, something I find extremely relaxing in all honesty. Like an artist with their brush, she runs her comb in several directions, changing the flow of my hair. She told me not long after I started coming to see her, she would give just about anything to have my hair color; deep black and thick, with shimmers of light bringing about a silver hue. Something she admits she can't duplicate with bleach and heat.

"I'm surprised you have any hair at all, with those eyes, and all that charm just dripping off you. Women must be lined up for days to have a turn." Growing up in the south, I had my fair share of talkative women. Miss Kiki was in a class all her own. Hell, even my momma would politely tell her to shut the hell up. For the next half hour, I had the privilege of hearing all the latest gossip; who was sleeping with whom in the shop, and what celebrities came in looking terrible. You name it, Miss Kiki had seen it since the last time I sat in her chair. I gave her a generous tip, a kiss to the cheek, and my word I wouldn't wait so long to see her again in the future. With a wave of my hand, I welcomed the sounds of the street, before making my pilgrimage to the glass tower I called my second home.

When I was younger, I recall my dad saying he wished there were more hours in the day. It wasn't until I was sitting in this very seat, clicking away on my computer, that I finally understood what he meant. My calendar was bursting with events I'd never attend, meetings I had to ask colleagues about, and dates I'd broken with girlfriends; all to be sitting alone in my office on a Friday night.

My cell has to be nearly out of battery life, from all the text alerts I've received. It's the weekend, and I was due to be downtown in a bar with the rest of my friends. I'm one of those crazy guys who swears up and down they will stop what they are doing, just give them ten more minutes. I have a million and one excuses for ignoring the ping of my cell; the haircut I needed, my backlog of work, and the inability to leave my desk on the same day I arrived.

I'm wrong about my phone battery, when the ringtone I've assigned for my granddaddy fills the room, giving me the first valid excuse for a break in hours "Hey, Granddaddy." Leaning back in my chair, the light from my desk illuminates the chess set perched on a table across the room. When I was seven, Momma drove us boys over to our grandparent's house. As usual, they were sitting on their front porch playing a game of chess. I walked over, and asked Granddaddy if I could play. He pulled me onto his lap, showed me the pieces, and then explained what moves they each could make. It was then, during those sessions, he began to teach me how to be a man. "Austin, all southern men drink good bourbon, and treat their ladies better than the Queen of Sheba." It was the beginning of a special bond between the two of us. Not a day has passed that we haven't had a game going. He would show me how to play, all the while sharing with me the pearls of wisdom he had collected over the years. Most of them I follow, some…Well, I'm not sure they apply just yet.

When I entered high school, he and Nana bought me the set which I keep at work. They had taken a trip to Australia, and during one of Nana's shopping excursions, she'd found the ebony and ivory set in an antique store. Daddy came home from work one afternoon, with a box tucked under his arm. Inside was the marble board, in a deep green with black veins and gold flecks, each piece wrapped in tiny plastic bubble sheets. Where other kids crawled around on their knees with trucks and cars, I sat at a table, admiring the details carved into the pieces.

"Austin, you still workin'?" Granddaddy was the one who taught me to work this hard, so I knew he had something up his sleeve. When I graduated college, I created a program where we could continue our chess game, even if one of us was unavailable. Adams Lighthouse got wind of my invention, and wanted me to write the program for production. I said no, this was something I had made just for granddaddy and me.

"Nope, just sitting here waiting for you to make a move." The chuckle that echoed over the line told me he knew better. I suspected he was ready to make a big move, maybe even win this game tonight. I switched my screen from the code work, which would wait until Monday, to the game we had been playing for three days now.

"Queen to H4." I watched my monitor, as he moved his piece into place. At first I rolled my eyes at his amateur move, until I saw my error. I had left my king unprotected.

"Check," he said smugly.

"Motherfucker!"

Had the chess pieces been real, I might have tossed them across the room. There's no way around it, the master had won once again. "You left your king unprotected! I tell you again and again, never leave a fox in charge of your hen house, and never leave that king to protect himself." He was right, he had drilled it into my head over and over. Too bad I hadn't quite learned that lesson yet.

Turning my chair around to face my window, I could see the Brooklyn Bridge in the distance. Tiny orbs of lights, as the cars moved back and forth across the span, reminding me of worker ants on a mission to feed the queen. I remember with absolute clarity the first time I crossed the New York landmark. At the time, I was convinced I was trying to make a name for myself, putting some distance between the man I was expected to be, and the man I wanted to be. Years later, I've realized they are one in the same. Lessons like this had to be learned by experience, and not handed down like an heirloom chess set.

Now, as I watched those headlights, it's a different bridge I see; one I have fond memories of back home. Like the first time I watched Dylan gasp for air when he'd challenged Chase to a race across the bridge. Or the day they ran side by side as we spent a few hours together before Chase went off to boot camp. I remembered how I had my first kiss with Jacqueline Moore at the very top of the bridge, still all knees and elbows, without an ounce of charm at the time.

"Speakin' of hen houses, how's your girl, Keena? Turning back from the window, I lowered my shoes from the edge of the desk, reality finding me once again with that question. Keena, my current girlfriend, had just moved into my newly purchased condo on Park Avenue. She was beautiful, not a stitch of common sense in her entire body. She was working as a cocktail waitress in a bar on the East side, a place my buddy insisted I had to visit. Keena gave me her number, and I of course called her. The sex was hot, and I was horny. It had just evolved from there.

"She's...Keena." Granddaddy and I spoke in depth one evening, as I was about to meet my friends. I chose to duck into a coffee shop, and told him pretty much everything. Keena had the legs every wet dream required, blonde hair, with curls so perfect you'd swear the angels above gave them to her, and an hourglass figure so precise, you could set your watch to it. Unfortunately, that is where her attributes ended.

She had no formal education, and furthermore, no desire to attend college, or even a trade school. Having a conversation that didn't include what the Kardashians were wearing was beyond her. Her time was spent watching reality television, so if you didn't follow the trends, which I didn't have the spare time to do, there was nothing she could follow and talk about

"You thinkin' of puttin' a ring on *that* finger yet?" Granddaddy was not one to beat around the bush. He made it clear he wanted to see little feet running up and down his front steps. He came from a large family, and expected all of us to follow suit. Another area I wasn't sure was going to apply to me.

"No, Sir." The one thing I did know about Keena, she wasn't the girl I thought about when I pictured my forever. I needed a girl who desired knowledge, as much as I did, and who possessed the same passion about something, as I did, like Chess and computers. I didn't care what it was, as long as it was something real. Reality television did not qualify.

"You're treatin' her right though, aren't you, Son?" My daddy and granddaddy not only told us, but also showed us, how to treat the ladies in our life. Keena wanted for nothing, just as my momma and nana did not want for nothing. She had full access to all my credit cards, keys to my car, and cash given to her weekly. Even a maid came to the condo to clean, and laundry was sent out.

"Yes, Sir."

"She still watchin' them soap operas?"

That's what he called Keena's reality shows. He knew my DVR was full of them. She would stop everything, including sex, to watch the misfortunes of the lives on the television. She raved on and on about how they seemed to have the perfect life, all while fighting with cheating husbands, and bad tabloid reviews.

"Day and night." There was no use in trying to hide the frustration in my voice. I had allowed this to happen, encouraged her when she lost her job, told her she could stay with me. I would take care of her.

"Well, you know how I feel about it. But you're a grown man now."

Granddaddy had a way of changing one's perspective, and steering them to his way of thinking. Or maybe it was just his way of helping you listen to the voices in your gut, telling you which way to turn.

"I know, and trust me, I've thought about it. But I want the woman I decide to marry, to make me a better man, not one she feels the need to change."

"Austin, I've lived long enough to know everyone does a little bit of growing when they find the one that's right for them. The key is to want to change, to be the better person."

He was right as usual. I knew Keena wasn't wife material. Hell, she wasn't really girlfriend material. But, she was what I had, and I would treat her decently until the relationship was over. Things were okay with us. She didn't complain about my long hours, and had never asked for more than I gave her. But maybe I wanted someone to nag me, to show me with their actions, they really cared.

"How did you know Nana was the right girl?"

"That's easy, she told me."

He also possessed the ability to bring you out of yourself. To show you how an ounce of laughter, can do a person a ton of good. With granddaddy, seriousness was saved for the courtroom or the Senate floor, not for conversations between families.

"Austin, when the right girl for you comes along, you won't need to ask if she's the right one, you'll know it. Until that happens though…" He didn't need to finish his thought. Treating women well was more than just showering them with gifts, and making sure the bills were paid. It was being honest with them about things that mattered. Leading a girl to believe there was a future wasn't something a gentleman ever did.

"Keep treating her right," he warned me. "Hey, you know next weekend is the Azalea run."

Every year in Charleston, the city would host the Azalea festival, complete with a run over the Ravenel Bridge. The first year I moved to New York, I flew back home to run it with Dylan. I looked over my shoulder at the bridge I wouldn't walk across if you paid me. It made me miss home even more.

New York was sizably larger than Charleston, but it couldn't compare. While there were ample activities here in the city, I longed for the slower pace, and graciousness of Charleston. I missed the way everyone knew me, wished me a good day, and meant it.

"Is Dylan running this year?" Even as I asked, I could not imagine him missing the opportunity to run.

"He and Carson. You know they would love to have ya."

Carson was more of the kick ass, cool uncle, than a family friend. He kept Dylan in line, and didn't let him get too full of himself. A full time job, in and of itself. I love my brother, don't get me wrong. I envied the way he could move from girl to girl, without a second thought, no feelings, and no promises. I just wasn't that way. I allowed my heart to lead me, instead of my dick, like Dylan.

"I've been thinking about Charleston quite a bit recently."

"You know, Austin, it's never too late to come back home."

I didn't know it at the time, but those would be the last words of advice I would ever hear granddaddy speak.

Chapter Two

Lainie

Courage is not the absence of fear. It is the ability to face it, overcome it, and finish your job.
- Billy Cox

"Come on you chicken shit."

My palms were sweaty, and my heart was racing so fast I was afraid it would pop out of my chest. Bouncing back and forth on the balls of my feet, I felt like a runner getting ready for the Olympics. It's the third time this month I've stood here. Praying for the courage to just do it, and get it over with.

Concrete lions stand sentry to my goal, mocking me with their blank faces. Where the fuck were they when the attack happened? Checking out a pretty skirt like most of the men on this street? Several pedestrians have looked at me with questioning glances, wondering where my shopping cart and crazy hat were.

I refused to stop trying, to give up. To allow a spineless coward of a man make me crawl under the covers, and hide from the world. I was sick of seeing the pity on Claire's face. Tired of her placing her life on hold, so she could secure my hair, as I vomited.

Never in my life have I ever let a man have an ounce of control over me. Not when Thomas Cowart said I couldn't use the tree swing over Parkers Cove back home in Kentucky. He told all the kids the swing was too short to make it over the water. Too bad for him, I weighed less, and sailed over the water to the other side. He cried all the way back to his momma, when he landed in the muddy water.

Not when Griffin Powell chased all the girls around the schoolyard with a garter snake. I watched the evil glint fill his eyes. As he went from screaming girl to screaming girl, thinking he was something, as he shoved the head of the poor snake in their faces. Fucker screamed the loudest of all, when I took the snatched the snake from his grubby fingers, and yelled at him for holding it too hard. He ran like the devil himself was chasing him, once I put the snake in his face.

Griffin told the principal what had happened. *"Lainie, don't you know when little boys tease little girls it's because they like them?"* Mrs. Culpepper tried to tell me, but I knew better. I got sent home that afternoon, with a note to my mother, for telling the principal she was wrong about the actions of mean boys. They didn't do those things because they liked the girl, they did them because they got away with it. Momma had worn out my backside that day, reminding me she had taught her girls better.

Candy Perry was as beautiful, as she was clueless. She had told me and my younger sister, Heidi, to always have a man by your side. To do everything in your power to keep them happy, and coming home. She even taught us how to cover up the bruises which may accidentally find their way to our faces. My challenging Griffin on the playground, had gone against everything momma had taught me.

I had taken those lashes, and then wore a dress for a week, due to the welts I had on my legs from them. I didn't cry or flinch when she'd lowered the strap. I didn't think twice either, when I hit her new boyfriend, Bucky, a month later when I came home to find him standing over her punching her in the face. I'd just picked up the frying pan full of hot grease, and smacked the fucker in the back of the head.

My sister, however, took our mother's words of wisdom to heart. She wore her dresses as short as the school would allow, and flirted without any inhibitions or self-respect. More than a few times, she had been caught sneaking in after curfew, with one of the local boys in tow.

It was the summer after her sophomore year, when a friend from down the street, invited her to a church revival. My sister wanted to impress our mother's latest boyfriend, Steve, an older guy, who'd invited momma to his church in the next county over. His shiny red car and full time employment, blinded both Heidi and Momma, from realizing he was a real snake.

Heidi skipped off to that revival where she met a man by the name of George Garvin. Mr. Garvin was ten years her senior, wore a suit and tie everywhere he went, and was an extremely religious man. According to Heidi, he walked over to introduce himself and with a single handshake. It was love at first sight.

He came over to the trailer that Steve had rented for us, and let Momma know he had feelings for Heidi. While my sister was ready to toss her panties and run off with the man, George was much more reserved. He insisted on several rules for their relationship. No kissing, holding hands, or being alone in the same room, until Heidi was of age.

For over a year, George would come by the house. The one he'd helped Momma to find. It seemed there was a reason Steve attended a church thirty miles away. His shiny red car and good income, was needed for his addiction to child pornography. At four o'clock one Thursday morning, the county sheriff had busted down the trailer door, arresting Steve on a parole violation. With no money to call our own, we were looking at eviction.

George made a big production about it, telling Momma she was being punished by God for her wicked ways. Heidi sat there like a bobble head, agreeing with everything he said. When George handed her the keys to a new house, Momma suddenly saw the light, and agreed with him too. George may have been a God-fearing man, but he used his ability to provide for Momma as a way to weasel his way permanently into the family.

Momma sat just as proud as a peacock when he would stop by, playing the dutiful chaperone. Smiling as if the King of Persia was in her living room, instead of the man who was old enough to date her, instead of my sister. He would bring Heidi gifts, and pick her up for church. Finally, on her eighteenth birthday, he asked her to marry him. He carted her off to the justice of the peace, and in less than ten minutes, secured himself a young bride.

After the wedding, George decided Momma and I needed saving. I was home from college long enough to spend a final summer, and see my sister get married. George tried to tell me I needed to stick closer to home, get a job, and start doing right by my family. He assumed I was partying, smoking, and running around, instead of studying my ass off, like I was.

Momma didn't care for it either, which unfortunately, caused a rift between her and my sister. For the first time since I could remember, Momma had to get a job, and support herself. For the last six years, she has worked at a nursing home, cooking in the kitchen for the residents.

George decided he and Heidi would start a ministry, bringing

Jesus to the world. Last time I'd heard from her, they had rented a building in Tucson, and opened a homeless shelter and soup kitchen. She and George barely spoke to one another anymore, as she had been unable to get pregnant. He told her it was because she wasn't a virgin when they got married. She was miserable, but he paid her bills and she wore his ring. She would never leave him, as she believed the bullshit our mother spewed.

With me, all the talk of keeping men and sacrificing yourself our momma preached at us, had the complete opposite effect, showing me what I didn't want. I would never depend on a man to pay my bills, or feed and clothe me. I was not opposed to having a man who complimented me, but if he were making my life worse, he would be given his walking papers.

So, instead of hooking the first guy with a job and a great smile, I studied my ass off. I got into Caltech, where I studied even harder. With the campus population mostly male, I had to fight my way into projects, and out of requests for threesomes.

Having that same fire I did as a young tomboy, I paved my way around the campus playboy, Kennedy Fraser. Kennedy coined himself a great catch. Being born into a bathtub of money, and a guaranteed job with his father's company, it was nothing to see him pointing to young giggling girls, and lining them up for his pleasure.

His parties were legendary. Anything you craved to dull your pain, he had, sitting on a waiting table. Security always managed to get lost when it came to responding to noise complaints at his address.

Kennedy and I had one class in common. A core class I had to pass to graduate. Professor French assigned a project to design a webpage with a theme we didn't agree with. The page had to attract viewers in a positive light, without screaming how wrong the subject material was. With a twist, he assigned partners; people in the class who he'd established had no common ground.

I decided Mr. French hated me, as he flashed my name on the overhead, a back slash separating my name from Kennedy's. I didn't give a flying fuck who he thought I could work with, this was something I was going to do alone.

Kennedy stopped me in the hall after class. He insisted we could meet at his apartment, professing it would be quiet, and the internet speed better than the free campus broadband. I had dealt with men like this douchebag; one's who towered over me, for my entire life. They smiled those perfect smiles, saying the words they read, and practiced to make girls swoon. He may be made of money, and walk around as if he owned the place, but he was about to lose big time. As this girl could not be bought, or won over, with cheap words and empty promises.

Imagine what his face looked like, when I told him I'd rather be eaten by a pack of wolves than to be alone with him. I'd been writing code for computers since I was able to type. Designing a web page turned out to be a walk in the park. It gave me a new direction, and another check mark to make me more marketable in the shrinking job market.

However, Kennedy didn't just step aside and let me walk away. Unfortunately, my refusal of his invitation became a challenge for him; more than just getting into my panties. For the remainder of our time at Caltech, nearly every project which was publically posted, we competed for; some I won, some he did.

A week prior to graduation, I overheard him speaking to some of his douchebag friends, telling them his older brother was sleeping around with a competitor's wife. Apparently, they were biding their time until the old fuck died. Then planned to have Kennedy come in and run the company, taking it to a level the current owner refused. I was about to walk away when he said my name, followed by, "She is gonna wish she would have sucked my dick."

I graduated second in my class, Kennedy didn't even make the top five. I had three companies offering me positions. Two were big name companies, Adams Lighthouse and Philip Conway, both owned by men with questionable ethics. The third company, Craven and Associates, was run by a woman. She promised me nothing, other than a paycheck twice a month, and great benefits. I didn't think twice as I packed my stuff, and moved to Charleston.

So here I stand, like a prizefighter, before his next opponent. I hated having this fear; walking past the place where a man took my sense of security, by placing his hands on me when they weren't welcomed. It made me feel weak. I didn't think twice when I was a little girl. Taking on boys with snakes, fat assed jerks who couldn't jump, or beating the shit out of a grown man, while telling another to eat shit and die, when he tried to boss me around.

But this…Facing my fears is different. A part of me can't believe I was being such a wimp about this. The other, the frightened little girl, wanted to run home and sleep with a night-light, and teddy bear.

"Fuck it! Rome wasn't built in a day."

Just like the multitude of times before, I accepted defeat, and ran to my car.

CHAPTER THREE

Austin

The biggest mistake I've made in my life, is letting people stay far longer than they deserve.
- Unknown

I was edging to that moment between dreams and waking. When you can see pictures fading away into wisps of memory, always leaving you confused by their meaning, and wondering what crazy item you ate the night before to cause them. Not to mention those irritating rays from the sunlight, which drag you the remaining distance to full consciousness.

I could hear irritating voices from across the room, arguing about something whose outcome will not change the fate of the free world. I knew it was too early for Keena to be enthralled with her latest reality obsession. It was something about arranging a marriage, or something like that.

Pulling my face from the confines of my pillow, I turned toward my alarm, the numbers on still blurry. I blinked several times, as the digits came into view.

"Shit!"

It was nine-fifteen, and my meeting with the division head was scheduled to start in thirty minutes. It takes at least that long to get to my office. I scrambled out of bed, my feet tangling in the white sheets. A brand Keena had whined about until I let her buy them. I'd have to skip the shower today, duck out at lunchtime, and then hit the one in the gym.

"Shh!"

Keena is sitting against the headboard of our bed, waving the remote in my direction, as she scolds me. Her breasts are still bare from the wild fucking we'd had last night. She'd just gotten off her period, and said she was pent up from going without. She didn't let me tell her no, before she dove on the bed, and onto my face. She had my dick in her hand, as she ran her cunt up and down my face. Sucking me until I was rock hard, and then flipping herself around, riding me through three orgasms.

"Fuck off, Keena. My alarm didn't go off, and I'm late."

Being late for anything is on the top ten list of things I hate. To me, it sets the tone for the whole day. There's no time to pour a cup of coffee, or eat a bowl of cereal. I'll need to text Walker, as soon as I get into a taxi about my situation this morning.

As I'm finally leaving the penthouse, I nearly take out my neighbor, Jeffrey. I don't normally see him since he's an acting coach, and works from home. Keeping complete opposite hours from what I do.

"Sorry," I hollered down the hall. As I ran for the stairs, my tie draped around my neck, and flapping behind me, as I sprinted for the exit doors. Taking the stairs two, and sometimes three, at a time,

I'm thankful for the shape I'm in. Having two brothers who thrive on physical fitness, helps give me the motivation I need some days to make it to the gym. I have to slow down as I reach lobby. No telling which nosey board member is lurking about, just waiting for a reason to complain about me. With only a few younger residents in the building, I've been warned this could happen.

I make sure to say good morning to the concierge and building manager on my way out, giving them no opportunities to report anything bad back to their boss. Mr. Clemens, the doorman, has a cab door open, talking to the cabby inside.

"Mr. Morgan."

I swear the man has eyes in the back of his head, as he calls my name. I hurry to jump into the back of the taxi, not meaning to be rude, but pressed for time. I've taken the liberty to learn as much about the people in my building as I can, knowing when something is out of the ordinary. Call me the eternal skeptic, but it does make me really good at my job. Mr. Carl Clemens, a high school dropout, who took over his job from his dying father, never married, and has a sister who lives in Jersey.

"Late start this morning?"

Carl and I have sat down a few times over a cold beer on my balcony. It's frowned upon to associate with the staff, but he is the one person who knows practically everything that goes on in this building.

"Overslept."

I admit, as he shut the door behind me, slapping the top of the taxi three times, as we pull away from the curb. Leaning back against the headrest, I feel slightly better that I will only miss about fifteen minutes of the meeting. Still, I fish my phone out of my pants pocket, and dial Scott's number, which goes to voicemail without ringing. I know for certain he is in the meeting, and realize I'm running later than I'd originally thought. There is nothing I can do, except send a text to my colleague, letting him know what's happened this morning. I've covered for nearly everyone on my team at least a dozen times, today they can cover for me.

The streets of the city are crowded with the early morning commuters. Thousands of men and women, just like myself, just trying to get to the fish bowl we all call home for eight hours. This particular cabby is making good time, and I'll have to tip him well for getting me to the office with about five minutes to spare. My calm is increased. The homestretch is laid out before me. I can see the street sign at the end of the block where he can drop me off, and I can make my meeting. Reaching down to pull my card out of my pocket, I feel around for my security pass, only to come up empty. In my rush this morning, I'd left it laying on the kitchen bar. Adams Lighthouse is quite serious about security. Without my security badge, even my own momma wouldn't be allowed to let me enter the building

"Dammit!"

My cursing captured the attention of the cab driver. As I explained my situation to him, he questioned if I would be averse to taking a different route back to my building. I responded by telling him there was an extra fifty in it for him, if he could get me back to this same intersection in less than twenty minutes.

Mr. Clemens gave me a puzzled look, as I exited the back of the cab before he had pulled completely to the curb. Taking the stairs three at a time, I'm again thankful for my moronic brothers, and their fitness obsessions. My hall is just as I left it, minus one Jeffrey Stone. No doubt he is overcharging some Broadway hopeful, to improve their chances of being the next star of *Les Misérables*.

As I open the door, I call out to Keena so that she doesn't freak out. She watches too much television, which causes her to have an overactive imagination. She will swear I'm some street gang member coming to kill her.

"Babe, it's just me. I forgot my badge."

I can hear the television in the living room. The guy from the store I purchased it from, cussed under his breath, as he lifted the heavy flat screen onto the bracket on the wall. In my mind, I pictured having my friends over to watch a game, the pizza and beer flowing freely. Never once has it happened, what with Keena constantly monopolizing the system.

It's evident as I walk around the corner, the television isn't the only thing of mine she had been keeping to herself. Bent over the mirrored coffee table, she'd bragged was just like the one she saw on an episode of something, was Keena with my neighbor, Jeffrey Stone, slamming into the back of her.

She was so engrossed in the show she was watching, and he was so enamored with his dick sliding in and out of her pussy, neither of them heard me come in. Picking up the lamp, which we never used, from the table beside me, I hurled it straight through the screen of the television. Sparks popped and flew, as smoke rose from the back near the wall. Keena screamed like she had seen a ghost and clambered off the table, knocking Jeffery off her, and onto the edge of the couch.

With my badge secure in my hand, I pointed my finger at the pair, kicked the ricocheted lamp, and sent it crashing into the glass door of the balcony. "Get the fuck out of my house, before I get back tonight!"

I didn't bother shutting the door as I left, giving the impression I wanted this exit to happen immediately. Keena screamed my name, followed by some bullshit about this not being what it looked like. Doesn't everybody say that when they get caught? Like it was some magic phrase to make you forget what you just saw. Next, she would blame me for not paying attention to her. For just giving her money, instead of time. Admittedly, that one was most likely true. Still, it didn't justify what the fuck just happened in there.

My taxi was still waiting, and the concierge was talking to one of the maintenance men, as I walked past. Without stopping my forward progression, I explained over my shoulder, "Miss Preston will no longer be a resident of this building. Make certain all of the staff knows she is trespassing if she is seen in the building after today." So much for my attempt at keeping my name out of the board's mouth.

My meeting was long over when I crashed into my office chair. By the look on my face, and the scarce greetings to my coworkers, they all steer clear of me. My office phone rang several times, but I lacked the motivation needed to answer it. Looking out my window, just as I had a few days ago, I now longed to return to the palm trees and brick streets of my hometown. I needed to distance myself from the people, and the bad memories this city has brought me. My cell vibrated in my pocket, mostly likely Keena with another excuse for fucking around behind my back. I have to pull the thing out anyway, as there are rules about cell phones, and where we can use them in the building.

My screen tells me it isn't Keena, but Momma, her beautiful face gracing the screen. Why can't all women be as good hearted and honest, as Priscilla Morgan?

"Hey, Momma."

Hearing her voice may just be the salve I need to mend the anger I feel inside. Quench the thirst I have for answers to questions, about just how women work.

"Austin, honey, are you at home?"

I didn't like the tone of her voice. Priscilla Morgan is a strong, vibrant southern woman, who can charm the pants off a priest in the middle of Mardi Gras.

"No, Ma'am. I'm at work already."

Maybe I'm wrong, and everything is fine. She has never had a set time for calling me, never needed one either. I'd move heaven and earth for my momma. No woman, in this life or the next, is more important than she is.

"Listen, I need you to do me a favor, Son."

Something is very wrong, she never approaches me like this. She always butters me up like a hot biscuit in July, before she asks what she wants.

"Momma, what's wrong?"

The line is silent; silence and Priscilla Morgan are not friends. I rise from my chair, grabbing my keys and jacket, preparing to hunt down the person responsible for making this woman's voice quiver. "Puddin', it's your Granddaddy…" I don't want to hear the rest of the sentence, and by the sounds of tears in her voice, she doesn't want to tell it either. "He passed away this mornin'."

When I was little, Priscilla Morgan saved me from a life of revolving foster homes. She took me in her arms, and swore to me everything would be fine. Even as a young boy, seeing everything I had, I didn't trust women. Granddaddy Van Buren took me by the hand, and walked with me nearly every day for a solid month, assuring me this family could be trusted. He showed me how to fish and skip rocks along the top of the water. He pointed out to me how by taking me from the home, she had chosen me and my brothers, out of all the other kids who lived there. Slowly, I had come around and was able to talk with her, kiss her cheek, and hug her at night. He became just as important to me as Dean, my daddy, did. Now he's gone. Who will tell me how to get past the betrayal of yet another woman?

Foregoing a trip to my penthouse, knowing the bitch would still be there, and I was not emotionally ready for conversation. Instead, I boarded a plane bound for Charleston with the clothes I wore to work, and sadness in my heart. The man I respected the most in the world was gone.

Chapter Four

Lainie

Sisters are angels who lift us to our feet when our wings are having trouble remembering how to fly
- Unknown

Being so new in my position, I couldn't even consider saying anything but yes when my boss asked me to go to San Diego. Our company was currently in negotiations to purchase a competitor. When she informed me which company she was after, I had to suppress a laugh. All the trash talking Kennedy Fraser did during college, only made him look like an idiot. As his father was recently arrested for alleged fraud. When the board learned of the allegations, they called for an audit. The results uncovered, were the reasons for the sale.

Once my plans were set, I called my sister, and asked her to come out and visit with me for a few days. I expected her to say no. To make up some excuse as to why it was a bad idea. She sounded so excited when she agreed. She said she would have to take a bus because George never let her have very much money. I offered to fly her here, and she accepted.

As I watched her walk down the hall to the baggage claim area where we agreed to meet, I had a rush of memories from the last time I had laid eyes on her. Nearly five years had passed since she'd graduated high school, and married George. Heidi had always been a pretty girl, taking after our mother in her pure beauty. Now, she appeared much older. Her once bouncy, golden hair, now laid slicked back into a low, messy ponytail at the nape of her neck. Her cheeks were sunken in, as if she hadn't eaten for weeks, and dark circles competed with the pallor of her skin.

Momma had always dressed us the best she could, with ribbons and bows, and matching sweaters in vibrant, pastel colors. Now, Heidi looked more like a nun, with her gray skirt and black sweater, both several sizes too big. Most of all, her sunken eyes made her look exhausted.

No words were exchanged, as we held one another tightly. The sounds of arriving flights echoing overhead, as we rocked back and forth. Love could erase the time we'd spent apart, and regrets we would never admit. She smelled off, like mothballs, and arthritis medication. Pulling back, I looked into her eyes; the sadness there chilled me to the bone.

"Come on, let's get something to eat."

The concierge at my hotel recommended an Asian restaurant a few blocks from the hotel. My company had given me a small allowance for a rental car, but I chose to use my own money, and got a convertible. I hadn't even made it past the first turn in the parking garage, when Heidi pulled the elastic from her hair, letting it fly free around her. She raised her arms into the air, after reaching over, and turning the stereo up as loud as she could.

Gone was the woman who stepped off the nonstop flight from Tucson. Replace with the young, vibrant girl, who never left the house without her lip gloss. As we traveled down the highway, the wind whipped her hair behind her, and Heidi danced in her seat. The words to the song forgotten, as she whooped and hollered, waving and blowing kisses, to cars we passed.

Growing up, we didn't have much of anything; except being poor, and each other. Sometimes, near the end of the month, before the food stamps came, we would dream of how good a package of Ramen noodles would taste. We would eat the last few crackers, even though they were stale or damp. When the powdered milk would get mixed with the last of the real stuff, it was just enough to make macaroni and cheese. I remembered how excited we would get when the government cheese was passed out at the local VFW.

Those days were long behind me. I haven't worried about a meal since the day I left for college. From the looks of her, it seems I can't say the same for Heidi. Once we sat in the restaurant, she pulled off the black sweater, revealing nearly skin and bone hidden underneath. She looked with a worried face at the menu. So placing my hand on hers, I assured her she could have anything she wanted, my treat.

It's nice to not only see my baby sister, but see her enjoying herself. Living as we did, survival was the only business of the day. Being able to sit and enjoy a meal, not worrying about saving half for a later meal, or if this was the only meal for the day, was something to treasure.

I allowed her to have her fill, enjoying everything she ordered, and a good portion of mine. Seeing her consume this much food and the condition of her frail frame, I questioned just how well her husband was taking care of her. During our phone conversation, she admitted they had closed the soup kitchen. George had wanted to devote more time to the ministry he was trying to build.

"So, tell me more about this new church?"

Heidi had ordered two desserts, a piece chocolate cake and a slice of cheesecake. Her fork was pressed against her tongue, the hot fudge too good for her to leave behind on the utensil.

"It's actually an established congregation, mostly older worshipers, and single mothers. A few youth, but not enough to start a group for them." Her eyes twinkled, and I knew there was something more there, something which excited her. "We have been blessed with a young musician who is excited about the choir." She lifted her eyebrows as she said the word musician. A classic move she learned from our momma. She believed you should always have a man on deck, one waiting in the wings, as you got rid of the one who warmed your bed. Each time we were about to be introduced to a new "uncle", she had the same look.

"I take it you're fucking him?" My words meant to bite. She had learned nothing from watching Momma run herself into the ground. Although it was her life, it bothered me Heidi was following in Momma's footsteps.

"Who, George?" She cast questioning eyes in my direction. The area between her brows puckered, and wrinkled.

"No, idiot. Why would I care if you're fucking your own husband? I'm talking about the musician."

Heidi never could lie for shit, neither could Momma. Where Heidi would curl her hair around her finger, momma would pick at her fingernail polish, then lie through her damn teeth. Right now, Heidi's fingers were headed straight for the windblown mess she was sporting. "It's not really fucking." With the fingers still hair free, I knew she was telling the truth. How long that lasted was yet to be determined.

"Then what is it? 'Cause oral sex is still fucking." I pointed my empty fork in her direction. I had gone with fresh fruit, instead of the sugar coma inducing mess across the table from me.

Heidi continued to cut her cake into bites, mixing each piece with a portion of cheesecake. Her eyes fixed on the movements of her fork; avoidance was a skill Candy Perry had mastered as well.

"Nothing has *really* happened." She shrugged, as she continued to build the perfect bite. My sister could justify just about anything. I could almost feel the excuse formulating in her mind. How she just fell on his hard dick, or she tripped and his tongue broke her fall by impaling her pussy.

"Might as well just tell me the truth," I leaned over the edge of the table, my arms crossed in defiance. "It's not like I'm going to talk with George anytime soon."

Heidi's eyes flashed to mine, her face remaining stoic, and pensive. "Let me ask you something," she leaned back in her chair, her dessert abandoned for the conversation. "How would you feel if the man who promised you the world, suddenly wouldn't touch you anymore?" Her eyes flicked between mine. The hurt she felt peeking out, overshadowing the exhaustion, which was covering her entire body. "You don't know what it's like to be taken to your marital bed, only to have your husband tell you sex is for procreation, not pleasure. And since you can't get pregnant, there's really no point in fucking you anymore."

Her voice told me this had been building; the pain wrapped around every word, said it all. The dreams she had of happily ever after, were now tainted with the harsh words of what sounded like a bitter, and possibly impotent, old man. Forcing her to seek the comfort and shelter, of a much younger, and perhaps more satisfying, man.

"Every Saturday he comes to the church, and has the choir in the palm of his hands. He inspires and lifts the members of the church up into the rafters, when he sings or plays the piano." The glistening of an approaching tear enters the corner of her eye. I can't sit in judgment of my baby sister, ignoring the pain, which seems to have consumed her. Reaching across the table, I extend her my unconditional love, with the warmth of my hand.

"He hugs me, Lainie," her voice cracks with her admission, and I can't fight the tears, which transfer to me. "He smells so good, like a man, and not a bottle of menthol. I know it's wrong." The tears are flowing freely. Releasing the pain from the guilt of either the actual sin she has committed, or the thoughts she has kept secret. "How long does God want to punish me for being a whore?"

As much as I hated Frances Greyson for hurting me, causing the irrational fear of I have of my own fucking shadow, I hated George Garvin for bringing even one tear to his wife's face.

"Heidi, honey, you're not a whore."

"But I can't get pregnant." Her voice cracked, revealing the true culprit behind the pain. Salty tears confessed what her heart feared, soulful regret for what she cannot have.

"Heidi, did a doctor tell you that or did George pull it out of his ass?" I was so sick of the pollution that man spread with his vile words, and outdated thinking. Backwater wisdom, full of invented forecasts in a world they could not explain. Heidi didn't have to answer. I knew he had convinced her of the price she had to pay for giving herself to another man. Even if she, and not his old ass, owned the loss of her virginity.

"Sissy, if whores couldn't get pregnant, then you and I wouldn't be here."

From early ages, Heidi and I knew the truth about our momma. The whispers, which flew around us from the other children, and hateful words spoken by adults when young sponges were present. The women of the town we grew up in would smile to her face, compliment her on her hair, or the way she dressed us girls. Then, when the church groups met, and the doors were closed, the evil witches would spread rumors like a virus.

"She did the best she could, Lainie. She had no formal education, just the face God gave her." This sounded more like my sister, defending Momma, no matter what the fight.

"You're right, she did. But she failed when she did what she did with all those men." I hated what I heard night after night. When she wasn't fucking the current guy, she was fighting with him. She'd provided nothing solid to form a healthy relationship on. Thus the reason, I had stayed away from anything long term. When I finally gave my heart away, I wanted to see it grow, not be repeatedly broken. I still had hope of finding my forever, of meeting the one we all dreamt about.

"I hate him, Lainie. I hate how he eats with his mouth open, and how he clears his throat before he takes a drink. He ignores me, and then talks about me in his prayers at church. He tells God that I am his cross to bear. But, he can't figure out what he is supposed to do with me."

I hated seeing one more woman in my family torn apart by the man they trusted, loved, and gave their bodies to.

"He won't touch me since we can't have a baby. Yet, he tells me that masturbation is a sin against God."

I can't help but snicker. Imagining George standing at the pulpit, screaming that God will make you go blind, if you touch yourself.

"Well, I don't know about it being sinful, but I do know I call out His name every time I do it." It was the needed words to lift the weight off the subject, bringing an end to the tears, and putting a smile on her face. "Heidi," I whispered, as I took her hand in mine. "What do you want to do?" Her brow furrowed, as she examined my question.

"Nobody has ever asked me." She admitted, her face lighting up with possibility. "I've always wanted to teach or work with little children. To be a voice for them, when they can't speak." Her honesty made me smile. I could picture her standing before a class room, molding young minds, on how things are made or work.

"But…"

There was always a 'but' when it came to my sister. A roadblock she created for herself. "George would never let me teach little children. He said he didn't want me putting ideas into their heads. I've always had to work in the church office, counting the offering, and answering the phone."

I shook my head, ready to give her ten reasons why George was a fuck-nut, and not worthy of anyone's time. "Lainie, can I ask you something?" Her voice stronger now, her eyes determined. I nodded, giving her the go ahead.

"You know I've tried things the way Momma told us to. Giving my man everything I had to keep him, right?"

"Yes, you more than me."

"Well I was thinking. What if I tried things your way, putting myself first for a change?"

I wanted to reach over the table, bring her closer to me, and hug the shit out of her. "I'd say, I'd be happy to show you how to live for you, and not everyone around you. I would love to introduce you to my best friend, Claire, who is the most giving, and wonderful woman I know. Together, we can teach you to be happy with yourself."

Her face filled with excitement. Her cheeks pinking from the rays of the sun she got on the drive over here. "Can I ask you another question?" Her voice pitched like a schoolgirl. The way she should sound, not like the decrepit woman she was dressed like.

"Of course."

"Do you know any good attorneys?"

Laughing, I stood from my chair, and then wrapped her in a hug, "Yes, an entire family of them. Even a District Attorney, with a killer smile."

Chapter Five

Austin

You'll only regret the chances you didn't take, relationships you were afraid to have, and decisions you waited too long to make.
- Unknown

New York was no longer my home, not that it ever really had been. It was just an escape from the chains I'd created for myself. A wild idea created by a fresh faced boy, with big dreams, and an even bigger ego. Being back in Charleston had reminded me of what being a good and decent man was all about. It also shed some light on a dark corner I didn't know existed, or perhaps it was just a very well kept secret, even from me.

I watched Dylan taking a girl into the bathroom, and marveled at his ability to fuck her among the filth left behind from nameless patrons before them. Using her to scratch the itch he had at the moment. He made no promises of anything. Both parties agreeing to get what they needed from one another, and then carry on with their lives.

Clearly, I was too young to settle into a long-term relationship, and give my all when so little was returned. Perhaps I was jaded after the death of Granddaddy, and the betrayal of Keena, or maybe I was just finally seeing the light. The more I considered it, the more I knew the decisions I'd made on the plane ride back to New York, were the right ones for me.

Once I was in the back of a taxi, I called a co-worker, whose wife was a realtor. She had helped me get my condo, and I knew she would get me the best deal in selling it. Next, I phoned Scott. He constantly harassed me to hang out with him, and the rest of my team. I figured since I was handing in my resignation, this would be the perfect opportunity to kill two birds with one stone.

After tossing the driver some cash, I stepped onto the sidewalk, and glanced up at the grey building that no longer appealed to me. Gone was the sweet smell of fresh cut grass, supper cooking, and laughter, shared between my brothers and myself. In its place was the dull hum of the city, car horns, and whistles. Was it that long ago I closed my eyes, and absorbed the sounds of this city? Relishing in the adventure it brought?

Carl held the door, and welcomed me home. I ignored the desire to correct him. This wasn't home, not anymore, and truthfully it never was. As the elevator took me back to my floor, I wondered if Keena had taken my demand seriously. Or would I find her camped out in the middle of the couch, engrossed in someone else's issues?

Glass still littered the floor where I had shattered the television. Various items of discarded trash confirmed that Keena had indeed moved out. She had left behind a tornado effect of old bills, and dirty clothes. But, she was most definitely gone. Glancing down at one of the discarded pages, I noticed her cell phone bill looked to be overdue. I smiled to myself, it was her issue now. While I waited for my flight to board, I had called all my credit cards, and canceled the ones issued to her. She was on her own, and now someone else's problem.

Scott sent me a message we would be meeting around nine at a club he went to last weekend. Olivia phoned with a potential buyer for my condo. They wanted to see it before it went for sale to the public. She explained the couple had been looking for something in my building for months now, but we're always getting outbid at the last moment. Six bags of trash and four boxes of dirty clothes later, I sat on the edge of my bed. I was taking great pleasure in deleting every single episode Keena had recorded on my DVR.

Pieces of Ice, the current hot spot on the Upper East Side. Blue lights glowed up the side of the brick building, which had once been a meat packing plant. Most clubs in the city didn't get interesting until well after midnight, so the line was non-existent when I pulled up. One entire wall of the open room served as the bar, with high polished countertops. The lights from the dance floor sparkled like stars around the room. Scott waved me over to the far corner of the bar. He already had a drink and a beautiful woman, who was not his wife, beside him.

"Hey, man. Didn't think you would really make it." He greeted me, as he stood, slapping me on my back. The blonde beside him flashed me what was probably intended to be a flirty smile, though it missed its intended target by a mile. She looked far too much like Keena, not a place I wanted to revisit.

"Nah, I told you I was comin'."

The blonde began to giggle, pointing her bright red fingernail in my direction. "You're from the *country*." Her eyes grew wide, as she scooted closer. I hated when people tried to imitate southern accents. Especially when they had never stepped foot out of the north.

They tended to sound ridiculous.

"Say that again, I just love a country accent." She purred, as she tried to touch my arm. Ignoring her request, I flagged down one of the waitresses, and ordered a beer. As I took a look around, I noticed a table full of women, all huddled together, as if they were planning to take over the world. Every once in awhile, one of them would poke her head up, take a look around the room, hone in on something or someone in particular, and then point it out to the rest.

When I was in high school, Granddaddy used to say, *"Beauty only gets your attention, personality wins the heart."* Chase had been pining over this girl, Vanessa. She was as pretty as a sunrise, but her heart was as cold as midnight. Her best friend, Gretchen, was sweet on Chase, but he didn't return the gesture. When the Sadie Hawkins dance came around, Chase assumed Vanessa would ask him. But, when Gretchen came round instead, he was upset. When Momma found out he was rude to a southern young lady, she made him walk over to her house, and apologize. Chase ended up going to the dance with Gretchen, and they dated for nearly two months. They broke up, not because Chase lost interest, but because she had to move away with her family. Where Vanessa was pretty to look at, she didn't have a lick of sense in her whole body. Gretchen on the other hand, loved to fish, and play the guitar, all the same things Chase enjoyed.

Looking at those girls, I could see the prettiest of the bunch, another blonde with big tits. I know I'm assuming she has titled herself as being the pretty one of the group, surrounding herself with her friends of lesser allure. She's convinced herself she comes out with them as a favor, getting them as many free drinks as she can. She's the type of girl Dylan would seek out, enjoy for a few hours, and then move on. I don't want the hassle of feeding her ego, pumping her friends with copious amounts of alcohol and empty compliments, so I've already written her off. There are two brunettes on either side of her. One who looks like she would rather be anywhere else, and the second looks like she was waiting for the floor to cave in.

Seated on the opposite side of the blonde was a raven haired girl. Where the other women have fruity beverages before them, she has the same brand of beer in her hand as I do. There's just something sexy about a girl who can drink a beer, and enjoy it. Perhaps sitting on the tailgate of a pickup, watching the stars fill the sky, and catching fireflies in an old mayonnaise jar. Not worried if her hair's a mess, or her shoes get covered in mud. Just happy being able to relax, and enjoy the simple life.

"Scott, I'll catch you later, man."

Getting a girl has never been an issue for me. Ms. Georgia was right when she said we were all just as cute as a toe sack full of puppies. Nana had warned us never to use our God given good looks to hurt young girls. I had no plans on hurting anybody, but I sure as hell planned on feeling pretty good in a few minutes.

With a cocky smile in place, I skirted around several tables, as I approached the ladies. Clearing my throat, I lightly placed my hand on the shoulder of the young lady I was interested in.

"Pardon me, Miss," I greeted. Using every ounce of baritone I had, something Keena said made her pussy wet. "Care to dance?" I locked eyes with her, and held out my free hand. The gasps of her friends could be heard over the music blaring from the speakers. I knew I could get any one of the girls at this table, but I wanted the one who didn't come here to get noticed. If I had to guess, I'd say she had turned down her friends offer to come out so many times, she couldn't formulate another plausible excuse. Dylan would have labeled her the wingman of the group, choosing the short straw, so her friends could get the guy they wanted.

She nodded, visibly stunned a man like me had asked her to dance. While I had no plans of making her a single promise, I would give her the opportunity to say no. Wrapping myself around her from behind, I tucked my leg between hers, and pulled her back against my chest. Boldly moving her hair away from her neck, I took the shell of her ear between my teeth. I had no time for bullshit, I wanted to fuck her, and get the memory of Keena out of my system.

"Wanna get out of here?" I whispered into her ear, turning her around to face me. Admittedly, I was using my looks to get her naked, but she still had a choice.

Nodding, she pulled me from the dance floor. "I have a room three blocks away." Waving goodbye to her friends, she never slowed, as we headed for the entry door.

Vivian was a twenty three year old visiting New York for her girlfriend's bachelorette party. She had recently found her boyfriend of three years with her cousin, in their bed. She didn't want to exchange last names or any other information, she had only one request. "Fuck me, hard."

Vivian, or Vi as she allowed me to call her, let me know up front that this was just sex. She wanted to forget the hurt her ex had caused, if only for a while.

"I got you, baby." I managed, as I slipped off her black silky top, revealing a matching lacy bra. She had decent sized tits, just a little less than a handful, but I wasn't going to be using them for long. Her nipples larger than I've seen, but again not mine to keep.

Sliding her pants off, her panties went along for the ride. Kneeling on the carpeted floor, Vi's legs spread with her glistening center on display. Keena very rarely let me eat her pussy. So, I raised Vi's knees to place them on my shoulders, took one last look at her, winked, and dove in.

"Wait!" She shouted, grabbing a handful of my hair in the process. "Are you sure you want your mouth there?" Her eyes were wide, as I leaned back.

"Let me guess, your old beau wouldn't go down on you?" Vi shook her head violently from side to side, her eyes still wide with surprise. Laughing, I grabbed her thighs harder, causing her to lose her balance, and fall back onto the mattress. "You better hold on tight then."

I'll never forget the first time I did this. We had just begun working on Chase's motorcycle, and the conversation had turned to pleasing women. Daddy and Granddaddy were debating the best way to win a woman's heart. After going back and forth with diamonds and trips, they looked at one another, and began laughing. "Eating her pussy!" They'd said in unison. Later that night, I had a date with Marcy Reece, my girlfriend at the time. Just as Vi was panting like a marathon runner, Marcy called on every deity she knew.

Sliding my fingers into her channel, her hips shot off the mattress, as I felt her walls contract around my digits. Holding her pelvis down, I made sure her orgasm was finished, before I kissed my way back up her body.

Vi let me get as far as her hipbone before jumping to her knees, and pulling at my belt and pants, until my hard cock sprang free. She may have never had a guy go down on her, but the girl had serious oral skills. Leaning back, I watched her lips circle the head of my cock, her right palm covering the top of my pelvis, while her thumb and fingertips found the side of my balls. Where most girls moaned as they sucked, Vi would lock eyes with me, and reached around to play with her clit.

Adding her other hand, slick with her wetness, to cover where her lips left off. Vi was no porn star, her movements were deliberate, calculated. She monitored my reactions, as the cue for her next move. Her rhythm was perfect, no teeth or gagging, not sucking too hard, or popping her lips. Once she had my cock all wet, she removed both hands, and slid my entire shaft into her mouth. Her eyes never leaving mine.

She is enjoying making me feel the warmth of her mouth, sending me to the brink, only to bring me back just as quick. Her legs are twisting. Her pelvis seeking friction that her fingers weren't delivering. She wanted my cock, and I wanted to give it to her. Vi pulls away, the loss of her warmth isn't welcomed, and I want to see how warm her pussy is. Could it compete with her mouth? She climbed her way to my hips, sliding my dick inside her. Not a word was said, as she closed her eyes, and rocked her body, as she rode me hard. I'm all about letting her have her fill. But, the combination of her tits bouncing, and how much her face told me she was enjoying this, left me needing to get mine as well. Flipping her over, I looked deep into her eyes and, with a smirk, slid back into her. "I recall you asking me to fuck you hard."

For an hour and a half, I turned her world around. Placing her in positions which left her gasping. At one point, she turned and knelt on all fours, silently asking me to take her from behind. When I left her with a sheet covering half of her body, I kissed her temple, and wished her sweet dreams. The sun was coming up, and my body was sated, yet exhausted, with Keena a distant memory.

Sunday, Scott phoned to see if I wanted to catch a game at the pub near his house. With Olivia bringing the possible buyers by in a few hours, I figured why not. Walking into the bar, I felt a few eyes on me. Sitting at the bar however, was a girl who lived in my building. Melanie Porter lived two floors below me. We had flirted casually, but we were both with other people. I didn't see Scott, so I headed to the empty seat beside her.

"Hey, Austin." Her flirting had increased. No doubt the word of Keena and I breaking up, had made the gossips around the building.

"Hey, Mel, what are you doing all the way over here?"

Her smile increased, as she picked up her drink, "Waiting for you."

I'll never look down my nose at Dylan again. Taking a girl, bending her over a bathroom sink, and fucking the shit out of her was a thrill. Worried someone is going to walk in and catch you, yet enjoying every thrust you drive into her. Knowing she won't be asking for anything come morning, even better.

Olivia called not two seconds after I left the bathroom. Her clients were serious about buying my condo, giving me a cash offer of seventy-five thousand over asking. Her news made my night, even better than the hot sex I'd just had. I wanted to share the good news, let my granddaddy know I was coming home. Hovering my thumb over his speed dial, I choked when I remembered; he would never pick up the other line.

"Austin, is there anything we can offer to help you change your mind?"

Not even an hour after I'd sent out my official notice, I had received at least a dozen phone calls. Each offering their own brand of curiosity, trying to find out why I was really leaving, and reminding me of the non-compete clause I signed years ago. This current douche was the company's new CEO, a real piece of work from what I understand. He only got his job because he was fucking old man Lighthouse's wife. He must have heard about the project we've been working on, maybe did a little research on his own.

"No, Mr. Frasier, I have my reasons, and I will be leaving at the end of the month." He returned with the same bullshit as the others, just using fancier words since they came from so high up. I wouldn't miss this, not one fucking bit.

My team had mentioned taking me to lunch for my farewell party. I tried to discourage them, but they wouldn't budge. Scott had chosen a decent restaurant with a loft style private area. He knew the guy who ran it, and got a deal on the food. Taking that call from Frasier had me running behind. Locking my computer and grabbing my jacket, I was nearly at the elevator when I heard a commotion.

Standing by the receptionist desk was Keena, who looked madder than a wet hen. Her hair was pulled back in what looked like an old bandana, her face absent of makeup, and her clothes looked like she had pulled them out of a cold dryer.

Her eyes grew huge when she noticed me. She raised her hand, with her index finger pointed at me like a magic wand, hexing me with a magic spell. "Austin Morgan." The last thing I wanted was to have my last day filled with drama. But with the tone of her voice, and the way she looked, I didn't see a way around it.

"Why did you cancel my credit card?"

"Excuse me?" I muttered, surely I didn't hear her correctly.

"I went to the salon to get my eyebrows waxed, and the stupid card wouldn't work. The lady said the card had been canceled."

Granddaddy taught us to take care of our girls, but Keena was no longer mine, and it was high time she figured that out. "Well, that's because I canceled it." I shrugged into my jacket, keeping my voice monotone.

"But you gave me that card to buy stuff I wanted." She really believed she could use my money after the shit she pulled. "And what did you do to all my shows? I tried to watch them, and the list was blank."

"Keena, I canceled the cards when you decided to jump into bed with our neighbor. I deleted all of your shit from *my* DVR, since *you* don't live with me anymore."

"But those were my shows, and I wanted to watch them." She was more upset I had deleted her recordings, than my taking away her ability to pay for anything; this woman had some serious issues.

"Then record them on your new boyfriend's equipment, and have him give you a credit card for your eyebrows."

Keena stomped her foot, like a petulant child throwing a fit. "I hate you, Austin."

"Feeling is mutual, sweetheart." I fired back, as I pressed the down arrow for the elevator.

"I faked it, every orgasm I ever had with you, I faked."

Her words were full of venom, but she didn't grow up with two brothers who sharpened their tongues daily. "Well, your blow jobs were as bad as your acting skills. You might want to have that acting coach of a boyfriend teach you a thing or two." She mumbled something, but the elevator door had already closed.

"Ladies and gentleman, welcome aboard flight 3209 to Charleston, South Carolina. Our flight time is…"

Looking out the window of my first class seat was like the beginning of my own personal celebration of the new chapter in my life. I watched as the ground workers scurried around with their tasks, loading the massive airplane with luggage and food.

"Excuse me, Sir, may I offer you a glass of champagne?" The pretty flight attendant stood with a white towel wrapped around a bottle of champagne, bubbles finding their way to the surface. I scanned her body quickly, as the thought of a quick minute with her in the bathroom crossed my mind.

"Absolutely," I smiled in return. She sat a glass down on the table, as another beautiful woman sat in the empty seat beside me.

"Make that two." The out of breath woman instructed.

I gave her an appreciative grin, she was even prettier than the flight attendant. As the drinks were poured, the woman beside me introduced herself. I didn't pay attention to her name, it wouldn't matter anyway. After the flight attendant moved on to the next guest, the woman raised her glass to me.

"A toast," she smiled. I noticed a large wedding ring on her finger.

Raising my own glass, I clinked the edge to hers. "To burning bridges, the ones your enemy needed in order to cross."

Chapter Six

Lainie

It's better to keep your mouth shut and give the impression that you're stupid than to open it and remove all doubt.
- Rami Belson

Leaving San Diego was bitter sweet. I enjoyed being with my sister, shopping, staying up late, and acting like the teenagers we never had the opportunity to enjoy being. While we sat in the hotel bar last night, she'd shared with me her application to one of the community colleges in Charleston. She was worried about the money they asked for to process her application, but I assured her I could afford to take care of her for a while. I bought her ticket from Arizona to Charleston, and gave her a little cash in case George turned ugly on her, and tossed her out like she feared.

"Heidi, if he does anything stupid, get yourself to the airport and call me. I'll get you on the next plane out."

She swore to me she would have a cop go with her to gather her things. Although I did try to convince her to just leave her old stuff there, and come home with me. She insisted she wanted to face him, when she asked him for a divorce.

She sat patiently, as I contacted Dean Morgan. He told her he had a new paralegal, Preston Daniels, who was always asking for extra cases. Dean assured her no court in the country would force a woman to stay in a marriage she didn't want. Mr. Daniels called a few minutes later, and he and Heidi spent over an hour discussing her case. He assured her he would be available the moment she stepped off the plane, and would file the paperwork personally.

As much as I enjoyed my time with my sister, I couldn't wait to get back to my life, and my friends. Hanging out with Claire was almost like having another sister. She and Dylan had been getting very close; he adored her, that was easy to see. Instead of calling her and possibly interrupting their sexy time, I sent her a text. It was safer that way.

Pulling into Dylan's shop, the sign which once read *"Iks"*, now looked really hot and completely badass, with *"Absolute Power"* in bright letters. The shop now suited the owner, displaying the same edge he possessed.

Dylan Morgan will forever be a hero in my eyes. Had he not reacted the way he did, I don't want to think about what could have happened. I've spent too many hours on the 'what ifs'.

Shelly, my counselor, refused to let me play the 'what if' game. She was an older southern woman, who was compassionate, yet firm during our sessions. She had a complete repertoire of more old time sayings than I'd ever heard. *"What if your Uncle Bob had breasts, he would be your Aunt Tilly."* The mental image of a skinny man, with chicken legs, a straw hat, and engorged boobs protruding from his chest, his beard only adding to the confusion, always had me giggling. It was her way of breaking the tension, and refocusing the session.

As I walked into the shop, I noticed Claire and Dylan right off. God she looked so happy, wrapped in his arms, and smiling like she didn't have a care in the world. Something in her eyes told me something big had happened while I was away. She might not be able to tell me now, but as soon as I got her alone, she would have to dish.

I hadn't realized Carson was in the room, until I heard the thump of his chair legs hitting the floor. He and Miss Georgia were the parents I never had. Claire had no idea how often Carson came over. He and I would just sit and discuss life in general, but there were also times when he would try and help me understand why people like Cash did what they do to people. He was comforting, yet kept his distance. He knew that I wasn't ready for any type of physical contact, especially from the male gender. He was a patient man, and made sure that when I was ready, he would help me. The first time I was able to hug him, I cried like a baby in his arms. He held me gingerly, letting me release all my pent up emotions, and then wiped the tears away when I was finished.

"Lainie, my darling, look at you," he whispered. As he slowly stretched his arms out to me, offering me a hug.

"Hey, Carson, I missed you." I smiled, while wrapping my arms around him.

"Missed you too, Darlin'. It's been boring 'round here without you."

He was full of shit. With the company he kept, boring would never be a description he could use.

"Hey, Austin, come on over here, I want you to meet someone." My smile faded, as I took in the man now standing beside Dylan. The resemblance was uncanny. Like two pieces of marble cut from the same quarry. Austin's hair was much darker than Dylan's, yet he had the same chiseled features, and muscular frame.

"Lainie, this here's my brother Austin." Dylan's smile was radiant, as he motioned toward his brother. A sly smile developed on Austin's face, and his hands found their way into the front pockets of his jeans. His face was dusted with just a dash of scruff, giving him a mysterious, and incredibly sexy look. It was his eyes, however, that took my breath away. Where Dylan had these deep, almost impossibly blue eyes, his brother's were an electric, soul reaching blue. Instantly, all of my attention and rational thought, were held captive within his magnetic stare "Austin, this beauty is my Claire's best friend, Lainie Perry."

All my recent inhibitions and fears, seemed to have disappeared. When I managed to tear my eyes from his, I found my hand cradled in his, soft skin against softer skin. There were calluses on the tips of his fingers. Whether from years of video games or keyboard use, I wasn't sure. "The pleasure is all mine, Miss Lainie."

Back when I attended Caltech, I worked my ass off to win scholarships the alumni offered to one student every year. It was enough money to pay my tuition, and give me a small allowance to use so I wouldn't have to work. When the finalist was announced, I never imagined I would actually win. There were three of us invited to the dinner. At the ceremony that followed, they announced the winner. The belly full of butterflies I felt before they called my name, gave way to absolute elation, once the check was in my hands. Providing me with the needed funds to allow me to graduate. That feeling was nothing compared to the warm feeling I felt in my gut, when Austin Morgan said my name.

There was no fear in my chest, no anxiety rising to the top, simply comfort, and contentment. His smile was so genuine and unforced; it was as if he truly meant it.

"Austin, you got any plans for tonight?" Dylan was once again wrapped around Claire, securing her to his chest. A place she admitted she loved more than anywhere else.

"Nothing I can't cancel." His voice so deep and mesmerizing, all while his eyes stayed honed in on mine.

"Carson, you wanna call Miss Georgia, and have her meet us?" I think it was Claire who offered the invite. But, with Austin still holding my hand, all rational thoughts were being rerouted to a file I would have to review later.

"Miss Lainie, it would be an honor if you would allow me to drive you to the restaurant."

Claire moved away from Dylan, sliding her arm around me. "Actually Austin, I haven't seen my best friend in weeks. She and I will meet y'all at the restaurant. We have things to discuss."

"So, where are we headed?"

Claire slid into the passenger seat, securing the seat belt, as she waved at Dylan and Austin, who chose to take their bikes. As incredible as Austin looked standing in the middle of the shop, that man was lethal with the way he was straddling that bike. With his jean clad legs, and Doc Martin boots, he made sliding a helmet on look more like a calendar shoot, than safety gear. But the crème de la crème, was when he slid his sunglasses into place, slow and torturous, like he knew I was watching. Dylan revved his motor, then peeled out into the intersection. Austin shook his head, but then followed after his brother.

"A place I've heard good things about, Five Loaves."

Claire told me to turn left at the next intersection, then settled back into her seat. "So, what did I miss between you and Dylan?" She couldn't run from me inside a moving car. I also knew she wouldn't be able to lie to me, or tell me I was imagining things.

"He said he loves me." Her eyes still on the road ahead, her admission not surprising me. Once Claire let that man in, she owned his soul. Dylan was exactly what she needed, and she him. They would be a dynamic team, able to conquer anything.

"About time." I hid my smile, although my lips twitched.

"What?"

"Oh, come on, Claire. The man gave up fucking everything that owned a pussy to be with you. His balls have been in your purse since the night you cleaned up his hand in the ER."

"I wouldn't go quite that far," she trailed off, watching the traffic light as it changed to green. She never commented on how I didn't freak out over the memory, or perhaps she was avoiding it. That would be classic Claire, putting everyone else's feelings before her own.

"I have some exciting news of my own."

Claire turned back to me, her face sharing my excitement, as she listened to my joy over Heidi moving to Charleston. "I'm so excited for you. You'll have to bring her by my house, so the three of us can go do something." I agreed. I wanted my sister and my best friend to become friends.

"So what do you think of Austin?" Her question didn't sound as if there was a hidden meaning. No emphasis on any particular word.

I tried my hardest to sound just as indifferent, "He seems very nice. But, is he like Dylan?" Maybe it wrong to lump them together, to label Austin a womanizer.

"He is really nice, and I think you will have a lot in common with him. He used to work for a computer company, Lightfoot or Light-something."

"Lighthouse?"

"Yes, that's it, Lighthouse." Claire nodded, snapping her fingers.

"Why did he leave them?" Lighthouse was an old company, with lots of financial backing, until the founder died. Last I'd heard, the new management, who ironically was my nemesis's brother, was running the place into the ground.

"Something about a program they canceled or something."

"Hmm?" If we had the opportunity, I would have to ask him about it.

I had heard of a program, very hush-hush, which could take control of a financial institution's password system. The holder of the program would be able to infiltrate the institution's mainframe, accessing all of their accounts. Essentially, they could delete accounts, transfer funds from one account to another, or open accounts. It was highly suspect why a program like that would be designed. As its true purpose would lean heavily towards illegal activities. It was originally designed to simply scramble passwords. If Austin was the original creator, he and I would have to sit and compare notes.

Austin and Dylan arrived before we did, and were standing in the parking lot. The pair of them looked like a slice of heaven with those jeans, boots, and ball caps flipped backwards, hiding their helmet head, I'm sure they could make popular. Dylan immediately moved to Claire's side, opening the door, and pulling her out. She giggled as he dove for her neck, whispering he loved her, as he kissed her gently.

"Miss Lainie." Austin offered as he opened my door, startling me slightly, extending his hand to help me out. A slight breeze brought his alluring scent in to fill my car, a mixture of leather, soap, and something I couldn't identify. Not wanting to appear rude or miss an opportunity to touch him, I accepted his hand with a smile.

"Why thank you kind sir"

I've never been one of those giggly girls, batting my eyelashes with unabashed flirting. Level headed and cautious was more my style. Examining people from afar, not jumping into relationships at the slightest smile, or show of attention.

"Have you ever eaten here before?" Austin Morgan possessed

one of those rich baritone voices, which defined men for me. I was never a fan of a guy who was still waiting for puberty to kick in. I wanted a manly voice, which would send chills down my spine, and swirl carnal notions around my lady bits.

"No, but Claire said it was a good place, so I'm sure it will be fine." I shrugged, as I stepped onto the curb of the restaurant. Claire came up behind me, pulling at my arm, holding me back to allow the guys to walk ahead of us. Men here in Charleston took the role of gentlemen seriously. I'd gotten used to it, and honestly, enjoyed the hell out of it. I waited for Austin to open the door, getting a closer view of the snug fit of his Levi's, which made his firm ass look really good. Casting my vision further north, I found the name and logo of the bike shop in the center of his back. As he turned in our direction, I nearly tripped over my own feet. Not only did he have the voice of many naughty dreams, his smile could melt mere mortals.

As soon as we stepped through the door, the aroma of charred beef welcomed me. It awakened my hunger, and focused my attention away from the hunk of man, who by the way the hostess's eyes were about to come out of her head, was standing at the door.

"Hello," breathed the hostess. A thick, younger girl, with a pretty smile and great skin, cleared her throat, and shook her head in an attempt to regain her focus. "How many will be dining this evening?" Her smile forced, her focus on me, and not the towers of seduction standing behind me.

"Eight," came a deep response from beside me. I turned my head slightly to my right, his height requiring me to extend my gaze up higher. Austin had his cell phone in his hands, ignoring the world around him, as his thumbs tapped away at his screen.

Who was so important he needed to text them now? Given the way he looked, and the reputation of his older brother, he was most likely sexting some girl. Did she ride on the back of his bike, fulfilling some fantasy he had about road head? More importantly, why did I even care? As if he knew I was looking, his eyes flashed to mine, sending a flirty wink in my direction.

"Are y'all with the Morgan party?"

Standing beside the hostess was a much taller, and strikingly handsome man. Broad shoulders, which could hold up the world, as our momma would say, and sparkling green eyes speckled with a hint of mischief. Just like Austin and Dylan, his Levi's were painted on—God's signature wrapping on a fine male ass. Black t-shirt, tight against a muscled chest, accentuating every chiseled line, and valley. His gaze held mine for a second, and then moves on to Austin beside me. Just as quick, he looks back at me. A half smile forming on his face, as he adjusts his stance, trying to appear just as sexy and confidant as he feels. It's a practiced move, I've seen it a number of times in various bars. Men will stand against the wall or the edge of a dance floor, looking for their intended target. Once the girl is located, the mating posture is engaged. Where most women I know fall over themselves to get closer to a man like this, it turns my stomach. You want to impress me? Open your mouth and speak intelligently. Don't brag about how many seconds your last keg stand was.

Ghosting fingers move across my shoulders, causing me to look to my left again. Austin had moved much closer to me, his left arm tucking me into his side. I wait for the panic to start, for the overwhelming fear to crash over me like a tidal wave bringing me under, but it never comes. The crushing pain in my chest never makes an appearance. In its place are the tingles from my heart racing, and the beginnings of butterflies in anticipation.

"We *are* the Morgan's."

I can feel the deep rumble of Austin's voice through the miniscule amount of his chest I'm touching. I can smell the left over leather of his jacket, combined with the unmistakable smell of man.

"Right, please follow me." The hostess picked up some menus, as we followed her through the restaurant.

I've seen my fair share of pissing matches in my days, been the reason for the fight on a few occasions, but this time felt different somehow. Our hostess has an arm full of menus, and a new smile on her face. Just as forced as the one she gave us earlier, her current one belongs to Mr. Green Eyes. Poor soul has it bad for him, and my guess is the feelings aren't returned. I'd love to warn her. To tell her to hold out for a guy who cared about her, and not fall for the bad boy, who would only rip your heart to shreds.

The restaurant is in an older building. Real hardwood floors covering the entire front of the house, and bright red brick with faded white mortar, covers the wall which separates the kitchen from the customers. In the back of the long room, I can see what looks to be a private dining area, and by the direction the hostess is headed, we are about to be seated in there. She stops at the door, moves to the side, and with an outstretched arm, invites us in.

Seated at the head of the table is the very handsome Dean Morgan, who stands as we walk into the room. Beside him, with her back to the large window, is one of the sweetest women alive, Priscilla. I've never told anyone what an incredible friend I'd found in Mrs. Morgan. She came to me almost in an angelic way, one morning when I was attempting to walk past the library. She held my hand, and told me stories of how she had found herself in a situation much like mine. *"Healing has no knowledge of time,"* she'd said. It was something her late father told her after one of her many failed attempts at having children.

Priscilla practically jumped from her seat, eyes bright, and the largest smile I've ever seen gracing her face. For such a petite woman, her hug rivals that of a linebacker. But it feels warm and welcome, as if she's sharing with you all the love she has. All the while, trying her best to increase the good in the world, banishing the bad into the depths of hell.

"Dean, have you ever seen such a beautiful sight as these two beauties?"

"Yes, Priscilla, every mornin' when I see your face."

Dean genuinely means what he said, not because he feels the need to show off or score points with his wife, but because it's the truth. He is madly in love with his wife. Someday, and I hope this with every fiber in me, I want to find a man who can give me his heart in a way Dean has done for Priscilla.

"What the heck are we, yesterday's leftovers?" Dylan moves around the table, a scowl on his face that I know is fake. He's a different man, no longer the angry cop who I met all those months ago. Still crass and a complete ass at times, however, just like his father, he is in serious love with a woman.

"Nah, you're just not as pretty to look at." As Austin waits his turn to shake his father's hand, I catch him looking at me. He owns it, not looking away when I catch him. He possesses the kind of confidence, which not many have mastered. Owning your shit goes a long way with me.

Priscilla squeezes my hand, and I've nearly forgotten she was talking to me. I shifted my attention from the man I have no business ogling, to the woman before me, who has a knowing glint in her eye. She saw Austin walk in with me, arm still around me appearing protective, and no doubt she witnessed our little exchange of not so subtle eye fucking.

"You're a very lucky woman, Miss Priscilla." Deflection has always worked for me in the past. While removing myself from sticky situations in order to save my dignity, and on a few occasions, my body.

Still looking over her shoulder, a smile she reserves for Dean, gracing her perfect features. "Oh, I wouldn't rule out any luck coming your way. You're not ready right now, but soon."

I'd love to have agreed with her, and confess I still held out hope for the perfect man to come in, and rescue me. Unlike the fairy tales

Disney paints for us, my hero came in, rescued me, and then fell in love with my best friend. Not that I would want a relationship with Dylan, the opposite is actually true. Dylan is the kind of guy I could hang out with, catch a ball game, while telling dirty jokes. Any thoughts of romance would send me to the bathroom hurling into the toilet. At this point in my life, I'm pretty confident my 'Mr. Perfect' took the wrong train, and is happily married with three kids in the middle of Kansas.

Dean motioned for Priscilla to come and join him in her chair. I took this as my cue to speak with him about my sister. To thank him for expediting the process in getting her away from George.

"Mr. Morgan, I know I've asked an enormous favor of you by helping with the divorce, and I can never thank you enough."

"Wait, you're married!?" Austin's outburst silenced the commotion of the others finding their seats. Dylan stood behind Claire's chair, trying desperately to hide the humor he found in his brother's reaction.

"No, Austin, her sister is." Priscilla reached across the table, placing her hand over her son's finger, which was pointed in my direction. Austin's eyebrows relaxed. It's a wonder they didn't disappear into his hairline, his eyes flicking between his momma, and myself. "Dean assigned one of his aspiring paralegals to help with her case."

Priscilla's voice seemed so gentle; I wonder if she told them animated stories when they were little. How effective was her discipline with them. Her mild temperament seemed to be something three rugged boys would trample into the dirt.

"Who's working the case?" Claire had shared with me how protective Dylan had become with her. She confessed she found it to be a double edged sword, incredibly arousing at the thought he wanted to protect her so fiercely, while completely infuriating when he assumed she couldn't take care of herself. I could see what she meant.

Dylan had assigned himself as my big brother, ready to fight the schoolyard bullies, who dared to pick on me.

"Preston has been one of the better men you've scared my way. He shows enough potential. I've given him this case, and have recommended him for the VanBuren scholarship."

I had read about that in the newspaper, a scholarship created by Priscilla. A full ride to law school in honor of her father. At Dean's mention of the scholarship, I noticed Priscilla's eyes begin to fill with tears. Digging deep into my diversion file, I fired my next question at Austin.

"Austin, Claire tells me you once worked for Adams Lighthouse. What did you do over there?" I picked up a slice of bread the waitress left as we took our seats. The aroma making my stomach grumble.

Austin switched his posture, glancing briefly at his water glass. "She's right, I worked on the Titan Project for the last few years."

"As?"

His eyes flashed to mine, confusion leading his frown. "A code writer?" His words were drawn out, as if he were speaking with a small child instead of an educated woman. Fire began to stir in my belly from his condescending tone.

"Really? You write code for encrypted programs?" I knew he'd worked on the program, I'd just assumed he was an accountant or part of their legal team. Austin didn't fit into the mold most code writers poured themselves into. The majority of members on my team wore sweater vests, and drove a Prius, not Levi's and a Harley.

"Why does this surprise you? Do I not look *smart* enough to build a program?" The cocky bastard was correct, he did surprise me. Although, never did I assume he didn't look smart enough to do anything.

"Before I answer your question, please, answer one of mine. What do you think I do for a living?" I asked, giving him a dose of his own medicine. I may not be a pageant winner, but I was no crypt keeper either.

Austin leaned back in his chair, the table remaining quiet, as he considered his answer. Claire nudged me under the table, anticipating his answer as much as I did. "I don't know. Fold sweaters over at Macy's?"

Like a bad taste in his mouth, his words landed on me full of insult and assumption. He wasn't the first man to think me too pretty to have a brain, and with little doubt, he would not be the last. "Good guess, but no."

Tilting my head in Claire's direction, I watched both her and Dylan, vibrating with silent laughter. Extending my outstretched hand in his direction, with a lot of pride in my smugness, I reintroduced myself. "Lainie Perry, Senior Software Designer for Craven and Associates. Pleasure to meet you."

Dylan let out a loud cackle, rivaled only by the howl coming from Dean. Poor Austin looked stunned, as if just being told Darth Vader wasn't really Luke's father.

"It's all right, little brother. Claire can help you surgically remove that size eleven from your mouth."

Chapter Seven

Austin

No relationship is ever a waste of time, If it didn't bring you want you want, it showed you what you didn't want.
- Unknown

I couldn't concentrate on the screens before me. I'd been studying the grainy photo Carson had sent me, before we took care of Cash. I needed to figure out who the girl was, and remove the seed of speculation I had about her identity. I was refusing to admit, even to myself, who the evidence was pointing to.

My mind kept flashing back to yesterday at lunch. I still had an issue believing Lainie did basically the same job I had back in New York. I'd never met a woman who could write code. Not to mention one so completely beautiful, and who could do anything except spend my money. I know how it sounded, but experience had formed that opinion.

When we walked into the restaurant, I had just gotten a text from Keena. She wanted to know if I could float her a loan until she found a new job. When I told her to ask her boyfriend, she texted back saying he'd thrown her out. I could have been a prick and told her to figure it out. Instead, I had a friend of mine get her a room in a hotel for a few days. I couldn't just toss her away, and hope she landed on her feet.

Then Jessie Wagoner walked up like he owned the damn place. Showing his cocky assed smile to the one of the few girls in Charleston he hadn't slept with. He had more bastard children running around the county than he could afford. Which was evident by the number of women who'd been to Daddy's office to file for child support. Son of a bitch knew he was being investigated, and tried to close his bank accounts. Which I'd managed to freeze, before he could.

He tried acting like he didn't know who we were, asking if we were with the Morgans. Motherfucker knew who I was. He got his ass stomped on the football field one too many times by either myself, or Chase back in the day. I won't even touch on how many run-ins he had with Dylan. But I sure as shit jarred his memory when I wrapped my arm around Lainie. Sending his ass a clear fucking message, to back the fuck off.

Oh, Lainie Perry…that girl has spirit and gumption; her sweet smile hides her tough as shit interior. But her eyes, her eyes tell me she is harboring something. A dark secret she's keeping, maybe even from herself. I must have looked at her for a good half hour after she told me she worked over at Craven. I'd considered calling Jackie up when I decided to move back home. It was more than just the no compete clause which kept me from picking up the phone. Just like Dylan, I needed a purpose. A fucking reason to endure the bullshit the world has waiting for us. Protect the ones who can't fight for themselves. Deep inside, I felt as if Lainie were fighting one of those battles, something maybe I could help her win.

"Austin?"

Momma had phoned me after we left the restaurant, asking if she could borrow a few minutes of my time today. She knew better than to think she would be bothering me. The woman was a saint, saving me from the system, and a life I wouldn't have survived.

"Hey, Momma, come on in." Standing for a lady was an automatic reflex Granddaddy had instilled in us. *"Southern girls are taught in the womb to accept a chair from a gentleman. If you ain't willin' to do it, they will stand there until the right one does."* Growing up, we took turns offering Momma a chair. A time or two we would forget whose turn it was, and begin pushing and shoving each other. She had this sharp snap, and when we heard it, we knew it was our only warning. Heaven help you if you ever heard that snap in church. It didn't matter if God was watching or not, your behind was about to get worn out.

"Momma." I kissed her cheek, taking in the comforting scent of her perfume. Just like most of the lady's in this town, Momma had a wardrobe of different fragrances. It seemed like a waste of money to me, as she'd worn the same scent every day of my life. Grasping her hand, I lead her over to one of the chairs facing my desk. She thanked me, as she always does, while I take the seat beside her

"Austin, I won't take much of your time, I know you're busy with all this." Waving her hand around my room full of monitors. "But I need to speak with you about yesterday." Her voice gave nothing away. No hint of disappointment about my reaction to Lainie, or my silence after learning the truth.

After Dylan offered Claire's surgery skills, I chose to sit back, and listen. I learned a long time ago most people will tell you more than you want to know, if you just let them speak. Not everyone uses words to tell their story. Some, like Lainie, have terrible poker faces.

Making slight facial expressions, as they listen to others speak.

Lainie had a deep love for her sister, Heidi. A love which outshined the affection I have for my entire family, which really said something. She smiled her perfect smile, as she asked Daddy to let her have the retainer bill for the divorce paperwork. Momma smiled with her own brand of pride, when he let her know he was giving her the family discount, which roughly meant this was pro-bono work. Lainie worried her brother-in-law would cause a ruckus when he was served, costing Heidi more time and money. Daddy had many offices across the country. He told her not to worry about anything.

When Miss Georgia and Carson arrived, poor Lainie was bombarded by red lipstick kisses, and complaints she looked too thin. Personally, I thought she looked pretty fucking perfect just the way she was. After he was seated, Carson leaned into Dylan, and whispered something. Just as we were about to order another round of drinks, Dylan sent me a text that Carson had just submitted his retirement letter. He would be joining our team full time by the end of the month.

"Austin, do you recall the trial your Daddy and Dylan were working on together when you first got here?" Priscilla Morgan was never one to drag out a conversation, and she was not one who believed in wasting anything precious- time and energy included.

"Yes, Ma'am." I crossed my ankle over my knee, my boots had become my best friends again. Dressing in jeans and Ropers was a big no-no in the business world.

"Do you recall anything about it?"

"A young girl was attacked, roughed up pretty good, over at the college, right?" How could I forget? It had opened the hail storm building between myself and Chase. With him moving back close to home, I didn't want to say too much until I could prove anything. I also wouldn't bring Dylan into it unless I had to. Keeping the family together was much more important, than being right about anything. So I wasn't too sure where Momma was going with this line of questioning.

"Yes, that's the one. Do you remember anything about the young lady?" I was puzzled by her question. Honestly, I was too wrapped up in the rotten onion I'd found, with each layer smelling worse than the one before.

Another thing about southern women, which always seemed to drive me crazy, was the large purse they strapped over their arms. Complaining to the hilt when they couldn't find the tube of lipstick at the bottom, or missing a call on their cell phone when they couldn't find it. Priscilla Morgan was no different. She had a purse large enough to carry a twenty-pound baby, and the crib he slept in. Reaching into the leather monstrosity, she pulled out a large white document.

"I noticed your interest in Miss Lainie yesterday." I was about to roll my eyes, and let her know I didn't have time to pursue a girl right now. "Don't think for one second you hid your staring from me, Austin William Morgan." I cringed hearing my middle name leave her lips. Knowing it was never good to have all three names, and the stern tone her voice had changed to. "Believe me, I know you think like Dylan most of the time. Trying on a new girl for size whenever the notion hits ya."

Since returning to Charleston, I have tried on a few girls for size. Enjoying the sweetness of the ladies round here. I made sure to tell them it was casual, no strings, and no commitments. I was also very careful. No unplanned, or unwanted children, running around for me.

"But the heart wants what the heart wants. Even if the timing ain't right." Placing the white pages on my desk, something told me I wouldn't like what I found written on them. "Now, Austin, I love Lainie like I love Claire, and I would never betray her trust. That girl has been through a tough time, and is still dealing with the fallout from what happened. While I would never tell her story, not even to Jesus himself, those pages tell the story. They are also a matter of public record, and any Tom, Dick or Harry could walk down to the courthouse and read them. Before you invest yourself in sniffin' after Lainie, take a good look at the story being told. If you can't help the situation and be something good for her, then leave her alone."

I knew by looking at Lainie she was changed by what had happened, that was expected. But as Momma left me to examine myself, and how I would move forward with the information she gave me, she left me with just one last piece of the puzzle.

"Austin, if you decide you want to see where this journey will take you, have lunch over at the coffee shop on King Street. The one with the outdoor patio. Tomorrow's special is shrimp and grits. I know you haven't had any since you've been back home." Even if the skies opened up and poured solid sheets of rain, I would be sitting on that patio tomorrow afternoon, as if my life depended on it.

Dylan and Carson came into the office, just after I finished reading the court transcripts. Somehow the fire Dylan had when he dealt with Cash had now been ignited inside of me. I knew the story. Dylan had shared every detail with me; I just never thought I would have a hand in wanting all parties involved dealt with.

Carson looked worn out as he entered my office. Dylan sat with his boot covered feet on the corner of my desk, his cell phone in hand, and a grin on his face. "Sources tell me, you have been tasting some of the local honey."

Not moving my eyes from my screen, as I installed a new program to help me figure out who the girl that picked up Cash from jail was. "Yeah, so?" Not giving Dylan the rise he wanted, since it was none of his business who I was 'tasting'.

"Listen man, I ain't your daddy, but this ain't New York either. Some girls you can fuck and forget." Dylan's feet hit the floor. His eyes serious, and his tone leaving no room to blow him off. "And some girls you better fucking forget, if you ain't serious."

Abandoning the program, I eased back in my chair, meeting Dylan's glare head on. My brothers and I have had our share of scrapes, bloody noses, cut lips, and a few broken ribs. We fight, smack each other around, and then hug it out. None of us have an issue when calling the other out on their shit.

"I take it you talked to Momma?"

"Nope. I talked to Claire, who talked to Lainie."

I tried to act aloof at the mention of her name. Nothing had happened, with the exception of a decision on my part to see this through. Well that, and a few text messages cancelling several planned hook ups.

"Okay? They're friends, what does that have to do with me?" I looked at both men with false contentment. A smoke screen I hoped would work.

Dylan leaned toward Carson, who leaned slightly toward him, his face revealing nothing, "Are you hearing this shit? Boy thinks he's being cute." A new edge wrapped around Dylan's words, condescending, with a boost of protectiveness.

"See, Carson, my younger brother thinks he can sit down to dinner surrounded by beautiful women, one of which I love dearly by the way, and think for one second nobody saw him salivating over the only single girl at the doggone table."

"Wait? Did I just hear correctly? You're in love with the girl?" Dylan had never been in love with anything, other than sticking his dick in any girl who would let him. I would have sworn he was severely allergic to love and commitment. I knew he had changed, the second he had asked for my help in closing down the bridge. Claire was a good match for him, and from the little amount of time I've spent with her, I can see she fills in the gaps for him. Calms him where he is wild, and brings to life the parts of him, which may have tried to die from his past.

"Yes, you did. I love my Claire to death." Dylan held nothing back, speaking with conviction, and honesty. He had discovered his feelings, processed them, and now bathed in their warmth. He'd also proven he was willing to go to any lengths to protect her. Even if it meant someone had to die.

"I love her enough to step in and say something when she's frettin' about her friend." Yesterday, as we settled the check, the four of us practically wrestling over who would be paying for it. In the end, the waitress ended up getting a nearly four hundred dollar tip from our check, as well as, all the cash tossed on the table to cover the tab. Claire had dragged Lainie off to the bathroom, like girls often do.

"Claire noticed the way you were looking at Lainie, and it worried her. She asked Lainie if she was interested in you, or if she needed to be sitting here instead of the two of us." The smart thing would have been to act as if I didn't care. Pretending as if the safety of the free world did not depend on the answer to Claire's question. But when it comes to Lainie, apparently I was stuck on stupid.

"So does she?"

Sophomore year in high school, Dylan made a bet with Norman Ledbetter that Chase could play the guitar better than his cousin, Cecil Ledbetter. Chase never made it known he could play any instrument, so Norman took the bet. Back then, we would gather in the middle of one of our daddy's pastures, crank up the music in one of our trucks, and have a party. That particular weekend, Dylan invited practically the entire school. Cecil spread the word he was gonna wipe the floor with Chase. Of course, once our little brother heard what Cecil was saying about him, he laid down a challenge himself. If he beat Cecil, then he would get his high priced guitar. If Cecil won, Chase would have to give up his guitar. Which was autographed by Johnny Cash, and a gift from our granddaddy.

Since the challenge took place on Morgan land, I became the emcee. We had Chase get in the back of one truck, and Cecil in the back of another, parked side by side. With Cecil as our guest, we let him decide who went first. Just like all Ledbetters around here, he wanted to go first. Cecil put his left foot on the wheel well, placed the neck of his guitar on his thigh, and then began playing his version of *Orange Blossom Special*. He worked that guitar like a county fair headliner; closing his eyes as his fingers strummed the chords, his face contorting with the emotions he was experiencing.

Chase was between girlfriends, and had his eye on a freshman, Nancy Mitchell, who had just moved to the district. She, however, didn't particularly find his charm appealing. The day before the competition, he'd stopped her at lunch, and asked her what her favorite song was. Then he made her an offer she found funny, yet couldn't refuse. If he won, using her song, she had to go to our parent's annual Low Country boil with him. If he lost, he would never ask her out again.

Apparently, Nancy was a big Nickleback fan at the time. Her favorite song included a guitar solo by Santana, *Into the Night*. Chase laid the strap over his head, tossed Nancy the signature Morgan wink, and preceded to, not only play the song, but also serenade the girl with his talented voice.

After every kid for two counties voted Chase had kicked Cecil's ass, Dylan walked over to shake Norman's hand. Norman, however, was a sore loser. He pulled Cecil out of the back of the truck, ranting about how the whole thing was rigged, and Chase had faked playing the guitar. So I jumped in, grabbed Norman by the shoulder, and suggested the best two outta three, just to be fair.

Norman agreed, but he wanted to choose the song Chase played. Dylan and I had both known he was building his own coffin. Chase loved two things at the time: playing guitar with granddaddy, and spoiling girls.

Cecil jumped back in the truck and played another tune. This time, playing a hit by the Charlie Daniel's band. Norman had a smug look on his face, as he'd watched his cousin hitting the last few notes. Chase cringed a few times noticing how Cecil had missed a chord or two, but never said a word. When the song ended, Chase looked over at Norman, silently asking him to do his worst.

"Sweet Child O' Mine."

Norman had apparently assumed since we lived in the country, we didn't listen to anything else. Or maybe he really thought he was on to something, and Chase had managed to fake playing a song, in the middle of a field, on the back of a pickup.

All his smugness faded away, as Chase's fingers plucked away, just as skillfully as the original guitarist. Every short skirt, wearing girl crowded around the bed of that truck, and began dancing and singing. For the second time that night, the crowd roared, and chose Chase as the clear winner.

Cecil jumped down by himself this time, turned toward his cousin's car, getting ready to leave. Dylan called down to him, asking him if he forgot something? Cecil mumbled something, before tossing his guitar in Dylan's direction.

Nancy informed Chase since it wasn't her song, which caused him to win, she didn't have to go out with him. Chase was upset for about thirty seconds, until Sabrina White came over to congratulate him, and see if he would let her see the guitar he'd won. Chase had never paid much attention to any of the White daughters, as their looks favored their father, and not the beauty of their mother. Still, when he handed that guitar over to Sabrina, her eyes had lit up like a kid on Christmas. Chase, being the good guy he was, saw the love Sabrina was showing to that guitar. He told her to take it on home with her, and keep it.

Misty Porter, who had turned Chase down a handful of times, had walked over and whispered in his ear. Something which made his eyes bulge, and ears turn red. Word around town was Misty had the talent to suck you dry in seconds. So, when Chase emerged from the thick pine trees along the edge of the clearing, Dylan asked the same question of Chase, that I'd just asked him about Lainie. Just as Chase knew how well Misty Porter could suck cock, Dylan knew I had an interest in Lainie Perry.

"According to Claire, she assumes you're just like me when it comes to girls." Smart assumption on Lainie's part. While I had recently tested the waters of Dylan's former lifestyle, I didn't care for it as much as I'd thought I would.

"So, I'm behind before I even start?" Claire doesn't know me all that well, not enough to say I'm a choir boy.

"Depends on if you're still planning to see Lexi Marsh." Carson, who had been silent until this point, tossed out the name of the one girl I hadn't heard back from. Lexi worked for Daddy, filing papers, and answering the phone. Everyone knew she wanted to marry big, and sit back with the easy life. She'd managed to hook one of the partners, only to find him cheating on her a few weeks after the wedding. I was leaving the building late one night, as she was finishing up some paperwork. We decided to go for a drink, and ended up in the bathroom of the bar. Afterward, she had invited me to go to Myrtle Beach with a bunch of her friends. I'd said I would, until I saw Lainie.

"Just like I told numb nuts here, I'm gonna tell you. Lainie isn't the type of girl you whisk off to fuck around with for a weekend. Given what has happened with her recently, she is a whole lotta gun shy. If you're looking for a place to stick your dick, go ahead to Myrtle Beach. But if you choose to be with Lainie, you better straighten your shit up."

Carson's warning landed on deaf ears. While the discussion of treating a girl like Lainie correctly was necessary for Dylan, it was like giving water to a drowning man when it came to me.

"Listen, I hear what you're sayin'. You care a great deal for the girl. It's admirable for you to come here, and make sure I understand that. But nobody is asking themselves an even bigger question: does she even want to be with a guy like me? I know you said she is worried about where I spend my nights, but that is just curiosity." I shrugged my shoulders. Looking at the both of them through honest eyes.

"I'd like to give Lainie what she seems to need the most, a friend. Someone who can make her laugh, and help her deal with the demons. Which seem to have been stealing her dreams."

Carson stood from his seat, took two steps around the corner of my desk, before extending his hand to me. "I'm gonna hold you to that." His grip was enough to tell me what his warning failed to do. Hurting Lainie was not an avenue I should ever consider walking down. It was a dead end, and Carson was the pitbull waiting in the last yard.

The sun was high in the Carolina sky the next afternoon. An untouched plate of shrimp and grits sat on the table before me. The waitress had refilled my sweet tea several times, as I waited to see what would happen across the street. She was nice enough, but a little too flirty for my taste. "Is there somethin' wrong with your grits?"

I shot her a quick look, apologized for my apparent loss of appetite, and asked her to take it away. Just as she pulled away the plate, a runner in all black, stopped in the middle of the sidewalk across the street. Her blonde hair glistened in the sunlight; despite the black ball cap she had shielding her eyes from the sun. She stood there bouncing in place, and at first I thought she was trying to keep her heart rate up. As I took a sip of my tea, the girl pulled her arms above her head, both hands clasped at the back of her cap, as she turned toward the street. I knew immediately it was Lainie.

For over an hour, I watched her switch positions a hundred

times. Having a war within herself about something.

"She's does this all the time." The waitress commented while refilling my tea again. "Stops there, and tries to go between the buildings where that girl was attacked."

The first time I sat behind a computer, and watched as it hummed to life, I placed my finger on the keyboard, and discovered a world I wanted to be a part of. Watching the spitfire of a girl stand like David before Goliath, I knew what Granddaddy really meant, when he said it was never too late to come home. Home was more than a place to rest your head; it was a moment to lose your heart.

Chapter Eight

Lainie

*Letting go means to come to the realization that some
people are a part of your history,
but not a part of your destiny.*
- Steve Maraboli

Heidi had phoned me early this morning. According to a call she received from Mr. Daniels, at the law firm, the divorce papers were on their way to the church where George worked. "I don't like the idea of you being there when he finds out you're divorcing him."

Last week when she let me know she'd arrived back home safely, she admitted he had been angry with her. Accused her of infidelity, and other sinful things. She denied he had become violent with her, but has made life much harder than it had been for her.

"He took away my car keys, and takes me with him everywhere." Thank God he didn't know about the phone I had gotten for her while in California. She kept it on vibrate, in the inside pocket of her blouse. "After I got off the phone with Preston, I started acting as if my period was starting." I could mentally picture the smirk on her face, and the eye roll she saved just for him.

When George was first chasing Heidi, he'd come by the house on a Saturday, when all three of us were on our period. Heidi was blessed with the most with terrible cycles; heavy bleeding, and cramps bad enough to stop an elephant. George found out when her bleeding got too heavy, ruining her dress in the process. He jumped up like his ass was on fire, spewing some bullshit about the blood of a menstruating woman being like a murderous man. After that he would stay far away from the house, when her monthly visitor came to town.

"He's leaving me here at the house, while he stays in the back office of the church, until the punishment is over."

"And by then you will be long gone." When I had found out about his yelling and name calling, I'd encouraged Heidi to leave the man the first chance she got. Her ticket had been emailed to her, and she had cash for the taxicab to take her to the airport. I even had Claire coming with me to welcome her to Charleston.

"I can't wait to start the rest of my life. Charleston is going to be good for me, I can feel it." It would be a close count to know who was more excited about her being here with me. Miss Georgia let me know she had an opening for a three bedroom in the building she managed, so we would be closer to Claire. A dinner was already planned to welcome her to Charleston, and thank everyone who helped get her here.

"I love you, Sissy."

"I love you, too, Lainie. I'll see you in a few hours."

It was pointless to attempt anymore work today. Watching the clock until her plane arrived, would be the most I would be able to get done.

I let my mind wander to this past weekend, and the conversation I had with Claire. It was clear by the way she was dragging me down the side of the restaurant, she had something urgent to tell me. As we'd passed several other patrons, she'd extended an apology to each of them, as we'd scurried past them.

"Don't think I didn't notice the looks y'all were giving one another." Claire accused. As she'd pushed me through the door, and engaged the lock, looking at me with a knowing expression.

"Who?" I demanded, looking at her through disbelieving eyes. Claire was bat shit crazy, if she thought for a single second I was tossing Austin any flirtatious looks.

"Really?" One thing about our relationship, it may be new, but it was built on honesty and trust. Claire has had my back since minute one, never giving me a single reason to distrust her.

"Okay, I admit, he is seriously gorgeous. But you have to agree with me, he is also Dylan's brother, and has been around the block a time or two." I know how much Claire battled with herself over Dylan's history, reminding herself how he interacted with women. Until Austin proved to me he wasn't a player, there would be no flirting, not from my side anyway.

"According to Dylan, he was in a relationship back in New York. She cheated on him, and he moved here." Her eyes flickered between mine. The amount of trust she had in Dylan was astounding. I envied her ability to be able to truly put his past behind her, and live in the moment with the man he was now.

"Now as far as him being like Dylan, I can't honestly say either way. Just don't judge him on who he is, until you get to know him."

She was right. But the conversation was pointless, at least I thought so. Until the following Tuesday morning, when my assistant buzzed me telling me I had a visitor in the lobby.

Standing among the security guards, check in desk, and a row of palm trees, was Austin Morgan. His dark jeans and designer sunglasses screamed New York, and not Charleston. His only saving grace was the hint of a t-shirt peeking out of his button up dress shirt, which was incredibly sexy hanging untucked.

"Mr. Morgan."

His blue eyes flashed with recognition, and his smile, which was already in place, grew tenfold. "Please, it's Austin. Mr. Morgan is my dad." He uncrossed his ankles, and stood up straight. He looked so different since the last time I saw him. All bad boy biker, and everything it entailed. Here was a man you could take home to your daddy, and show him the good Christian boy you'd found on your way home.

"Very well, *Austin*. What brings you by? Looking for a job after all?" I'll admit, I did a little investigating of Austin after our last conversation. While he was absent of any criminal record, and his credit was solid, there wasn't much else out there. He didn't own any property here in South Carolina or New York. Although, I did raise both eyebrows at the amount of money he'd sold his condo in Manhattan for.

"Is there somewhere we can speak a little more privately?" I hadn't noticed the noise level in the lobby had decreased to practically silent. Of the half dozen people standing in the lobby, most of them were listening close.

"Of course, follow me."

With the crazy hours, and even more bizarre habits some of the code writers kept, Jackie the owner, had a room designated for some down time. Furnished with a couple of couches, vending machines, and a coffee pot. You needed a code to get in, and since I was a senior staff member, I had one. Granted I'd never used the room, for fear of what kinds of things I would walk in on.

Entering my six digits, I glanced back at Austin, noticing his smile was still lighting up his features. Now that he was closer, I found he was wearing the same alluring fragrance he had the other day. Scruff added to his chiseled jaw line, giving his face that little something to turn up the heat in a girl's panties. Lips, which went far beyond kissable, rounded the base to full on sucking. Maybe being in a secured space wasn't such a brilliant plan after all.

"Is this better?" I motioned to the large open space, with my arms extended like a halo around me.

Austin's eyes roamed over the area, and then back to me. "It's fine, thanks. I just didn't want to compete for your attention back there."

Nodding behind him, I'm assumed he was referring to the busy bodies we had just left. If he was concerned with someone seeing us together, he just gave them more ammunition, by following me behind a locked door.

"So, if you're not looking for work, what brings you by?"

"Lainie." My name came out in a sigh. His entire upper body slumping, as he exhaled. He looked like a man who was about to hand out a death sentence, or a dear Jane letter. "One thing you'll find out about me is I am honest, and straight to the point." He underscored his words with his hands, in a sideways slice of the air.

"Dylan and Carson came by my office after seeing the way I was looking at you the other day. They are concerned I have less than honorable intentions with you." I swallowed hard trying not to have a complete freak out. If Austin had an issue with me, this could create a big issue between Claire and I. With Heidi hopefully in the air, as we spoke, I was counting on her help.

"You have to know you have a lot of people who care about you, and love you to some degree. My momma is your biggest ally when it comes to this family. As a matter of fact, she beat the both of them, in giving me a firm warning when it comes to disrespecting you. She told me to have lunch at a coffee shop across the street from the library."

He took a few steps closer to me, lowering his voice to a level, which made him even sexier. "Secrets are not something which leave the circle we have in our house. Loyalty is held pretty high, and breaking your word is an unheard of act amongst the Morgan men. I have no first hand knowledge of what you're dealing with, or what kind of battle you fight every time you close those beautiful eyes." The last three words were whispered in his gravelly voice, shooting straight to my heart, and lighting up my soul in the process.

"But I'd at least like to offer to be your friend." He stops, taking a deep breath, as he glances out the window across the room. "That's a lie, I don't want to be your friend." Shaking his head, his eyes still focused out the window. As ridiculous as it sounds, my chest feels empty. The sting of building tears begins, as I watch him shake his head.

"Austin, really, it's okay. Just because we share a few mutual friends, doesn't mean we have to be." Another lesson I learned by watching the world around me; just because you have the right to say something, doesn't mean you have to say it. It's always better to be the person who walks away with grace.

"No." The distance between us was suddenly reduced to nothing. His movement startles me, causing me to jump slightly, and place my hand on his chest. It was warm and incredibly solid, and I can feel the quick beating of his heart.

"I'm sorry, that didn't come out right. What I meant was, I want to be so much more than your friend. But I know you're struggling with what happened, and I'd like to help with that, too. If you will let me."

Heidi's plane had been delayed coming out of Denver. She phoned me just as I was about to leave work to pick her up. It would be another couple of hours before they could get her on the next plane. She assured me she was fine, and had made a new friend while waiting in the line for a connecting flight. "Preston left me a voicemail saying George had been served while meeting with the church Deacons."

I could feel the sheer joy in her voice, finally being free of the man who had enslaved her for all these years. Although it did bug me she was calling her attorney by his first name. "Okay, call me once you've boarded your flight, and are almost ready to take off."

Austin had wanted to take me to dinner, so we could sit down and get to know each other, without the influence of his family. When I told him I had to collect my sister from the airport, he understood, and offered to come with me. I declined, but made a date for later in the week. With nothing to do for the next several hours, I tossed fate a bone, and called Austin.

"Hey, did you get your sister okay?"

I could hear the clicking of his keyboard in the background, and imagined I was on speakerphone. As that's what I would have done. Did his office look anything like mine? Monitors on every surface that could hold the weight, placed there strategically by the person who would be using them.

"Her plane was delayed a couple of hours, due to mechanical issues with the connecting flight. So, it seems I have a few hours to kill."

"And you thought of me first?"

Chasing men had never been my style. If I wanted a guy around, I let one in. After the attack, this worked to my advantage, as a way to avoid male contact.

"Well, ya know how it is. You start calling the people on your contact list, and low and behold, your name starts with the letter A."

"So I win because I am at the top of the alphabet?" He chuckled,

"I can live with that."

"Is the offer for dinner still open, or do I need to look at the letter B?"

Hard laughter filled my ear. I imagined him pushing back his chair, as he tipped his head back toward the ceiling. Tossing down a pen or two, maybe even spinning in his chair.

"Sweetness, you better forget the rest of the alphabet. I'll pick you up in ten minutes."

When I was sixteen, I had my first real boyfriend, Clayton Thomas. He was sweet enough, and the tallest boy I'd ever met. But, so very shy. His younger brother came to the house one day, and told me Clayton was sweet on me. We held hands, shared a popcorn at the movies, and he would walk me home in the afternoon. It took him nearly four months before he kissed me on my cheek. That summer, his daddy had an accident and had to have surgery. So Clayton had to take over working the farm. He tried to come over as much as he could, but getting his crops in so the family could eat, was more important.

One day our neighbor made homemade ice cream, and I thought Clayton would enjoy something cold. I packed up a big container, and walked over to his house. When I got to the front door, I found his mother and little brother sitting in the living room, watching television. It bugged me that they were inside with the air conditioning, and Clayton was out in the field. Wayne, his little brother, motioned toward the back of the house. In the last room down the hall, I opened the door to find Clayton getting a blowjob from a girl I didn't know. I could have stormed out of there, or tossed the ice cream in his face. Instead, I told the story differently when school started back up. The girl became a guy, and everyone believed me. How the story spread after that, wasn't my fault.

When I was eighteen and getting ready for my first semester at college, the country fair was going on in Louisville. My friend

Samantha, got a car for graduation, and so we headed out for a road trip. We met these two guys who were also going to the fair, Justin and Matt. Samantha was in serious lust with Matt, which left me and Justin to spend some time together. We walked around the fair, and he tried to buy me a lemonade, but I refused. After we made the big loop, he said he had to go and do something, but hoped to see me later. I found Sam by the entrance to the entertainment stage, where she told me the guys were part of one of the bands. We found some chairs, and waited for the show to start. Sure enough, Justin came out on stage, and began singing cover songs. He spotted us half way through a show, and dedicated a song to 'the pretty girl who doesn't like lemonade'.

Justin was touring around with his band. But he called me all the time, and visited me on holidays, and long weekends. The first Thanksgiving we were together; he invited me to spend the holiday with his family. His momma was amazing, and I fell in love with his little sister. He took me around the small town he lived in, showing me off to his friends. At the end of the evening, we ended up in the back of his truck, where he told me he loved me, and I gave him my virginity.

The next summer Justin auditioned for a talent competition, and was picked up by the production company. I was excited for him and wanted him to succeed. But the harder he worked to fit into the band, the less time he spent with me. Eventually, he stopped calling, and I stopped writing. After that, I devoted every waking moment to getting my career.

Austin shocked the shit out of me by pulling up to my building in a truck. I had assumed, with his big city ways, he would have been driving an Aston Martin or something equivalent. He pulled up to the cover of the building, jumped out, and opened my door for me.

"Hey, sweet girl, long time no see." He sent me that damn wink Claire warned me about, when I called her earlier about seeing Austin. Well that, and to chew her out a little, for running her mouth to Dylan.

"Hey, handsome, goin' my way?"

"You do the leadin' and I'll follow." Something told me he meant that literally, and not just as an anecdote to liven the mood.

"All right, Cowboy! You promised me dinner, and I'm starving."

We ended up at *Sesame Burger*, my absolute favorite place to eat in Charleston. He told me about his first year at MIT, and how he worked really hard to fit in. I shared the struggles I had being one of the few girls at Caltech.

"Lainie, you are the first girl I've been able to sit and have a conversation with, which didn't involve some reality TV star." He made me laugh, and forget the panic which would creep up on me every once in awhile. He even told me these incredibly stupid jokes, I couldn't help but laugh at.

"You think you had it bad growing up? I was a computer geek who played chess."

"Wait, you play chess?" I watched his face fall, as if he hadn't meant to say anything. I instantly felt bad for causing the smile to leave his face. "I once tried to learn how to play, but I couldn't find anybody else who knew how." It wasn't a lie, when I was little we had gone to a thrift store for summer clothes. On the counter was this really cool chess set; the players were Civil War soldiers. I must have looked at that set for an hour before Momma dragged me away. I found a book on how to play, but no one would play with me.

"Well, I have an amazing set at my office. Anytime you want to learn, you come on by."

As we were about to order desert, Heidi called to say she was on the way. So he paid the check, and drove me back to my office. "I'd like to take you out again. I have a meeting with my brother tomorrow, but if you can…Will you stop by the shop after work?"

I would ask if Claire wanted to come with me, and bring Heidi along, so she could meet my family I'd found here.

"It's a date."

Chapter Nine

Austin

Only three things can lighten up a victim's feelings,
justice, revenge, or justice
- *Bradley B Delania*

"Carson said he would be a little late. He got some news about his retirement. I have a feeling it ain't good."

I loved coming to the shop. It reminded me of the time we spent hanging out with granddaddy, covered in dirt and grease, learning about how life really was. We were free to say what we wanted, no question was too bold, or subject off limits. It was like our own secret society. Held together by honesty, and blood. As I drove home last night, I caught myself wondering what Granddaddy would think of Lainie.

"Find a girl who is willing to cook your supper, clean your castle,

and straighten your short hairs."

I knew the majority of his words of wisdom, or granddaddy-isms, as Chase cloned them. Gave us advice our young minds could understand, while having the guy humor we all enjoyed, and remembered. I had no idea if Lainie knew how to cook, and honestly, I didn't care. When a girl can sit at a table across from you, dive into a rare hamburger, stacked high with all the fixings, and then wash it down with an ice cold beer, she pretty much secured herself a place on my list.

I couldn't help but watch her. Her hazel eyes, which seemed to sparkle with excitement, as she told me of graduating at the top of her class from Caltech. How her fingernails were painted with that white line at the top, clean, and well kempt. Her clothing professional. No tight fitting blouses, with her tits about to come falling out. While I appreciated a woman who can dress sexy, sometimes the illusion is better than being stripper pole ready. And while her smile was electric and body perfectly curvaceous, it was her incredible legs which hooked it for me. Long and slender, glistening from healthy skin, and proper grooming. When she excused herself to visit the ladies room, I imprinted every step she took into my memory. Appreciating the definition her workouts had created, and smiling at the way her heeled shoes accentuated her ass.

She was busy with Heidi today. Sending me only a few texts, and a picture of them on what looked to be someone's bed. Where Lainie fashioned after the 'girl next door' look, Heidi subscribed to the 'pure and natural'. Where Lainie wore freckles dancing across her nose, kissed by the sun as she enjoyed the outdoors. Heidi looked more like the older of the two, pale and tired, with scars from a hard life.

They had plans of visiting the campus today, buying Heidi the books she would need for her classes. I offered to come with them. To keep her mind off the library and the shadows, which haunted her. She declined my offer. As Claire and Momma were going with her, making a day out of it, with a trip to the mall and salon. If I knew Priscilla Morgan, the mall would turn into the shops she enjoyed, and the salon was exclusive to a select clientele here in Charleston. Momma prided herself on being an original. No measuring up to the magazine covers she skimmed through, as she killed time. I'd called ahead of time. Sure enough, Mrs. Morgan had the afternoon reserved with three guests joining her. I left my credit card, with instructions to take care of Lainie's and Heidi's expenses.

"Austin!"

Hearing my name being called, snapped me from the memory of Lainie, and the sight of her waving goodbye, as she drove off to the airport.

"Huh?"

"Did you hear anything I just said?"

I wiped the oil from my hands with the shop rag. My mind had wandered away from Dylan talking about Carson, and his retirement. "Yes, you said Carson was gonna be late."

Dylan shook his head, chuckling silently. "That was fifteen minutes ago." He tossed the rag in his hands at me. "You want to pay attention before you do some damage to that thing."

I glanced down at the oil, which now sat in a puddle on the floor. The screw still sat where I'd placed it on the lift. My mind was so preoccupied, I forgot to replace the screw. Now that I was back home, I had made a promise to myself to take my bike out as often as possible. As I tightened the screw carefully, a thought hit me.

"Hey, Dylan, does our paint guy do helmets?"

Dylan flashed his eyes in my direction, as he continued to work on the custom job. "He does. You thinking of getting somethin' new?"

I wanted to share pieces of my world with Lainie. Not just dinner, and the occasional movie. I wanted her on the back of my bike, wrapped around me, as I drove us down the highway. Along the back roads, while we lost ourselves. I wanted to cook dinner with her, as we laughed and shared stories of our day. Sit with her on my lap, as we competed for control of the keyboard, and see what kind of code she was capable of writing. For the first time in my adult life, I wanted to have a conversation, using big words I didn't have to define. To have someone who could take care of me, as I took care of them. And I wanted that someone to be Lainie.

"Yeah, I want to get somethin' new."

"Sorry to interrupt."

Audrey, the new receptionist Dylan hired, stood shyly in the office door frame. Dylan said she'd taken to the job like a fish to water, organizing the old files, and learning the computer system I created for us. He even raved about the coffee she managed to make come out of the old coffee maker she found in the back.

Audrey Helms, another southern born girl, who had been wronged by the men in her life. I hadn't shared with Dylan or Chase everything I had discovered from the background check I did on Audrey. While she worked hard to provide for herself, she also struggled with a few bills, which had recently gone into default.

Lucas Campbell, the name on the loans Audrey co-signed, was bad news. Records showed he was married to an Amy Campbell. A high school dropout from Biloxi, Mississippi. Amy wasn't much better in the character department. Three arrests in the past year, ranging from petty theft, to aggravated assault. Jail must have been a turn on for these two. Given their quickie courthouse marriage, was the same day they were both released from a Savannah jail five years ago.

Lucas had purchased a mobile home and a new truck, totaling just over one hundred thousand dollars. He never paid a dime on either one, and now the loan was in default. He had a list of priors including domestic violence, and not surprisingly, forgery. My guess is Miss Audrey never signed the loan papers. Maybe he took his wife to sign, with his girlfriend's credit, to seal the deal. While I'd never seen any marks on Audrey, I questioned if he strong-armed her at home.

One summer Momma took us to work on a campground in North Carolina. We were raised with the belief that while you can talk about the wrong which happens in the world, you can't complain until you do something about it. Daddy had been contacted by his branch office in Charlotte, asking for help with a shelter they had come across.

Our family went to do whatever we could to help. While we fixed a bad roof, and replaced several old pipes, what we took away was an experience I will never forget. Our last night there, Dylan and I were sitting beside the campfire, tossing in scraps of twigs and bark. He asked me if I'd seen the sign which hung in the meal hall? I hadn't, so he showed me where it was. *What you allow, is what will continue.* Reading those words changed the way I looked at the women around me. It solidified for Dylan his need to be a cop, and ultimately form this underground system we had.

Audrey came to us eager to please, with a low value of herself, and the weight of her world displayed on her shoulders. She came early every day, and stayed until the last possible moment at night. Her lunch consisted of a few crackers with either butter or jelly between them. A few days ago, I came by the shop on a Sunday afternoon to do some work on my bike. Audrey was in the bathroom, and nearly jumped out of her skin when I said hello to her.

Since then, she has been skittish, fumbling over her words, and apologizing for everything. We've told her a dozen times she can wear jeans and the company t-shirt. But every day she comes in with a long black sweater and skirt, which reaches her ankles.

"The boxes that were delivered for Mr. Chase have been put in s-storage." Her fingers were knotted in the fabric of her skirt, and her hair was falling into her face, shielding her eyes from us. "Except for...e-except for the long box that I unpacked, and hung the guitar on the wall."

Glancing over her shoulder, I could see his most prized possession on the wall. When Granddaddy gave it to him, Momma wanted to get a glass case for it. But Daddy told her a guitar was meant to be played and enjoyed, not stuck behind glass just because someone famous wrote on it.

Chase had all of his stuff sent here to the shop. Audrey had cleaned out the area above us, suggesting to Dylan he could rent the place out as an apartment. We all agreed it would be better used as storage, and a temporary bed, if we ever pissed our girls off too much.

Chase had made Momma cry when he told us he was done with the military. Since his announcements, I had been sending him several apartment listings in the area. I cringed when he mentioned having Harmony live with him.

"Miss Audrey, do you like Chinese food?" If what I suspected was true, she was using every dime she made to pay that cocksuckers bills. Leaving no money to buy food, or anything else. If Lucas was still claiming to be her boyfriend, he was failing miserably at taking care of her.

"Yes, Sir."

Dylan looked at me with a puzzled gaze. Surely he had noticed how thin she was, and how little she ate, if she ate at all.

"Good, cause I am craving some shrimp fried rice. Can you please take some money out of petty cash, head two blocks over to Mr. Wong's, and get us all some dinner?"

Dropping her head again, she started to turn around. "Miss Audrey?"

She stopped with a jerk, as if she had been electrocuted. She lowered her head, and turned back around. Dylan rose up from the floor, he too had noticed her reaction.

"Y-yes, Sir?"

"Audrey, take enough to order yourself a hearty dinner. Not just an egg roll and a drink. I wanna see a full box on your desk, and a fork delivering food to your mouth." Dylan and I both watched as she took a deep breath. No doubt the gears in her mind completely confused at the different way she was being treated here, as opposed to the way she must suffer at home.

"But…"

"No buts. If our Momma found out we didn't take care of you, she would make us find a switch from the tree out back."

Audrey had experienced a small dose of Priscilla Morgan. According to Dylan, she came by the shop one morning to find Audrey on her hands and knees, scrubbing the back room floor, so she could put Chase's boxes in there. She had accidentally managed to spill a bottle of gear grease when she was moving things around. Momma went off on Dylan for not having first helped Audrey move the heavy box, and second, for not having nicer supplies on hand for Audrey to use. Just like everyone who has encountered the woman in full form, Audrey straightened her back, and headed out the front door.

"Somethin' we need to talk about?" Dylan's brow furrowed, crossing his arms against his chest.

"The list is long." Shaking my head, I made sure Audrey was inside her car, and out of earshot. "I can't say for sure, but that girl is hiding from something, or someone."

Dylan cast me a look, pulling the stool from behind the lift. "Such as?"

"Such as, she's working to pay for the boyfriend's toys, while he is married to somebody else. You can't possibly look at her, and not have questions."

Dylan glanced over his shoulder, wheeled the chair over to the fridge. "I noticed. I suspected the first night I met her. She was scared of her own shadow." Pulling two beers from the fridge, the light from the inside illuminated the anger on his face. "My arrogant ass assumed it was because she wanted to ride my dick." He twisted the cap off his bottle, sliding the second in my direction. "I've seen the boyfriend, drives a lifted, newer Silverado. He came by the shop one morning, demanding money from her. I stepped in to make sure everything was all right. He took the money, and peeled out of here."

Dylan's phone vibrated in his pocket. By the smile on his face, I assumed it was Claire. By the shaking of his head as he read the screen, I knew it was. "You waste no time do you, Austin? Haven't known the girl more than a minute, and you're already taking care of her."

We had the same upbringing, the same core values, so I wasn't sure what his issue was. "Why wouldn't I? You take care of Claire, Daddy takes care of Momma, and I take care of Lainie. I'm sorry to say, Chase is taking care of that bitch Harmony." Even saying her name made my skin itch. She was rotten to the fucking core. I just had to prove it and open Chase's eyes to the shit she was pulling.

"Well, for one, I love Claire. Daddy is married to Momma, and Chase, well, he's an idiot. Lainie is a girl you met a week ago, or has something happened I don't know about?"

There was no denying the smile the thought of her brought to my face, or the feeling I got in my chest when he said her name. While I didn't love her, I cared a great deal for her. "Lainie is my girl. I won't label her as my 'girlfriend' because we aren't in the seventh grade. But I've canceled every date I had planned, so I could spend my free time with her. I've told her how I feel, and we are dating. Not that you didn't already know all of that because you gossip like an old woman, since you've gone and gotten yourself a girl."

Dylan laughed so hard he nearly fell off the stool he was rolling around on. We tapped bottlenecks, as Dylan made a toast.

"To the beautiful ladies who stole our hearts. May God have mercy on their souls."

Audrey returned a short while later, three bags of food in her tiny hands. Dylan fussed with her for half a second, as he took the load from her. "Next time call us when you're pulling up, and we'll come out and help you." Defeat was immediately written all over her face. Dylan, the dumb ass, didn't always consider not everyone was used to his crassness.

With the poor girl trembling so bad her hair was moving, I tossed Dylan a look, then moved in for damage control. "Darlin', pay him no mind. Our Momma dropped him on his head one too many times. I never meant for you to carry all this by yourself. Next time we'll come out and help you. Just send us a text or call, okay?"

Dylan handed her an open beer, then gave her a side hug, adding a simple kiss to her temple. For the first time ever, I watched as the skin on her cheeks pinked, and a smile graced her lips. This girl owned a beautiful smile. Too bad there was no one to give her reason to keep it alive.

When Audrey finished her dinner, we loaded her car with leftovers. As we watched her drive away, Dylan pulled out his phone, pressed a few buttons, and then slid it back into his pocket.

With my eyes still fixed down the dark street, "Do I want to know what that was about?"

Dylan turned to walk back up the drive. "Just a tip to a cop friend of mine. I just remembered where he can find a guy with an open warrant."

Carson came in twenty minutes later with a case of beer, and a worry line you could park a truck in.

"What's wrong? They close the Dunkin' Donuts on your beat?" Dylan faked a dive to avoid the slap he assumed Carson was about to deliver. When none came, he set the beer on the top shelf, closing the door without getting any beer.

"I wish it was that fucking simple." Dylan kicked a chair in his direction, as he took the rolling chair to his left. "Georgia had a letter waiting for me when I got home. The investment company our broker used, has mysteriously lost my retirement money."

I hated hearing this; bad investments made by inexperienced brokers. Now the man had only his pension to retire on. "Aren't those types of services insured?"

Leave it to my ass of a brother to know nothing about investments.

"No, I mean the account has been wiped clean. There's no trace of the money ever existing." My interest was piqued. Carson's face was red with rage, as Dylan reached in for a cold beer. "I called the company. They insist they have never had an account with me. They also said there is no way anyone could tamper with the system, as the passwords change every day." He twisted off the cap, his face contorting with the force he used. "Without that money, I'll be working until I'm eighty." He tossed back the bottle, emptying over half in one gulp. Carson was family, and Morgan's take care of our own.

"Come by my office in the morning. Bring any account numbers; pay stubs, anything you can think of, so I can start digging up a trail. It's impossible for money, letters, anything to disappear from the internet, without leaving tracks to follow. It might take me a little while, but I will find your money. You have my word." I closed my hand around Carson's shoulder, squeezing him just like I would one of my brothers.

"We need to get the details of the Frank Benson case ironed out." Dylan reached into his pocket, pointed his cell phone at a monitor, and brought the screen to life. "Preston has the divorce papers ready to be signed. Austin has arranged for all the money in his accounts to transfer to Francine's name, and I have cleaned out the pole barn on my property. According to the weatherman, this weekend will be perfect weather for hog boilin'. Now, according to Francine, he has a business trip scheduled for Thursday through Monday. Austin looked up his tickets, which are actually first class to Jamaica." Each point shown across the screen, I stood in wonderment watching my brother in the role he was destined to live. It was so hard for me to recall the ass of a man he was just months ago. Now, he's passionate about what he is doing, has a girl he loves, and looks so damned happy.

Our plan was simple. On Thursday, I would pick him up in a town car we'd rented. Carson would be in the back seat waiting to have a come to Jesus meeting. We would take him out to Dylan's property, and return to him the level of pain he has inflicted on his wife all these years. Francine didn't want him dead, but the man was certainly going to pray for it.

"I'll let Claire know I'm doing a parts run. She'll know to keep Lainie busy. Miss Georgia is going to be out of town with Francine at a spa. Anything else?"

Each of us looked at the other. When no one had anything to say, I took it as my cue to start.

"Actually, I have something I need to show you guys. It's about Harmony."

Chapter Ten

Lainie

Life begins at the end of your comfort zone
- Neale Donald Walsch

B eing called into the boss' office before you even put your purse down is never a good sign. Even though I knew I had done nothing wrong, I couldn't ignore the feeling of dread, as it coursed through my chest. Jackie Craven had worked hard after her father died. Taking the community college education she had under her belt, and continuing on where her father left off. Being a woman in the computer software field is tough enough, owning the company, near impossible.

"You wanted to see me?" I knocked softly on her open door. Jackie's head was down, her focus on the papers littering her desk. Where most executives had top of the line furniture and a corner office, Jackie was completely old school. With a desk her father got at an auction, and an office she shared with her assistant.

"Hey, good morning, yes, I did want to see you. Come in, and close the door." Her tone told me what my mind already knew, the issue wasn't with me. When I first took the job as designer, I had received a lot of flak from some of the guys on the team. But just like Griffin Powell, and his tiny snake, I gave those boys a taste of what I was capable of.

Jackie leaned back in her chair, her hands folded, with her fingers locked around themselves. "Lainie, tell me what you know about Kennedy Fraser?"

Memories of college classes spent listening to him brag about a girl he fucked the night before, and sometimes, the minute before class. The numerous projects where he'd paid some broke kid to do the work. But my favorite had been the underage girl who'd fumbled into one of his parties, only to return four months later with a positive pregnancy test, and an irate father.

"The man on paper, or the man I tolerated for four years?" I wasn't willing to risk my job, or reputation; on the chance she was his current fuck buddy. This business could be cutthroat, with near constant competition for the next best thing.

"Maybe I should tell you why I need to know. Save you time on what to leave out, and what is important for me to hear." She adjusted her position, with hands on her desk, and green eyes locked with mine. Jackie was a pretty girl with her cinnamon hair, and tanned skin. A curvy woman, but not obese by any measure.

"A little over a month ago, Frasier Global had all of its assets frozen by the Federal Trade Commission. Their CEO, was arrested for insider trading with his parent company; a pharmaceutical company which was about to release a new antidepressant." I would have given anything to see Kennedy hauled off to jail, crying like the punk ass bitch he is.

"Lucky for us, I have a very good friend who let me know the company was being sold for an insanely low price. With the clients they carry, purchasing the company was never in question. While I've agreed to keep the majority of the staff on, I've received an email from Kennedy, who would like to keep his job as well. So, tell me, what do you know about the Frasers?" Jackie returned to her prior relaxed position. With no qualms about the truth insulting her, I began my tale.

"Well, let's start with his family. Especially since you get your moral compass from the ones you call family. The eldest brother, Simon I believe, used his looks, and apparent big dick, to ensnare the wife of a competing company, Adams Lighthouse, until the founder's death. At which time he assumed on the role of CEO, and from what I hear, just lost his top coder." Jackie's eyes become saucer in size, and her mouth opened with a gasp. However, her brow quickly rose, and she tossed out a question, interrupting my train of thought.

"Where did you hear this, Facebook?"

"No, I happen to know Austin Morgan personally. He has opened his own business right here in Charleston. Although, I don't think he is writing code."

"Wait, you say you know Austin? But you don't know if he is still writing code? How good a friend is he?"

I thought of Austin, and his quiet smile. The one I tell myself is reserved for me. He has this cute little wrinkle in the middle of his bottom lip, begging me to touch it with my tongue. I enjoy the way his hand feels against the edge of my hand, respecting my need for space. "Pull up the security camera from earlier in the week, you will see us in the lobby of the building."

With three clicks of her mouse, and several flicks side to side with her eyes, she scans the scene on the monitor before her, "Good God, he's hot! Is he single?"

In poker, you never reveal your hand. Avoiding any twitches or bouncing of your leg, which could give away your cards. I've never been good at games, or keeping my face emotionless. Well, except for the whole resting bitch face. I'm an expert at that one.

Austin had made his feelings quite clear. He wanted to be much more than a friend, and while he maintained restraint in the restaurant and the car ride to and from, he'd presented himself as a man with intent. Friday, when we had our plans hijacked by the take no prisoners, Priscilla Morgan, I discovered just how serious his intentions were.

While Claire and Dylan had tiptoed around the inevitable, Austin had sent out what in his mind, was a clear sign she was his. Too bad for Dylan, his attempted Bat-signal was used on someone who was in no position to be saved. In my case, however, since I'd grown up with a momma who used men to their fullest, I was able to decipher the unspoken words most men understood. When Austin's momma stepped in, I sat back and let it happen. I said my please and thank you's, not because I wanted to use Austin or his momma, but by refusing their generosity, I would have insulted them. An act you never do with a southern woman, or the man you have decided to take a chance on.

"He is seeing someone. A girl his momma has already met." Meeting the parents, at least in the majority of southern families, is a big step. Men can and do have their fill of girls they enjoy for a time, and then move on to the next. However, once they introduce them to Momma, the game changes. Granted, I'd met Priscilla before I met Austin. But Jackie was in the dark as to the fact that someone, was me, and the circumstances around the meeting of said momma.

"Figures, men who look that good don't stay single long." Jackie spoke the truth, especially when we are talking about the Morgan men. Every one of them was built like the cover model of a bestselling romance. I'd watched first hand, as Austin had pushed up the sleeve of his shirt, granting me a glimpse of the hard work he did in the gym.

"Anyway, once Lighthouse lost their top earner, I heard they went looking for some new blood. Someone who could finish what Austin had started."

"The Titan Project?"

"Yes," I affirmed.

"Rumors have circulated for a while the project was being abandoned. With the security risks involved, it would be near impossible to get a buyer." Jackie scoffed. Like most people who had no hand in the invention, having the need to make themselves feel better.

"Who told you this?"

"Kennedy Frasier, actually. Lighthouse came to them around the same time the Trade Commission began snooping around."

"Of course he did. Kennedy knows Lighthouse is scrambling since they're down the original writer for the program. Why buy today for a few million, when you can get it next week for a few grand? Austin would have signed a non-compete, which by industry standards is six months. After which time, Kennedy thinks he will be looking for work. Why not offer a man who may be down to his last penny a life ring? Hire him for a little more than he made previously, buy the program for a song, and BAM! You've become king of the hill."

Jackie sat back in her chair. A look of disbelief all over her face. Was she more surprised I knew so much, or I knew the game Kennedy was playing? "Too bad for Kennedy his plan went up in smoke when his company was sold off, and the original writer isn't hurting for money. Not for a long time, if ever. Since Kennedy is never one to give up, and he has no idea Austin started his own company, he is going with plan B."

"Which involves coming to work for me?"

"If that's what he wants to call it. Plan B is to come here, get the program, and the writer in the same day. Then he is the golden boy once again. Able to sit back, and order people around, like he has his entire life."

Jackie looks bewildered when I'm finished, and I'm not sure she believes me. If Kennedy were to come work for her, it would leave me in a position to possibly seek employment elsewhere. Which would put a rather huge damper on my life here in Charleston.

"I'll be heading to California tomorrow to meet with the employees who are remaining with the company, including Kennedy. I need you to keep things running around here. Which is why I'm promoting you to Director."

There is no way I've heard her correctly. Receiving two promotions in less than six months is almost unheard of.

"This isn't going to be easy for you. Just beyond that door is a stack of hungry managers, who think they have big enough balls to run this company. Even if I tell them to follow you, at least half of them are going to fight you, go against everything you say. I'm going to need the girl who graduated at the top of her class, stood up to the big boys at Caltech, and showed them what she is made of."

If it wouldn't have made me look like a three year old, I would have jumped across the desk, and hugged her. Jackie was a woman of action, not promises which would be forgotten before the sun set.

"I've never been afraid of the bullies on the playground. I learned a long time ago they're mostly talk, with very little action."

"That, right there, is why I chose to hire you the day you first interviewed. And my decision to appoint you Director was made the second my offer was accepted to purchase Frasier Global. Now get out there, and get to work."

Rising from my chair, the elation bubbling like Mount Vesuvius about to erupt. I'd worked hard to get to this point. Beaten the odds of my white trash upbringing.

"Oh, and one more thing." I glanced back at her over my shoulder, struggling to keep my smile in check. "Tell your boyfriend if he ever wants a job, he can come talk to me. I'd hire him in a second."

Stupid lack of a poker face.

"Fucking voice mail."

Jackie was right. When the announcement came out I had been chosen for the spot, a lot of grumbling could be heard. Being seasoned in ignoring the bitching of men around me, I made it clear I would continue to run things as Jackie requested. When we broke for lunch, I tried to call Austin to share my good news.

He had mentioned he was going to be hanging out with Dylan today, but I didn't think that included turning off his phone. I found my sister sitting surrounded by textbooks, and her new laptop, engrossed in her studies. Refusing to disrupt her, I headed to my bedroom, and quietly closed the door.

"Hey, stranger."

I took a chance I was catching Claire at a good time, not certain when she would have a break at work. I had to tell somebody the good news, with Austin still not answering, I was out of options.

"Hey, Bestie." I tried to curb my excitement, which was an incredible feat at this point. I had this overwhelming desire to jump up on the tallest building, and shout to anyone who can hear how I did it. I'd jumped into the big boys club, and kicked some serious ass.

"I'm not disturbing anything am I?" Last thing I wanted to do was to disturb her during sexy time with Dylan.

"Not at all. I just got home from work, and Dylan is on a parts run. So I have a free night." Hold the phone, if Dylan was on a parts run, then where's Austin? "Parts run, what's that?" A large part of me slipped into the place where so many have gone before. Where rational thoughts are forbidden, when fear and doubt are greeting you at the door. Rooms full of smoke and mirrors, allowing our deepest fears to become real.

"Oh…um…" Her hesitation shattered the last remaining barrier, making my heart pound in my chest, and my throat feel as if it were swollen shut. "See, Dylan is really picky about who he has make parts for him to use on his bikes. With this new contract, he's been going up, and supervising the build of the newest part." While I was a terrible poker player, Claire was an even worse liar. But why? What could have possibly happened in a week, which would give her the need to lie to me?

"How far away is this shop? I mean, to be away overnight seems a little extreme." Maybe it's a character flaw, but I have this incessant need to dig and dig, until I unearth the truth. Especially if I know the person is lying.

"Not really, the part is complex, and time consuming. Why risk having an accident, if you can crash in a hotel room and be safe?"

"Makes sense I guess, but why drag Austin with him? Seems like he would be capable of supervising by himself." *Unless that isn't where they really went…*

"You forget, Austin owns thirty three percent of the business. He's in the shop almost daily working alongside Dylan. Why wouldn't he tag along for some guy time?"

"I guess you're right. I've never really been around the caliber of man the Morgan's are."

"Lainie, you have nothing to worry about when it comes to Austin. The man is completely nuts for you."

Easy for her to say, she was in on the deception.

Chapter Eleven

Austin

Pain makes you stronger. Fear makes you braver. Heartbreak makes you wiser. So thank your past for your brighter future.

"It's still lying."

"No, it's not. I will be in the same fucking room with you."

"It's semantics. Which is still a fucking lie!"

"If it is bugging you that fucking much, call her up, and tell her the whole truth. Or stay the fuck home, and Carson and I will handle it."

Some would argue the choice I had made to join with my brothers, dealing with the career criminal, wife beaters, and general scum of the earth, automatically placed me in a position where having a relationship was too selfish. Being a martyr came with the uniform of loner, absence of a companion, while roaming the planet in search of justice. It sounded more like the script from one of those comics they've made into a movie lately.

Having the desire to do the right thing isn't a curse, but neither is finding the person who makes you happy. They're the reminders of why you continue to take the ones who care so little for human life outside of their own, and make the world a safer place.

Dylan was correct. I didn't actually tell Lainie a lie. I told her I would be hanging out with Dylan, while he finished a project. Which was completely true. This was Dylan's project, and although my role was quite small, I wasn't one hundred percent certain I could trust Lainie with the truth. I couldn't take the chance she was one of those people who would look at what we were about to do as a crime, rather than a form of justice it was meant to be.

"How did you tell Claire?"

Dylan stopped folding the rope we would use to suspend Frank from the beams of the barn. "Claire was the driving force behind my decision to do this. Watching her kicking that fuck in the face, releasing the fear she had inside, made me want to keep it away." His normally blue eyes were alive with a passion and fire, I had never seen in him. Even when he'd solved his first case as a detective, he didn't show this much emotion.

"What I didn't count on was Claire being so fucking smart." He pointed his finger in my direction, as he picked up the rope with his free hand, winding up the tangled mess. "Which sucks for you because Lainie is not only smart as fuck, she knows how to get around the internet, just like you."

I wasn't worried about the internet. While Lainie is smart, I've seen her work. She's good at designing and making clients happy with dancing webpages, but she has never created a firewall or attempted to navigate a wormhole. I'd covered my tracks well, so even the most advanced hacker couldn't figure out how to follow me.

"You don't have to worry about her discovering me like that. I know she did a search on me, she found what I wanted her and everyone else to find." Dylan shook his head, but didn't meet my eyes. I knew my brother, and the silence he used to ponder what I'd said, before choosing his words carefully. After the last piece of the rope was secured, he placed it in the back of my truck, his hands on the tailgate.

"Right now things are new with Lainie. She's still dealing with her demons, courtesy of that dirt bag criminal who you helped send to hell. You may not have known her at the time, but you saved her, and you will continue to go out when the occasion arises to save someone else's Lainie. Not because you want to, but because that girl's name is already tattooed around the skin of your heart." Dylan has never been a profound speaker, with his normal use of the word fuck limiting his vocabulary. Clearly Claire had awoken more than just his callused heart, but also his sense of loyalty and valor.

"Sometimes we have to break a few rules, and leave out a few truths, to keep the ones who live in here sleeping soundly at night." He tapped his chest over his heart, as he ended his sentence. My brother has always been the protector. From the first day we entered each other lives, he had taken on the role.

"Don't wait too long to trust her. Girls like Claire and Lainie," he shook his head as a smile of longing appeared on his face, "Well they don't come by very often."

Men are simple creatures really. Give us something to drink, something naked to look at, and we're happy. Do both at the same time, and we will do anything you ask of us. Using this principle, getting Frank Benson in the back of the town car, and keeping him there was easy.

Slipping his regular driver a few hundred dollars to get in the back of a van with a naked girl happened in a matter of seconds. Too bad the girl was a member of Vice, and he was now on his way to county jail for solicitation.

Frank came out of his South of Battery home, with his briefcase in one hand, and his cell phone in the other. Like the fuck stick he is, he didn't even glance at his driver, as he slid into the car. They were well around the first corner, before he realized a masked man was sitting in the car with him.

Carson may be over fifty, but the fucker can move. He had Frank tied up like a hog off to the slaughterhouse, before they made it to the next block. With a ball gag in his mouth, and hands and feet tied behind him, Carson smacked his ass, as the fucker pissed his pants.

"What's this? We heard you liked it rough." Frank closed his eyes tight, as the tears began to roll.

When Granddaddy died, he divided up the land he owned in northern Georgia between us. Nearly one hundred acres of hunting land we used almost every year when we were little. Daddy even had a little cabin and barn built on it, and since Dylan still went hunting in the fall, he got the section with the buildings. Once we switched cars, placing Frank in the back of Dylan's truck, we headed for the Georgia border.

"You gonna be all right with this one?" Carson asked, looking at my face for any sign of hesitancy.

I was wondering when he would ask me this. Reading Franny Benson's diary had indeed stirred up some old memories. Although my memories were just still shots of moments from my past. I had contacted a private detective, who was able to dig up information on my biological mother. Veronica Porter, the middle child of six girls, not a single one of them having the same father. Ronnie, as she was known on the streets, started turning tricks when she was fourteen. Becoming pregnant with me a year later, and refusing to give me up or get an abortion, she kept on doing the only thing she knew.

Ronnie fell in love with a man by the name of Teddy. A big old guy, who her pimp hired to watch over his property. Trouble was, Teddy was also a meth head. While he was busy getting high, a guy Ronnie was giving a blowjob to, didn't feel like paying her. Instead of just leaving the room, he pulled out a knife, and stabbed her fifteen times. He never noticed me curled up with my blanket in the bathtub.

"More fuel for the fire man, more fuel for the fire."

Dylan had pulled his four wheelers out of the barn, allowing more than enough room to pull his truck in, where no one could see what was going on. While we were in the middle of nowhere, we were also still in the south. People around here looked out for strange things going on, and since deer season wasn't for another few months, there was no real reason for us to be around.

Carson jumped in the back, as I shut the barn doors. The smell of human shit and piss hit me, as I too jumped in the back of the truck. When we loaded him in the bed, we covered him with an old tarp. Dylan stayed within the speed limit, and we had no reason to stop.

Dylan turned on the propane gas for the hog pot. A large brick enclosed cast iron pot, in the corner of the room. Granddaddy loved to hunt wild boar, so he had one custom built. With a cherry picker winch to hold the massive boars we had seen, while hunting for deer.

Carson tossed Frank out of the truck. He landed with a thump on the dusty floor. Dylan took the knife Chase had given him a few years back. Some SEAL issued thing a buddy in Afghanistan got for him, and cut the soiled clothing from his body, leaving him bound and gagged. "*Treat him as he treated me,*" was Franny's only request.

With the fire roaring, bringing the water to a scalding hot rolling boil, Dylan came over with the pulley he had attached to the highest beam in the barn. Securing the rope, which wrapped around Franks ankles, Dylan hoisted the fat fuck upside down into the air.

Carson and Dylan each took a machete from the wall of the barn. Sitting on a small milking stool, Dylan pulled out Franny's diary, and opened the first page.

"Frank Benson, you stand accused of mental and physical abuse of your family. How do you plead?"

Frank started jerking, and mumbling around the ball gag. Wanting to give the man a voice in all of this, I walked over, and removed the device.

"I have money!" He began shouting. "Lots of money. Tell me how much you want, and it's yours, just don't kill me." He begged, like the bully on the playground who pushed the wrong kid. Now he was sorry, a moment too late.

"We ain't gonna kill ya." Dylan taunted. Slapping his open palm with the side of the blade. "But you're gonna wish we would have." Making his point obvious, he runs the blade from just below his pelvis to the middle of his stomach, bright, red blood streams down his body, as his cries fill the air.

"Frank, do you know what this is?" Dylan waved the diary back and forth in under his face.

"No." Frank shakes his head back and forth, sweat and spot glistening on his face.

"This is the diary of a woman, who for the past twenty plus years, has suffered at the hands of the man who swore to love her." He made another slice parallel to the first. Frank's body shaking with a combination of fear and pain, bouncing from the movement of the blade.

"I've read this diary from cover to cover, several times over the past few weeks. And let me tell you," another slash, another scream.

"The more I read, the angrier I get." This time he grabbed a sock, with what I suspected had a rock or a bar of soap inside, using it like a whip to lash across his legs. He will bruise internally. A trick Dylan learned from tryouts for quarterback in high school.

"Seventy two times she went to the hospital for stitches. One hundred and six times she suffered a bloody nose at your hands. Seven times she has been treated for gonorrhea. I lost count of how many times she was chained to the bed at night, or the broken bones she's suffered because of you."

Carson had waited patiently, as Dylan read off his crimes. The water had started to boil over in the corner, so he motioned for Carson to get some of it. "With all the abuse you gave her, all the times you laid a hand on her, which didn't make her feel like a lady, nothing struck me more than the time you turned up the hot water in the shower, and held her head under. Sending her to the hospital with second degree burns."

Carson returned with a pole in his hand, a steaming towel wrapped around the end. "Let's see how you like it?" Frank passed out from the pain he felt, as Carson laid the boiling hot towel across his dick and balls.

By the time the sun came up, Frank had signed the divorce papers, agreeing to all of Franny's terms, and was returned to an apartment she had rented for him to live in. None of his cuts required stitches, his burns were no worse than too long in the sun, but the memory of the pain would last a lifetime.

After Dylan dropped me off at my office, I wasn't ready to tackle the next file on my desk quite yet. I climbed the steps to the roof top, a cup of coffee in my hand. Standing on the gravel cover, my view of the bridge unobscured. It seemed like a life time ago I'd thought of this view, and how much I missed it. Now I could stand here in the South Carolina sun, fresh air across my face, surrounded by family and a girl who deserved to be treated like a piece of fine china.

Pulling my phone from my pocket, I knew she would just be getting up. But I had to talk with her, apologize for not being honest with her. I could feel the dread fill me, as my phone vibrated to life. The screen read Dylan, and I knew instantly this was going to be bad.

"Hey, got a call from the Silver Dollar Pawn Shop. Guess who tried to sell a diamond ring?"

Chapter Twelve

Lainie

If there comes a time in your life when you've taken one step forward and two steps back, take one huge lunge forward, so you're four steps ahead, and don't let anything let you take that step back.
- Unknown

"You've been in town for a minute, and you already have a friend?" I teased my sister. The once shy girl who'd questioned if going back to school was the right thing to do. It took some words one of my professors gave to me to bring the smile and hidden confidence back. *"Education is the one thing no one can take away from you."*

"I have several friends, but Ginger is the one who I get along with the most. She has this really great boyfriend who is always buying her stuff, paying her bills, and driving her around." Heidi wore the spark in her eyes. The one responsible for the demise of many a great woman, too trusting for their own good.

Maybe I worried too much, imagining her jumping from one bad situation to another, each one worse than the previous. I feared the worst, as it was all she really knew, the only way she had ever learned. While I can't be a mother to an adult woman, it doesn't stop me from wanting to protect her from the harshness in life. Like a toddler, curious about the hot stove, I wanted to keep her from experiencing any unnecessary pain.

"I know that look, Lainie, and I'm not stupid."

She's right, she isn't stupid. But, she is naïve, and far too trusting. George had kept her hidden from the real world, showing her only the parts he wanted her to see.

"I know you're not." I walked closer to her. Taking her hair between my fingers, and recalling the glee she had when Priscilla wrapped an arm around her, as we exited the elevator to the salon. The wonderment in her eyes, as she took in the massive chandelier hanging from the ceiling, and floral arrangements welcoming her with their exotic scents.

As children and young teens, we never had the resources to enjoy any time at the salon. Clipping bangs and creating curls happened on the front porch, as the neighbors watched, using dull scissors and dime store setting gel. Living on my own had afforded me the opportunity to patron that particular salon many times. Heidi had lit up the room with her wide expressive eyes and contagious smile. As she was primped and powdered, hair shampooed with professional grade products, and hair colored to look as if the sun had kissed selected strands, erasing the dullness living under George's thumb had created. Gone was the girl who'd stepped off the plane, wearing dull gray, with school marm hair. In her place stood a twenty-three year old college student, with cut hair and stylish clothing. A clean slate to take over the world.

"But as your older, and much wiser sister, it's my job to keep you grounded. Dull the shiny toys men use to try and sway you away from your dreams."

"Lainie, not all men are like that, like some villain out to kidnap me." I would love to place all the ignorance of life on George's shoulders, to chastise him for not allowing her to live. But she is just as much to blame for closing her eyes to the news on the television, or the homeless people she fed in the soup kitchen. While her knowledge of the world is limited, it's not empty.

"You're right again. But it's been my experience to treat them all as if they are lying sacks of shit, until they prove otherwise." For the first time in the conversation, I was speaking to myself, more than I was advising her.

Austin still had not called, and I refused to chase him. Despite what Claire said, I didn't understand why he had so quickly changed his mind about me. Parts run or not, you could take a minute to call or text the girl you claim to have an interest in. Claire and Austin thought I was this computer geek, constantly absorbed in graphics and code. But what I've never shared with either of them, was that the summer I lost my virginity to Justin, was also the time I spent covered in grease and sweat, as he showed me how to change the cylinders on his bike. He had called them jugs, and I'd smacked him good, when I thought he was talking about my chest instead of the part. Surely Austin was familiar with the same reference, using the play on words to his advantage. Lainie Faith Perry may have been born at night, but it wasn't last night.

"Well, I'm not even divorced yet, and trust me, it will be a long while before I even consider bringing a man into my life." She closed her book and collected her notes. She had been using the student center on campus, just because she could. I couldn't fault her. If a man had basically imprisoned me, I would want to get out, and see the world too.

"Ginger is giving me a ride home later. Do you mind if she comes up?"

"I've told you before, this is your home too. Feel free to have friends over, just keep the guy friends to a minimum." I tapped my hip against hers, sending her into a fit of giggles, as she left the house.

With Heidi gone for a few hours, a bottle of wine, and a hot bath were calling my name. My neck and shoulders throbbed from all the recent tension I've allowed in. All unnecessary stress I didn't need, or desire. Maybe by the time the water was cold and the bottom of the bottle was in sight, this week will have magically fast-forwarded. Something told me I had yet to hear the end of Kennedy Fraser. He didn't give up in college, and challenged me at nearly every turn. I seriously doubted he would give up now.

When Heidi first moved in, she had an abundance of free time. She took some of that time, and re-organized my kitchen. Pulling open drawer after drawer, I searched for the key to open my bottle of good dreams. Just as I lay my hand on the silver slice of heaven, the buzzer sounded. It had to be Heidi, as it's not the sound from the security door downstairs.

"Did you forget your key?" I twisted the knob, the corkscrew still in my left hand, and expecting to see my blushing sister on the other side. Instead, with sheepish looks on each of their faces, stood Claire, Austin, and Dylan.

"Nope, never had a key." Claire stepped forward first, kissing my cheek, as she passed. Her face was still shining with the happiness she'd found with Dylan, which don't get me wrong, I'm excited for her. But I'm trying not to be angry with her, as I have no proof or justification for those feelings I had planned to drink away.

Dylan and Austin both wore forced smiles and exhaustion, in copious amounts.

"Mr. Morgan." It's the nicest thing I could say to them. When

I wanted to scream at them about how disgusted I was with these two sacks of shit liars. How even though my dealing with Austin has been in small doses, his betrayal weighed heavily on my heart. I opened the door just a smidgen wider, hoping they could take the hint their welcome had been extinguished. I looked at the wall behind Austin, refusing to meet those blue eyes of deception.

"Lainie, we need to talk with you. Please, just listen, and if you're still mad, we will all leave you alone." Claire's voice was the same as when she was trying to rationalize with Priscilla. Reaching out with her left hand, she asked me to join her on the couch, while Austin and Dylan remained standing near the door.

"When we talked the other day, about where these two had taken off to, I could tell you didn't believe me." I remained still, having agreed to listen to what she had to say. I'd always known Claire to be such a confident person, seeming to always have the right words to say.

"It wasn't that long ago, I stood in the very same shoes you're in now. Angry at what I thought I saw. Avoiding asking any questions, for fear the truth would send me into a place I didn't want to be. Broken in half by a man I felt so foolish for giving that kind of power to." I bit the skin of my bottom lip, afraid to show how the truth of what she was saying was affecting me. I swallowed hard to fight down the tremors in my chest. Scared as hell the pain would trigger tears to form behind my eyes.

Claire rose from her seat, sliding in beside me, and engulfing me in her slender arms. "Do you remember how you felt when the judge sentenced Greyson to such a short time in jail?"

How could I forget? Sitting in that courtroom, listening to all the people I knew having their character examined, as if under a microscope by a poor excuse for a human. Believing for a moment, the judge would see past the deceit and lies coming from Greyson's mouth. Thirty days for stealing away the confidence I'd worked so hard to build for myself. Planting fear inside of me, causing me to be too frightened to walk between two buildings, and for a man to touch me, offering a hand as gentleman often do. Compounding it by meeting a man I could accept simple, kind gestures from, only to find he too has his own brand of deceit.

"I'm sorry to drag this up, however in order to explain what happened—is happening—we need to dig up some old graves." I had no issue talking about what happened, with help from my counselor. I'd been able to dissect the attack, label it into separate files. I've been working on the final stage of putting the entire situation to rest, although what I'd assumed to be the easiest, has actually been the most difficult.

"When the verdict was read aloud, we sat together with our hands clenched, waiting for the Judge to return to the bench saying he was only kidding, and then give Greyson a life sentence." My eyes closed without my permission. My throat seemed to tighten, and panic rose in my chest just, as it had in the days, which followed.

"Want to know what I remember?" Just like the moments spent sitting on that hard bench, anticipating the whole thing was a big joke, she held my hand tightly in hers. "I remember getting a call early one morning from my best friend, demanding I turn on the television."

I had been woken a few hours before from a sound sleep. The first one I'd had in many months. Not by a nightmare or anything like that, but from a strange feeling of calm. Unable to fall back to sleep, I got up, and started doing some work on the computer. Turning the television on for white noise. Calling Claire was done on autopilot, wanting to share the news that my nightmares could stop, the devil had returned to hell.

"The relief was so full in your voice, it caused me to hurry to the television, and marvel at the news the man who had hurt so many, was now dead." Knuckles cracking across the room, reminded me *he* was still here. Remaining silent, as if he has been read his Miranda rights, choosing to keep his guilty words to himself.

"Lainie, I know you felt relief when the news was announced. Who wouldn't?" Her features turned serious. Her reassuring smile fading into something far less pleasant. A warning of bad news on the horizon. "I bet in all the excitement, you never questioned a few details surrounding Greyson's sudden jump off the bridge. Missing information even the police didn't search for." I could feel Austin move closer. My breathing quickening at his nearness. He was the first man to make me feel so incredibly safe, and yet set my heart into a rhythm, which makes me sweat.

"Did you ever ask yourself why the security cameras never showed Greyson walking up the pedestrian path? Or the lack of any cars traveling up the bridge, but none coming down? How the Coast Guard cameras showed the bridge still as a stone? Nothing, not even a piece of lint, falling off the side?"

Claire was wrong, I did question those things, but not enough to release them into reality. I didn't care why he'd died, and as selfish as that sounds, he was brimming with evil and nothing, except for death, would change that.

"And why, if the police knew about this yet had no answers, why would they not open an investigation?"

"Claire, you forget there was a report of a power surge, causing the cameras to fail. My guys were all talking about it. How they had run diagnostic tests on our equipment to rule out any damage to our system."

Austin came into my peripheral vision, his hands in his pockets again, something a few of my guys did when they couldn't find something to do with their fingers. "You've run that path with me. It's over a mile from the parking area, to the center of the bridge. The surge would have lasted a few minutes, tops." First time Claire called me to run with her, she was so excited about the pedestrian path; I told her it was going to kill us both. By the time we'd made it to the cement benches at the halfway point, nearly thirty minutes had passed.

"Lainie, you know computers."

Third year securities class, Professor Logan who owned the cool-as-fuck teacher title, known for showing up in jeans and a band t-shirt, ball cap always on his head, consistently told us; *computers are just like a running engine, it needs a constant fuel source. Take away the juice and it won't work.* Another kid beat me to the punch and asked about battery power, saving the earth with solar energy. *"Dude, it's a computer, not your girlfriend's vibrator. You can use a battery backup, but batteries lose power by the second. Anything over about ten minutes, and your computer will start dropping features, recording ability is most commonly dropped first."* Later that year, he showed us how to break a video feed, when a popular movie featured an override of a government system. *"The issue is breaking a firewall. Once you get past the gatekeeper, you can do anything you want. Most companies have them, some of you may even work as code writers for security companies."*

A cold chill ran down my spine. Having a single malfunction within a company is normal. Multiple events at separate locations, separate organizations; you had a better chance at seeing the two branches of government agreeing on something, than that happening.

Unless…

"You blindfolded the gatekeeper." My accusing words hung in the air like the fog in the morning after a heavy rain. Austin was the only person I knew who could break that many firewalls, and maintain a dummy feed. It was much like juggling knives and bowling balls, while watching a two year old who is reaching for the flames of a roaring fire.

"You fed a dummy to the server, making the system appear to have a surge." My eyes squinted, looking at Austin in confusion. Why would he do this? Why would he risk getting caught, and sent to prison for a long time?

"Why?"

Austin stood tall, facing me like the man he was, mouth opened slightly and he started to speak. "Be—"

"For us, Lainie," Claire interrupted. "Dylan found me kicking the shit out of Greyson, after he caught him stalking me outside the hospital. He was coming after me because I stood up to him, and belittled him in front of his street thugs. He knew the law had failed you, and me, and every woman these two love." She finished, pleading in her voice for me to understand. "They had to do something to make him stop."

And I did understand, more than anyone could imagine. Had she forgotten we were both girls from Kentucky, raised around men who never considered involving the local sheriff when shit went down? Taking care of those who'd wronged them, being the judge, jury, and executioner. Folks where we came from had a term for it, Southern Justice.

"When I was eleven," I focused my eyes on Austin's blue ones. "I came home one afternoon to find my momma on the kitchen floor with her boyfriend, Bucky, straddling her hips, while punching her in the face. I managed to grab a skillet off the stove, and cold cocked him in the back of the head. I knew I wasn't strong enough to do much damage, but I knew who could."

Austin moved closer, taking slow, deliberate steps toward me. He needed to hear how I understood why they did as they'd thought best. "Larkin Biggs, the man who managed the trailer park we lived in, came around on his four wheeler every day to check on us. I knew if he was home, he would take care of Bucky, who was screaming for me to come back. I ran as fast as my feet would carry me, right up to his porch. Larkin opened the door, calmed me down, and then grabbed his double barreled shotgun." I reached out with my open hand, laying it gently against the rough scruff of Austin's face. His warm skin felt so good under my cold hand, and all the accusing thoughts I had earlier, seemed impossible now.

"Larkin dragged the guy out of our house, leading him to the wooden shed he kept the lawn equipment in. After Momma told him what happened, several of Larkin's family came out, and helped to set up a rope in one of the trees." There were no suggestions to call the law, or for someone to take him to jail. They would handle this as they always had; themselves.

"One of his uncles had served in Vietnam, and he had a chair set up with Bucky tied to it by the time we got over there. I stood beside Momma, as Uncle Beau took a pair of pliers, and removed every one of Bucky's fingernails, from both hands. Then they let Momma slap him until she had her fill." The final thing they did, before they let him die in pain and agony, was to take away what was most precious to him. Larkin had turned to me, as he brought his knife down on the man.

"One of the other men took his hunting knife and cut Bucky's jeans off. Leaving him only in his white underwear. Larkin looked over his shoulder at me, and said loud enough for everyone to hear, that this was for me. When he moved away, Bucky's white underwear was a dark shade of red from all the blood rushing out. His dick was shoved in his mouth, keeping his screams silent."

New found joy began to migrate across Austin's face. His signature smile timidly making an appearance. Austin's smile spread across his face, at my understanding.

Such a handsome man. With eyes holding such power, they could make a woman forget why she was angry in the first place, which is where I am now.

"Wish we had Larkin with us last night." Forget the eyes. The vibrations of his voice created goosebumps to form on my shoulders and arms. Patches of discolored skin rose to the surface under his eyes. I hadn't noticed it before, but as I scanned his olive skin, thick eyelashes and delectable lips, his lack of sleep began to tell on him.

"Thank you." Two simple words containing bottomless meaning.

"I wanted to tell you about last night, but I wasn't sure I could trust you with something as serious as what we had to do." I understood what he was saying. We had known each other for the briefest of time, not even defining what was happening between us.

"I'm sorry for the thoughts I had about you." His face pulled back, looking at me with confused expression. "When Claire told me you and Dylan had to supervise the bike part, I assumed it was a play on words for seeing a girl naked."

Austin's eyes bulged in shock, shaking his head in disbelief. "Wh—what?"

Dylan pulled Claire to his lap, hugging her tightly, as if worried she would disappear. With his face in Claire's neck, he mumbled a single word, which gets a smack from Claire, and a snorting laugh from me.

"Jugs."

"What?" he questioned, as he grabbed her hand from smacking him again. "Jugs are what we call the cylinders inside a bike engine and what you guys have—"

Claire pulled away from him, extending her index finger in his direction. "Don't you dare." Dylan smiled at her, turning her anger into something she must find funny, as she laughed into his neck. Dylan took advantage of the diversion, and swept her up, heading for my balcony.

"I'm sorry you had to spend the night in confusion and anger. My only intention was to protect you." Honesty colored his eyes. The penetration no longer sexual, but of the profession of truth. "I'm not used to feeling this way." He lowered his eyes to our hands, which were clasped together, and I'm clueless as to when they found one another. "If you've forgiven me, I'd like to ask something of you." I searched his face, for what I'm not certain. Austin is the definition of hero, giving selfishly of himself for the benefit of others. Willing to risk imprisonment, for standing up for what he believes in.

"There is nothing to forgive. You were doing something to make the world a better place. I should be thanking you for taking one of the monsters, and sending him back where he belongs."

"There are a lot more monsters."

"And you're going to deal with them one by one."

"Not if I have to sacrifice you." He took my face between his hands. Warm skin, creating a heat in my body, and a new desire in my belly.

"How do Dylan and Claire do it?"

"Well," he responds, bobbing his head back and forth. "That's where the term 'parts run' came from."

The fog which I placed in the room earlier, lifted with the warm breeze of his honesty. "I can live with that." And I could. He has a call to do the right and just thing. To pick up where the chains of injustice restricted those who they had sworn to protect.

"We won't go without a solid plan, background checks, the works." He assured me, and I believed him. More importantly, I trusted him.

Yet, something he just said stuck out. "Who's we?"

"Well, there is Dylan and I, Carson, and our little brother Chase."

I'm shocked to hear Carson is in the mix, but reassured as well. He is the king of the protectors, and my adopted father. "Really? Carson? That wasn't expected."

Austin takes my hand again, playing with my fingernails, reminding me I need to see my girl soon. "Yeah, he came to us right after Chase tossed Cash off the bridge, said he was tired of the red tape." He is very brazen in his word choice. I ignored it, and concentrated on the calluses of his fingers, as they glide across the back of my hand.

"Lainie?" He whispered softly. The only other sound in the room was the beating of our hearts, reaching out to touch the other. Basking in the newness of this relationship. "Can I kiss you, please?"

Four weeks ago, I wouldn't have been able to sit here, this close to a man, and allow him to touch me. Could I let him kiss me? When I don't reply, Austin takes his free hand, and uses his bent index finger to pull my chin closer to him. I can smell the coffee on his breath, and feel the heat of his body, as he closes the distance between us. As if sensing the buildup of nerves and desire, he licks his lips before pressing them gently to mine.

His graze is soft, patient, and welcome. Although brief and innocent, it's also a small teaser of possibilities. Austin is a man of extreme passion, a wealth of knowledge, and after the exchanges we'd shared today, the owner of my soul.

As he moves in again, the patio door swishes open. We turn to see Dylan pocketing his cell phone, a scowl on his face.

"Sorry to be the motherfucking cockblocker, but that was the pawn shop guy again. Guess who just tried to pawn a ruby and diamond ring?"

Chapter Thirteen

Austin

"Nothing too easy, or done too quickly, is going to be right. It takes time to create perfection, whether it's your tea or the love of your life."

"I told her, I couldn't help her without a valid ID." Dylan explained on the way over, how he had left his information with the pawn shop owner to call him if the girl who tried to pawn our momma's silver showed up again. In his years as a cop, criminals sometime developed a pattern, going back to certain places if they think they can fence what they steal. This girl, who we both suspected was Harmony, had apparently returned to the shop.

"She tried to argue, but I pointed at the sign." Above the gentleman's head, in bright red letters on a white background, were the words *Must Present a Valid Photo ID to Pawn or Redeem. NO exceptions!* "She batted her eyelashes at me, and even tried sticking her tits in my face."

Gordon Cooper, one of the daytime managers, was a pleasant enough man in his late fifties. With his Grecian formula dark hair, and gold jeweler's loop, he was ready for a throwback party, or trip to the strip club.

"She tried to tell me we had bought from her in the past, and never asked for an ID. But we get all kinds in here, one sob story after another." He waved his hand in the air, a look of disgust on his face.

"Real shame too, that ring had a Burmese ruby with diamonds around the stone, very rare and very expensive. I would have given her five grand for it."

Frustration fueled anger began rising in my chest. Pulling out my cellphone, I scrolled through several emails I had recently received from Chase. Locating the one I needed, I turned the phone to show Mr. Cooper the photo. "Like this one?"

Chase had confided in me he had purchased a ring from a shop near his base. He asked me not to say anything to Momma or Dylan, saying he didn't want either one of them to freak out. I, of course, questioned him as to why he was giving her a ring so soon? He explained it was just his promise to come home to her. He planned to replace it with a diamond, once he got out of the Marines.

"Yep, just like that." Gordon nodded. "It's stolen, aint it?" He leaned on the glass counter, looking at the screen as if the ring would pop out of the image, and into his hands. He was practically salivating at the hope of having it in his huge sausage like fingers.

"No, Sir, it ain't stolen," Dylan resolved.

Gordon let us know the girl had left in an older model Camaro. A Hispanic guy behind the wheel, driving like a bat out of hell. "Did the guy have any markings you'd remember? Tattoos, birthmarks?"

Gordon pondered for a minute. "As a matter of fact, he had a tattoo of a crown." Pointing to the side of his neck, tapping the skin three times indicating its placement.

Judging by Dylan's reaction to the news, he had an idea of who we were dealing with. "Hey Gordon, do you have security monitoring?" If my suspicions were true, I could compare the footage in the store, to the grainy photo I've been studying for weeks.

"Sure. We have closed circuit. The recorder is locked up in the back."

We passed Gordon a few bills for letting us copy the video to a thumb drive I always carry. After again asking him to call us if the girl returned, we jumped back into Dylan's car.

"Wanna tell me *why* you have a picture of that ring in your phone?

"It's not what you think, I can assure you." I hated keeping things from my family.

"So it's not a ring for the slut our baby brother is fucking?" Without taking his eyes off the road, he pressed a few buttons on his console. I chose not to answer his question until his phone call was over. Instead, I listened to the ringing coming through the speakers.

"Carson."

"Hey, old man. Tell me if Largo, or Kevin North, is a current guest downtown?"

"What did the fucker do this time?"

"He may be in possession of stolen property. Also, check and see if there were any reports of a stolen Camaro recently." Dylan shifted gears as he moved around traffic.

"Let me check, and I'll call you back."

Dylan ended the call without saying anything, something Momma would have fussed at him for. It would seem it was time for us to compare notes, to get a better handle on this situation. Where I felt awful for going back on my word to Chase, something told me this went deeper than just some girl on a stripper pole.

"Chase bought a ring for Harmony, said it was just a place keeper for the real ring he is planning to give her." Dylan shook his head, pressing the accelerator harder. The speedometer spiking with the increased speed.

"Who is this Largo?"

"Largo is a street thug we arrested a few months back. He's a local gang banger wannabe. The tattoo on his neck is a symbol for the Latin Kings. Last I saw him, he didn't have the diamonds on it. Meaning he hadn't taken the final step to becoming a full member."

Dylan pulled off the highway, headed in the direction of Claire's apartment. "Hey, Dylan, I need to go to my office, and have a look at this video against the photo of the girl." I also needed to take a look at Chase's financial records, to see if any money was being syphoned out.

"You don't want to see Lainie first?" He questioned, astonished.

"I do want to see her, but this is important. Besides, I have to be careful with her, take things at her pace." I could feel Lainie trembling slightly when I'd kissed her. She needed me to be patient, and I would, no matter how long it took. I would wait for her to be ready for us.

"When is Chase due back in the states?" Dylan knew when to back off and when to pursue. Lainie was special to me, and had been through a lot lately. Had it been Chase sitting in this seat, talking about Harmony, the situation would have resulted in blood shed and harsh words.

"Not long."

Dylan pulled the car into the parking lot of my building. Just as he pulled into a spot, I looked at him. "Listen, Dylan, don't say anything to Chase. I can't prove the ring is the same one he sent to her, and you can't prove the two girls are the same." Parking the car, we were just about to open the door, when his phone rang.

"Morgan."

"Largo is not a current guest of the county, but a stolen Camaro was found in Mount Pleasant. We are still processing it for prints." Dylan slumped his head against the headrest, removed his sunglasses, and tossed them on the dashboard. "Thanks, Carson. Call me with any developments."

"You got it, man." Dylan ended the call, but remained in his seat. He was tired, we both were, but finding the answers we needed overruled hitting the sheets. Something deep inside was nagging, telling me all of this was somehow connected, but how? If it was Harmony who had tried to sell Momma's silver and now her own ring, what did she have to gain from it? Besides money? If she were to sell the ring, surely Chase would ask her about it when he got back. Lastly, how did this Largo fit into all of it?

As we entered the building, Momma was heading out the door, her arm secured around Daddy's elbow. I kissed her cheek, and let her hug the piss out of me, then Dylan. "I have the best news! Chase just emailed us. He will be back in the states by the end of the week!" I knew what this meant; Priscilla Morgan was about to throw a party. The radiance she normally displayed increased tenfold at the idea her baby boy was headed home. If only she knew a snake waited in his bed, coiled, and ready to strike.

Daddy reminded her they had an appointment to keep. Pulling her toward the parking lot, allowing us to get to my office, and the answers I hoped to find. Hopefully we could save Chase a world of hurt and ridicule, as Momma would not hold her tongue if she found out someone was hurting one of her boys.

I slid the thumb drive into the slot, fast forwarding to the location we needed. It would take a minute or two for the program to compare the photos. As I waited, I took a peek into Chase's bank accounts.

"Hey, you still play this?" Dylan stood across the room, a chess piece in hand, taking care to set it back gently. "I haven't since Granddaddy passed. But I plan on taking it over to Lainie's, and teaching her how to play." The thought gave me a rush, showing her a part of me I though might die with his passing.

Chase's bank had a joke of a firewall. Less than two minutes after I started, I had everything on three screens. Looking through months and months of back bank transactions, nothing seemed out of the ordinary, until about two months ago.

"Look at this," I told Dylan, pointing to the numbers on the screen. "Three thousand dollars has been paid to Armstrong Properties in Mount Pleasant." Dylan pulled his phone back out, his fingers flying across the screen. "Armstrong Properties is a property management group for three complexes here in Charleston. The Grove, Hummingbird Point, and Whippoorwill Valley."

I took down another firewall, this time with Charleston Power. It provided me with a little more of a challenge. "Wouldn't you know it, Chase Morgan has an account with the electric company for a condo in The Grove." Pretty impressive for a man who is half way around the world.

"Hasn't he been looking for an apartment in Parris Island?"

"Oh, it gets better," I opened the last webpage. "He has opened three credit cards in the last month, all with Harmony as an authorized user." Dylan glanced up from his phone, his eyes full of fire. "Tell me you're fucking kidding me?"

"Nope, and it gets even worse. Every single one of them is maxed out from cash withdraws."

Dylan pocketed his phone, and turned to look at my wall of screens. Staring him dead in the face was nearly thirty thousand dollars of debt. How is that possible?

"Look at this charge." Dylan moves closer to the screen, pointing to a charge made four weeks ago. It's a jewelry designer. The IP address telling me it's an online company, and probably some back alley shop in Hong Kong.

"Looks like Harmony purchased something to go with the ring Chase got her."

Dylan looked back over his shoulder, "Or copy it."

A ping sounded from the recognition program I had comparing the photos from the pawn shop, and the first stolen car. The angle of the closed circuit is terrible, focusing on the merchandise at the back of the store, and is black and white. The first photo is grainy, and I'll be shocked if we ever identify her.

"Anything?" Shaking my head in the negative. The angles were just too muted, bringing us no closer to the truth then when we started. It's completely frustrating. I'm tired, and pissed, and even with all my equipment, I can't figure this shit out.

"Come on, let's go see our girls."

It's the best suggestion I've heard all day. I need to get back to Lainie, talk to her about how to proceed from here. Maybe sneak in a few more kisses, minus the interruptions from the outside world.

I boxed up my chess set. Knowing it will give us time to talk, and give her something else to think about, instead of the craziness in her life.

"What are you doing?" Dylan has never been the patient one in the family. Being an early riser from the second he was born, the way he sped through everything, included climbing the ranks in his job.

"I told you I was taking this over to Lainie's. She wants to learn how to play."

Dylan's smirk made me want to slap the fuck out of him. I tried sampling the waters the way he had, a different girl every day. While the feeling was great, and the sex satisfying, it still left behind an emptiness. Maybe that's why he stayed with Claire. He finally found a home, filling his own. In his mind, I should head over to Lainie's, bust down the door, and fuck her until she couldn't move. But that wasn't me, and it certainly wasn't Lainie. We would write our own chapters, live up to standards we create…together.

Seeing the smile on my girl's face as she opened the door, made the frustration of lack of answers go away. The sunlight from the window behind her created an angelic glow around her. Although she didn't need the help of the sun to be an angel, she managed that all on her own.

"I brought my chess set, I was hoping you had some time to play." Raising up the box to show her, as she sidestepped to allow me in. I loved her house, with the tall windows and the early Charleston style. She'd confessed she had just moved in a little over a week ago, but you would never guess. Her style wasn't flowers and fuss, just soft fabrics and comfort. If Dylan could have heard my thoughts, he would have handed me a tampon for my vagina.

"Are you sure you have time to teach me?" She moved a basket, full of remotes to the side, making an area to set up the board. "It may not be every day, but yes, I have time." Shooting her an assuring smile, the one she returned would stay with me for days.

"Have you had supper yet?"

"No, I usually grab something from a drive thru."

"Make you a deal, you get the board ready, and I'll make us supper."

Setting up the board took no time at all. The smells which found their way to me, became too much to resist. Trying like hell not to appear to be a crazed stalker, I peered around the edge of the bar to find Lainie peeling a potato. Back and forth she used the blade to remove the brown peel, her eyes focused on the root vegetable.

"You know, if you're gonna stand there and watch me, you can always come in and help." I wasn't even embarrassed she had caught me. I could watch her all day. The way her hips swayed to the music in her head, or how she relieved an itch with the back of her hand.

"You may want to reconsider, I've been known to burn water."

Her eyes flashed to mine, as she stopped peeling, dropping the potato into the empty sink. "How did you survive in New York?"

Laughing nervously, I rounded the wall of the kitchen, not certain I wanted to revisit my time up north. "It was easy, a deli on nearly every street corner, and a different restaurant beside them."

She continued with her peeling. "What no girlfriend to bid her way into your heart by way of your stomach?"

The thought of Keena removing herself from the television screen long enough to open the fridge was quite comical. Detaching herself from anything which didn't give instant gratification, or something to tweet to her friends about, wasn't on her radar. My silence gave Lainie the wrong impression, as she began to apologize. "I'm sorry, I didn't mean to open a closed grave."

I reached over to touch her face, her petite chin soft between my thumb, and index finger. "Keena, the girl I lived with in New York, wouldn't know how to turn the stove on, much less cook on it." I lowered my face slowly to hers, searching her eyes for any hint of warning. "She never cared if I ate or even came home, as long as she had cable and a big screen."

The timer on the stove gave us the indication that something she was preparing was finished. I ignored the intervals of beeping. Concentrating instead on the pair of lips against mine, soft and supple, with the perfect amount of pressure. Wet fingers skimmed across the skin above my shirt collar, and into the hair at the back of my neck. Her ample chest pushed into mine, signaling I could deepen if I chose. I pulled her closer, my arms wrapped around her, losing myself in the essence of her.

"Lainie, the stove has—"A feminine voice breaks the spell, but I refused to let her go. "Oh, God, I'm sorry." Heidi appeared in the kitchen, silencing the offending alarm. Lainie was first to let go, stepping around me to open the oven.

"It's fine Heidi, we were just about to have supper. Are you hungry?"

I leaned back against the sink because I'm clueless as to what to do. In my time, I've been caught by a few siblings, a couple of pissed off dads, and one nearly blind granny.

"Is Ginger still here?" Lainie continued, as if nothing happened. Maybe this wasn't the first time she had been caught either,

"No, her boyfriend had car trouble, and he felt bad because he couldn't give me a ride home like he promised. So he called me a taxi, and paid for it." Shrugging, as she starts to cut the rest of the potatoes in the sink.

Glancing in Lainie's direction, the look on her face tells me this isn't welcomed. "Heidi you should have called me. I would have picked you up."

Heidi turned back around, her face contorted in anger. "You didn't sleep much last night and besides," she nodded in my direction, "you had company." A mischievous smile formed on her face.

Soon we were sitting at the bar, a full meal before me. The only woman who ever took this much time to cook a meal for me was my momma. I would never tell her, but Lainie made a meatloaf which would rival hers.

"So do you need a ride to campus tomorrow?"

"Nope, Ginger said she would have her car tomorrow. But I do need to give her some money for gas. I mean, she lives all the way over in Mount Pleasant."

At her words, I drop my fork, sending it clattering to my plate. "I'm sorry," I quickly pick up the lost utensil, continuing with my dinner. Heidi smiled the same grin her sister had. My long night and day were suddenly catching up with me.

"Austin you look like you're ready to drop. We can start chess lessons another night." As much as I wanted to argue, to stay here wrapped up in the feeling I get from being around her, I did need some rest.

Chapter Fourteen

Lainie

What men desire is a virgin who is a whore
- Edward Dahlbert

It's funny how we never stop to consider how life truly goes on around us. When we take a day off, stay wrapped in the warm sheets, life still rolls on. My boss Jackie is a prime example of this, sitting in California enjoying room service, while I run her company.

I hadn't heard a single word from her since she left; no email, no messaging, nothing. Even though everything was running well, I've left her a message assuring her of this. While I'd planned on working this weekend, anticipating her unannounced return, those plans were canceled by a single phone call.

Priscilla Morgan phoned very early this morning, letting me know an invitation to attend Chase's welcome home party, would be arriving later today. Heidi was also included, but I already knew she had a test to take on campus. Priscilla agreed a test was important, but also left no room for not showing up. Evidently, wanting to impress your boss doesn't score high enough for her acceptable excuses chart. Would I ever have the self-fortitude to hand out orders like she did?

Claire had called me shortly after, too late to deliver her warning to expect the call. "Dylan told me Harmony was invited, only because Priscilla doesn't want any drama. She made him and Austin swear to keep their mouths shut."

Austin hadn't shared with me his dislike for his brother's girlfriend, so Claire told me the story of meeting the family for the first time. "She seriously wore a mini skirt to meet the parents?" I recalled the length of a few of my momma's skirts. Ones she wore when it was time to find a new paycheck; a term she used for the man who would pay her bills for a little while. She'd dress the way they wanted, until she got bored of being told what to do, and then she went searching again.

"Apparently, they suspect her of being dishonest with Chase. I'm not sure what about since Dylan doesn't want to involve me." Now this got my attention. While Dylan has been known to be crass, he was also known to be an excellent judge of character. If he's questioning something Harmony is doing, then I agreed blindly.

I'm not sure what I expected when Claire and I pulled up outside of the Morgan home. I knew from living here, Mount Pleasant was a more affluent section of Charleston. But nothing I could have dreamed up, would have prepared me for the real thing. I've never been to Italy, so I had nothing to compare, other than what little I'd seen in pictures and movies. But, I wouldn't have been surprised if the Morgans had a Tuscan villa shipped over. With sand colored exterior walls, a terra-cotta roof, and four majestic columns reminding you this is the south; the house seemed to go on and on, with pristine landscaping, bordering the richness of the area.

I imagined having three little boys running wild around the massive yard, playing cops and robbers, allowing their young minds to roam free. How many celebrations of birthdays, anniversaries, and spelling bee competitions had been held here? Even the victory parties, for well-played football games.

Claire entered the house as if she'd done it a thousand times. Walking toward the back of the house, where the sounds of an established party were already in full swing. Music and laughter blending into one beautiful song, with lyrics everyone knew.

As grand as the entryway was, full of character and charm, the back sitting porch left me with a new appreciation for men with visions, and skilled hands to make them into reality. A stark white wood porch ran the length of the home. Tall palm trees danced in the wind. Creating a backdrop for the inhabitants of the four empty rocking chairs to enjoy. Full and healthy ferns swayed back and forth from their perch on the under hanging. Reflections of light danced off the choppy water of the lake behind the house.

Austin and Dylan stood beside the largest grill I had ever seen. A beer in one hand, as they laughed to whatever story the cook was in the process of telling. Red, white, and blue covered every surface, with a massive banner, welcoming Chase Morgan home again.

I scanned the sprawling lawn, noticing a pool off to the left side, with several young people enjoying the refreshment it brought. I knew the second I saw Harmony, exactly who she was. Gray tank top, tied just beneath her breasts. The knot was completely tacky against the brand of jeans she'd painted on. I'd created a webpage for the ostentatious Michael Avery. Women paid unfathomable amounts of money to purchase his jeans, each coming with its own serial number, like a fine Italian purse. You had to know someone, or be someone, to get an appointment with him. Having the webpage was his way of showing off what he could do. Either Harmony knew the man personally, or she spent some serious time on her knees. Continuing with her tacky ensemble, just above her million dollar jeans, sat her belly button ring, glistening in the sun.

Just as Harmony came with her own neon sign, Chase Morgan had no problem catching a few eyes as well. Dark hair, just like the other men in his family, his cut short, still reflecting his military service. His face clean-shaven; with the same cut jawline I enjoyed on Austin. Chase may be the baby of the family, but he is taller than his brothers. Khaki cargo shorts, and a tight red t-shirt, never looked so good.

"Careful, Austin at two o'clock." Claire snickered, becoming my voice of reason, and resident drool monitor.

"Hey, just because I'm seeing Austin, doesn't mean I have to quit appreciating the rest of the male population."

Harmony chose that moment to look our way, almost as if she could hear us, and wrapped herself around Chase's free arm.

"Hey, Sweetness," Austin whispers in my ear,. Kissing the side of my cheek, as he wraps me from behind, it's my favorite way to be touched by him. His warmth was a welcome addition, even in the heat of the day.

"Hey, yourself." I'm instantly glad I didn't fight Priscilla on blowing off work. Dylan joined us, dipping Claire back in a silly kiss. The movement allows me to see a young girl standing off to the side of the yard. Its evident she is alone and feels out of place. I imagine she's debating hiding in the bushes or just going home. "Austin, who is that?" I asked, before I can stop myself. Both he and Dylan look to where my attention is.

"Oh, that's Audrey, she works in the shop."

She is pretty in that natural kind of way; no need for makeup, or heavy hair products. Her clothing is appropriate for the event. A knee length skirt, white tennis shoes, and three quarter length blouse. She wasn't advertising any attributes, or giving away free glimpses of where her panties came from.

"Momma likes her, and spent the better part of an hour reassuring her she was welcome." Austin takes my hand in his, squeezing it tenderly, but my attention stays fast on Audrey. "I'll be back"

I'm not sure what it is about Audrey that calls out to me. She isn't being picked on or harassed, and she isn't in danger of being hurt. But as I move closer to her, I glance around to see what she is looking at so sternly. She too has noticed the trampy Harmony; much like a monkey on a bicycle, you have to see it to believe.

"Hi, I'm sorry, you don't know me but—" The last thing I wanted to do was frighten her. It's clear; to me anyway, she could use a friend. "I'm Lainie Perry, Austin's girlfriend." Her brown eyes take me in, almost as if she were deciding if I'm one of the good guys, or a friend of the circus performer.

"Hello." Her voice was timid, like she's trying it out for the first time. Her eyes flash to the ground, and then she thinks the better of it, bringing them back to mine. "I'm Audrey, Audrey Helmes." Her extended hand shook, and her tiny fingers were cold, despite the rising temperatures.

"That's not a name you hear anymore." I surmised, trying to keep her talking, and her tremors to stop.

"My mom was an Audrey Hepburn fan. She watched her movies everyday until the day she died." She spoke so proudly of her mother. Not like some people when you mention a loved one who has passed, and you instantly feel bad about mentioning them.

"Much better than mine. My momma let the nurses who were in the delivery room name me." True story, Momma was told I was a boy, but when I popped out with no stem on the apple, she had no clue what to name me. So she let the nurses give her their favorites.

"Really?" Her laughter filled the air. A welcomed richness, which enhanced the feeling, instead of annoying the hell out of me.

"Oh, yes. You know it's too bad we don't get to choose our own names, since we're the ones stuck with them for our entire lives." Nodding her head in agreement, her eyes flicking past me.

I turned slightly, knowing exactly what, or rather who, she was looking at. It was hard not to if you asked me. "You'd think she would know how to dress if she's acquainted with these people."

"She should be ashamed of herself." Her words were rushed, and she immediately slapped a hand over her mouth. "Oh, my gosh, I'm sorry. I never should have said that."

"Why not? It's the truth."

The look on her face was priceless, eyes huge, and glistening with the beginnings of humor. "But it's rude to say. My granny would have a few things to tell her, walking around with all that skin on display. Why there is food being served, for Christ's sake."

Audrey was an absolute delight, definitely a girl I could have a great time with. "You won't tell Mr. Dylan I was talking bad about Miss Harmony, will you? He's been so good to me; giving me a job and a car, and letting me work as much as I want. I don't mean to listen to his conversations, but sometimes he talks so loud it's hard not to." One thing about Audrey Helms, once you got her started, the girl could talk.

"I hear how she's taking advantage of that soldier. Poor man, off serving his country, and she sits back, spendin' his money like they was married."

Dylan may not have wanted to involve Claire in his issues with Harmony, but I was getting an ear full from Audrey.

"Why just a few minutes ago, she was chewing Mrs. Priscilla's ear 'bout how now that Chase was home, she could have her over for dinner in their new home."

"Wait, Harmony and Chase are living together?"

"Yes, Ma'am. Harmony said it loud enough for practically the whole country to hear. Mrs Priscilla went right off and into the house, Mr. Morgan close on her heels."

I looked with wide eyes over at Austin, his face dropping as he came closer.

"Afternoon, Mr. Austin." Audrey greeted in her heavy southern accent. I didn't know where she was from, but I bet it was so far south they had to bring in sunshine.

"Miss Audrey, are you enjoying yourself?" My Austin, kindness in his every word.

"Yes, Sir. Your Mom didn't have to invite me, but I wanted to thank her anyway." Audrey wasn't looking at Austin; she had her eyes firmly planted on the third Morgan brother, longing in her voice.

"She was just here somewhere." He searched around the yard among all the guests.

I reached over to get his attention, I wanted to have a hold on him when I let him hear the news. "Austin, your momma was upset by the news Chase and Harmony have moved in together."

Dylan heard me; he wasn't even three feet away, as the two brothers looked at one another. "Excuse us." Austin announced, as he and Dylan moved away.

Claire must have overheard as well, she was now on the other side of Audrey. Watching as the guys approached Chase, pulling him aside, and began speaking. At first it was Austin, and everything seemed calm. Then Chase pointed at himself, and then Harmony. "Fuck you, Austin!" Chase shouted, loud enough to silence the people around them. He grabbed Harmony's arm, stomping into the house.

Austin and Dylan remained standing, watching the couple retreat into an open door. As conversations resumed, Priscilla and Dean returned. It's evident they are both angry. She notices us, tells Dean something, and then walks over to us.

"How are my favorite girls?" She leans over to kiss Claire's cheek, then mine, and finally Audrey's.

"I wanted to thank you for the invite." Audrey begins, but was shushed by a head shaking Priscilla.

"You are a breath of fresh air, just like these two."

"You may want to take that back when you hear what just happened." She gives me a concerned look, one I don't deserve. "Priscilla, I need to apologize as I may have just ruined your party."

I watched her eyes roll, as I tell her what just occurred. "Lainie, honey, if anyone needs to be apologizing, it's that harlot for showing up with her tits on display, and her hips hanging out of her too tight jeans."

The phone in my pocket began to vibrate, pulling it out; I hoped it was my sister with good news about her test. I excused myself to take the call, as Austin and Dylan came over to stand by their momma.

"Hello?"

"Lainie, its Murphy with security. I need you come by the office as soon as you can. There are gentlemen with badges here to see you."

"What kind of badges? Is it the police?"

"No, Ma'am, they're from the government. They asked for Jackie, but ain't nobody able to get ahold of her. They asked for the person in charge, that being you."

I looked over at Austin who was looking at me with worry. The last thing I needed was to cause any more issues today. "Okay, Murphy. Tell them I'm across the bridge, and I'll be there as quickly as I can." I ended the call, and Austin is at my side in an instant.

"Babe, you okay?" His comforting hands are on my face. I've come to love when he touches me.

"I'm not sure, that was one of the security guys who says I need to get over there right away."

"Okay, I have my bike here, but I can ride you over." I'd love nothing more than to jump on the back of his bike, but he needs to stay here and fix whatever is wrong with Chase.

"No, I'm fine to drive over. Besides you need to stay with your family. Fix what's wrong with Chase."

Claire is getting a ride home from Dylan, leaving me to head on over to my building. When I arrive, there are three black SUVs in the parking lot. Grabbing my security pass, I enter the building. Standing around the desk, phones to one of their ears, are four men in suits.

"Are you Miss Perry?" The shortest of the four questions. His blonde hair is slicked back with some sort of hair product, his tie is slightly askew, as if he's been picking at it.

"Yes, Sir."

He pulls something out of his pocket, showing me his silver badge, and government issued ID. "Ma'am, I'm Brad Parish, an officer with the Federal Trade Commission. Are you familiar with a Jacqueline Craven?"

"Yes, Sir, she's my boss, and the owner of the company."

"Have you ever had any dealings with a Kennedy Fraser?"

"We went to college together. What is all of this about?"

My heart was racing, as the man who was on the phone walks over. "Afternoon, Ma'am, has Officer Parish informed you of your rights?"

I nearly passed out. My rights? "I'm sorry, did you just say my rights?" My legs are trembling, and I can feel the edges of my vision fading to black.

"Yes, Ma'am, this is an ongoing investigation." His tone is gruff, as if this is keeping him from something more important. His poor attitude is enough of a reprieve that I'm able to think around the panic.

"No, I have not been told much of anything, and I wish to pause this conversation until my attorney is present." I don't wait for them to agree or disagree. I want to call Austin, have him here to take the bad feelings away, but he isn't the Morgan who attended law school. Two rings in and he answers the call. I can feel the panic return; he picks up the distress in the cracking. "Lainie, say nothing to them. I'll be there in a few minutes."

I hang up the phone, and continue to ignore the four men. Scrolling through my contacts, I locate Jackie, and press send. But the ring never comes, instead I hear the announcement the number has been disconnected. I know it can't be right, so I try it again, with the same result. Thinking she's had to change her number from possibly a lost phone, I scan my email, but there is nothing from her.

Looking out the window to the parking lot, my heart jumps as three solid men are walking toward the building, from an all too familiar truck. They all have sunglasses covering those eyes. But I can tell the one in the middle, the one who holds my heart, is pissed. I want to run to him, toss myself into his welcoming arms, but I know I can't do that. I have to show these guys behind me I don't have any involvement, other than professional, with the dynamic trio who have just walked into the door.

"Afternoon, Miss Perry, pleasure to see you again."

Dean Morgan had an air about him, confidence he could sell in buckets. Professionalism abounding, and a million dollar smile, wrapping it all up in a nice looking gift.

"Who is in charge here?" Dean wastes no time in pulling out his identification, showing the feds exactly who he was.

"Hey, pretty lady." Dylan stands strong, his flirtatious nature helping to ease the nausea I felt.

"I'm so sorry." I whispered. Austin ignored the situation, and took me in his arms. I needed it, the comfort of his touch, his smell, and whispers of everything would be okay.

"Miss Perry?" I cringe at the sound of my name, although I shouldn't since I've done nothing wrong.

"Can you explain to Officer Norris why you are here instead of Miss Craven?"

With Dylan on one side, and Austin on the other, I tell them of her purchase of a fledgling company, of surveying what they have, and giving Mr. Fraser an opportunity to keep his job.

"Miss Perry, I'm sorry to tell you this, but we are seizing Craven and Associates. Effective immediately."

Chapter Fifteen

Austin

The saddest thing about betrayal is that it never comes from your enemies... It comes from friends and loved ones.
- Ash Sweeney

I now understand how Dylan felt the day he found Cash following Claire. While Lainie was in no danger of being hurt physically, the look of terror on her face both broke me, and stirred a rage I've never felt. When Daddy got the call from her, he pulled Momma out by the pool to talk. I knew something was up by the look on his face. The second I heard her name, I was ready to kill. I couldn't get Dylan's car to go fast enough. I didn't care if the cops tried to pull me over. I was going to get to her.

I'd assumed seeing her face would tamp down the rage coursing through my veins. But, watching those four men, using their position to fill her with fear, caused the anger to reach ultimate levels. Dean Morgan was a man who helped people who had been wronged. But when it came to family, he went the extra step, using every loophole he could. Lainie had done nothing except her job. With nothing but her time vested in the company. Those fuckers had no cause to treat her the way they did, and if I knew my dad, someone in Washington would be answering for it.

After we left the building, Lainie asked for something stiff to drink. Dylan told her there was a bottle of Hennessy in my desk she could have. It wasn't quite the icebreaker we needed. Dylan admitting he hadn't been to McGuire's in months, not since the last time he'd met Carson there.

"I wonder what ever happened to Dr. O'Leary and his bride?" The question hung in the air. I wasn't interested in taking her to the bar, there were more pressing issues to deal with.

Daddy kissed Lainie as he headed into his office. He said Momma and Claire were on their way over, and he would entertain them until we could find some answers.

"Oh, my God." Since meeting Lainie, I've often wondered what she would sound like, as she said those three words. Granted it would have been different circumstances, and she would be under me, but I'll take it. She is more than just my girl; she is a fellow computer junkie.

"Austin, this is incredible." I had the same reaction when I finished this room; using the equipment I wanted, and placing the monitors in the order I found the most useful. But seeing the smile return to her face, rather than the fear of an hour ago, I would do anything to help keep it there

"Come on, have a seat. I'll make you a drink, and then I'm going to crack a few firewalls."

Three drinks later, a rosy cheeked Lainie twisted back and forth in her chair, as I used my copy of the Titan program to break into

Adams Lighthouse. Someone had been updating the system, Scott I suspected, by the trap doors and double walls.

"You know, I never understood why they always use a skull and crossbones at the junction wall. Why not something really scary like, a 3D rendition of Freddy Krueger?" I wasn't positive if it was the whisky talking, or her inner thoughts unfiltered. But as I cleared the final gatekeeper, an idea began to formulate.

Lainie reached for the bottle, but as the door opened and our troop of friends entered, she changed her mind. Momma was across the room at lightning speed, hugging Lainie tight, using words she reserved for the times she was really angry.

"Dean Alexander Morgan, you make sure those bastards pay for making my girl cry. You put them under the jail, do you hear me?" She stomped her foot to drive her point home. *"When a woman is screaming and yelling, you have nothing to fear. It's when they act very calm and collected that you should sleep with one eye open."* I can practically hear my granddaddy saying those words. His wisdom about life was something I missed the most.

"Love, I've already contacted Senator Graham's office. He is opening a formal investigation first thing in the morning."

While Momma threw her hissy fit, and Daddy appeased her, I managed to find what looked to be the financial records for Craven and Associates, as well as Frasier Global. "Babe, didn't you say Jackie went to California to purchase Fraser Global?"

Lainie moved away from Momma, pushing her chair beside mine. "She said she had purchased them, and was going out there to look at her new assets." She could see the same screen I saw, the same numbers, or lack thereof, that I did.

"That lying bitch!"

Carson and Georgia chose that moment to walk into the room. Lainie ignored them, as she continued to read the screen.

"Care to share or do we have to guess?" Lainie and I looked at each other, shrugging. We continued, as I recalled something I had been working on for Carson.

"Hey, Carson, can I have your social security number?" If what I suspected was true, I was about to open Pandora's box.

"Austin, can you tell us something, please?" Momma had lost her fire, which was a good thing, as she was too much of a lady to act amuck. I continued clicking, not to be rude or disrespectful, but because I had encountered a series of hidden doors. Lainie pointed a few out I'd managed to miss, while reassuring the room we would explain everything in a moment. Finally, after opening more doors than I ever have, I had the final piece to this puzzle.

"Okay, first, Carson you recall the investment company you used to handle your retirement money?" He crossed his arms, standing firm behind Miss Georgia. "You were told the account never existed when you went to set up your allotment, and they were correct." I clicked a few buttons, sending information to the largest screen I had, so everyone could see as I explained.

"When the account was created, it was while the firm used the old system. Years ago, Adams Lighthouse developed a program, which allowed the company to go in and randomly change passwords. It also gave them the ability to move money around while the codes were scrambled. Now, Adams Lighthouse had a change of leadership when the founder passed away, leaving his grieving widow to run the company." I sent the photos of the widow, and her lover to the screen as well.

"Since Lighthouse's wife was having an affair with Jonas Frasier, the eldest son of Frasier Global, she appointed him CEO."

"Now, in the software community you have two companies which dominate the industry, and a third, which once upon a time, was a solid second. Now, years ago, you could own as many software companies that you wanted. But in the last ten years, legislation, and fear of dangerous monopolies, have made it illegal to have your fingers in more than one pot. As a matter of fact, the long arm of the law extends to the workers in that you have a mandatory waiting period to switch companies. That way trade secrets can't be stolen in the still of the night, again creating this super monopoly."

Lainie reached over interlacing her fingers with mine, a happy and content smile gracing her face.

"When the widow Lighthouse let her bed warmer take charge of the company, she gave him forty-nine percent of the company in the process. He neglected to tell his sugar momma he already had fifteen percent vested in Frasier Global, which is a direct violation of the Federal Trade Commission. Now, old man Frasier tried to move around some stocks, making it appear the percent Jonah owned was on the pharmaceutical side of the house. But he wasn't quick enough and the feds caught on. With both companies now in trouble, the youngest son, Kennedy, dreams up this brilliant plan to buy the program I invented for pennies on the dollar He decided to fly under the radar as an ordinary programmer, working in the only remaining company until the dust all settled, and the designer of the program, namely me, was flat broke and panhandling. What he didn't expect was not the fact said designer had a nice little nest egg and wouldn't need his help. No, what he didn't expect and neither did his wife of the past eight months, Jackie Craven, was that Lighthouse didn't own the rights to the Titan project."

Carson moved closer, his hands palm down on my desk. "So who does?"

Looking at Lainie, very pleased with myself for making her smile return, and for the idea which had solidified in my head. "I do."

I looked back at my friends and family. "You see, Adam Lighthouse knew his whore of a wife was fucking around with Jonah. He called me during a holiday weekend, and sold the rights to me for a quarter. No one ever checked on the patent, and no one had challenged it. When Jackie sent her golden boy to his brother to purchase it, it was discovered he didn't own it. This triggered the chain reaction where the feds again got nosey. Jackie went to California, not to see her new company, but to join her husband who was making final arrangements to flee the country. Not only was Jackie lying about her marital status, but also the fact her father had been operating in the red for years. She filed bankruptcy three months ago."

"So where does that leave me and my retirement money?" Carson had worked hard all of his life. He and Miss Georgia deserved to travel the world, or relax on her beloved front porch.

"It's sitting in your bank account, that's why I asked for your social security number. I took your money and all of the money they stole in the past few years, and transferred it into a file, which will be easier to hand over to the authorities. I also alerted the TSA manager in New York City, that Mr. and Mrs. Frasier are due to board a plane in an hour."

Momma left the room, coming back with a bottle of champagne, and several glasses. "Today was scheduled to be a celebration. First, my youngest son returns from the desert," she started. Popping the cork from the chilled bottle, filling the first glass, and passing it to Claire. "My oldest has finally found the girl of his dreams," she passes the second to Dylan. "And my middle has used his gift and love of computers to save the livelihood of several perfect strangers and some dear friends." She filled the remaining glasses, passing them around, until everyone has one in their hand. "I'd like to propose a toast," she smiles, raising her glass while encouraging everyone else. "To doing the right thing, even if it hurts to do so."

I knew she was talking about more than what had just happened. She was talking about the argument Chase and I had, when I'd confronted him about moving in with a girl after not knowing her for a second. Also giving her access to his accounts and paying for her to live in a condo well above her station. He had responded in a clipped tone, telling me to stay out of his business, and to leave Harmony alone. Further embarrassing us by screaming at me.

Lainie had only a sip of the champagne. A wise decision based on the amount of whiskey in her system. Dylan and Claire gathered the empty glasses, biding us goodbye, as they had plans for the evening.

"Claire, before you go, I'd like to get together this week for lunch. You, Lainie, and that lovely girl, Audrey." I had no clue what Momma had up her sleeve. But it was clear, Priscilla Morgan had an agenda, and something big was about to go down.

After everyone left, I took Lainie by the hand, and led her over to the sofa I've slept on at least a dozen times. I cradled her in my arms, feeling euphoria just being this close. This wasn't something you could ever find in a pill or bottle.

"I'm glad you were there today. You came running when I needed you." Her fingers ran up and down my arm, the comfort going both ways.

"I'll always come when you call." I meant it. She was the girl I had been waiting for, and all the girls before her, were just understudies.

"I do need to talk to you about something." I felt her flinch, so I turned her around to face me.

"You know Dylan has the bike shop as a diversion for what he and I really do, right?" She nodded her head, eyes searching my face. "Something you said earlier about icons for firewalls not being scary enough got me to thinking." The skin between her brows wrinkled in confusion, as she sat up, facing me completely.

"What if you came to work for me? Designing web pages and scary firewalls. Doing for me, what the bike shop does for Dylan."

Chapter Sixteen

Lainie

*Don't talk, just act. Don't say, just show.
Don't promise, just prove.*
- *Unknown*

I had little choice other than to accept Austin's offer, so I agreed. Being responsible for Heidi and myself, I needed a job. I worried working with him would change our relationship, but two weeks later everything was running smoothly. Not wanting him to regret offering me the position, I insisted we have separate offices. When Priscilla found out, I came into a newly furnished office. Complete with mirrored finishes, soft white surfaces, and four very large, very welcomed monitors. Courtesy of the handsome man who was currently arguing with one of his clients.

My first assignment, design a webpage for Absolute Power Motor Sports. It seemed simple enough, present a theme, which shouted badass man on two wheels. I managed to create three different options, all featuring a hot, half-dressed girl who helped to answer any questions the viewer needed. Dylan chose certain elements of each one, yet eliminated the cliché girl, which surprised me.

"*Motherfuckers can find hard tits somewhere else.*"

After I finished Absolute Power, other companies got in contact with Austin, wanting to have a similar page created. Austin took their money and smiled, as I decorated the internet with diamond plated backgrounds, and bold letter fonts. I'll admit, it was fun to sit back and allow myself to play around.

While Austin had agreed to keep our working relationship separate from our personal one, he also went the extra mile to make me aware of how much he cared. For example, last Friday he sent me a bouquet of wildflowers, their happy faces arranged in a dark vase. The card attached, spelled out his desire for a date. The flowers he used as an opening line.

Lainie,
I know a place where these grow wild.
Let me show you tonight.
Austin

The characteristic I loved most about Austin was his ability to know where I will feel most comfortable. Words could never define how sexy he looked standing beside his motorcycle, in my favorite faded jeans, black boots, and logo shirt. Working in his office, afforded me the luxury of wearing jeans when I chose. While I enjoyed my skirts during the majority of the work week, every Friday, I slid into a pair of jeans I'd had long enough to make them feel like pajama bottoms.

Sitting on the seat of the bike was a bright red helmet, which matched the paint on the motorcycle. As I got closer, I noticed the tiny letters, which formed my name in script, emblazoned on the side.

"What's this?" Uncrossing his arms and ankles, he shoved himself away from a reclined position. "Well," reaching for the helmet, his fingers gripped the straps, and his hand disappeared inside. "I have plans of having you on the back of this quite often, and need you protected."

Hearing the words and absorbing their meaning, I accepted the truth of his intentions. While he may have meant the danger I faced from the accidental contact of the road or elements, my heart sighed a little, allowing him to take ownership. It was deep and powerful, with the possibility of crushing me, and there was no way I could turn away.

I've watched Austin work a computer as if it was an extension of himself. Fine-tuned hand and eye coordination, in a beautiful symphony of speed and skill. I handed over my safety, and giving complete control to his skills as a biker came easy. Just like the keyboard, he commanded the power of the vibrating machine under us. No one could argue he was a walking billboard for sex under normal circumstances. However, the feel of him between my thighs, the way he squeezed my hands when we stopped at a traffic light, or how he rubbed my knee before he dug into the throttle, increased his sex appeal tenfold.

I could have remained attached to his back all night. No conversation was needed, only observing the scenery as it passed by. Down city streets where men stopped what they were doing, pointing in our direction, admiring the sexiness of the bike as we went on our way. Modern highways turned into dirt roads, which ended in fields of billowing grass. The sun setting in the horizon, cast the last few rays to the countryside beauty.

Austin allowed me to get off the bike first. His gloved hand providing a solid hold, as I placed both feet back on the ground. Taking my new helmet from me, his already hanging from the silver handle bars. His hair oddly sexy, regardless of the restraints from his safety gear.

"Where are we?" I wondered, as I shook out my not so sexy hair, wishing I had worn a hair tie to work. I used my fingers to drum life back into the flattened strands.

Something to my left reflected in my vision, causing me to turn. It's a small pond with a wooden dock running about half way down. Dusting the west edge of the water is a patch of wildflowers, just as he'd promised to show me.

"Well about six miles in that direction," he pointed across the expanse of the pond. "Is the entrance of my brother Chase's land. And about ten miles on the other side of that road we just left, is Dylan's property."

I looked around in the directions he pointed, appreciating the beauty, which surrounded me. There is a long tree line, which borders the pond. I could almost picture a log cabin nestled in the pines. A simple front porch with rocking chairs facing the water, giving its inhabitants a place to reflect, and enjoy the beauty of nature.

Austin interrupted my ridiculousness, by taking my hand. He walks us through the high grass. I cringe for a moment thinking of the number of snakes coiled up in the camouflage of underbrush, hiding from the heat of the sun. I'm grateful when our boots hit the wood of the deck, and no snake scurried out from hiding.

"It's beautiful here." And it is, a peaceful lullaby of silence being separated from the city. Picture perfect in nature's unduplicated painting of untapped landscape. Bull frogs singing their own version of appreciation for the endless beauty.

"I agree, which is why I brought you out here." His hands are back in his pockets, a sign he is nervous about something. He's also rocking back and forth on his heels, a complete contrast to his normal in charge demeanor. "I called an architect about a month ago. He sent me an email yesterday with a rough draft for the home I want to build here."

"This land is yours?"

The rays of the sun highlighted the healthiness of his hair; giving life to the scruff he had allowed to grow. Austin was blessed with an olive skin tone, flawless even in the harshness of the sun.

"Yes, Granddaddy gave each of us a portion. This was where I learned to fish and skip rocks. I even fell off the end of this dock once, had to have six stitches in my arm." He pulled up the sleeve of his shirt revealing a faint, linear scar, under the edge of a tribal band tattoo. My fascination with tattoos in general overrode my manners, as I reached over, running the tip of my index finger along the black lines.

"What's your tattoo of?"

Austin pushed the sleeve of his shirt the rest of the way up. A look of pride taking up residence on his face. "It's silly really," he grinned. Pushing the edge of his cotton shirt up and away from his deltoid, giving me a clear view of the intricate details of the piece of art.

"Granddaddy was always giving us these lessons in life, words to live by I suppose. But this one time, he took the three of us out to his house, pulled out a bottle of Hennessey, and gave us all these bracelets made of paracord. There was this metal plate in the center that had 'faith' written in the center. He told us to always have faith, to carry it with us, and as long as we had it, things would be okay."

Black lines curved and circled like wild vines, attaching themselves to his arm. I'd seen enough back alley tattoos to know if a man had ink completely around his arm, he had either been shit faced drunk at the time, or had balls made of steel. Knowing Austin like I did, my money was on the balls.

"I kept hitting mine on the edge of one of my keyboards, so I had this done."

There in the middle of the entanglement, in scripted letters was the word faith. "My middle name." The words came out in a breathless whisper, leaving my body before any rational thoughts could be formed.

"I know, kinda cool, don't you think?" Austin had a new look about him. Where his words reflected that of a kid who just discovered *GI Joe,* his eyes spoke of something else. Something deep and with more meaning than he was prepared to share. It gave me a tiny sliver of hope. A secret longing for the desire I haven't shared with anyone, or admitted to myself. I've allowed him to become this ball of wonderful, filling the hidden crevices of my soul.

"So, this house you want to build." I broke away from the heaviness, redirecting from a conversation we had approached far too soon. The last thing I wanted to have happen between Austin and myself was to fall into a falsehood, confusing the feelings associated with a long absence of affection and heartfelt emotions. A move I would've called normal, if we were talking about my momma or sister.

Austin went on to describe his home. Complete with hardwood floors, crafted from the trees which would need to be cleared to make room for his house. His excitement was almost contagious, causing my face hurt from smiling so much.

As the sun finally dipped behind the trees, casting its final orange and purple rays across the sky, small shimmers of light peaked between tree branches. Austin and I sat on the end of the dock, toes in the water, watching as the ripples carried off to nothing in the mass of water.

"You know, this is one of my favorite things to do. Sitting back and enjoying the small moments we're usually too busy to observe. You know what would make this even better?" Austin turned his head in my direction, those blue eyes of his seeming to sparkle in the fading light. "A blanket on the tailgate of your truck, and a cooler full of beer?" I wanted to add a mayonnaise jar full of fireflies, but chickened out at the last second.

As the final remnants of the day faded into the night, a flash of something brightened his face. Leaning over, invading the small space, which separated us, he placed his fingers along my jaw, and pulled himself even closer. In a moment filled with electricity, his lips brushed against mine. Soft caresses of promises of what I hoped to come.

Laying in my bed later, my lips still tingling from the connection I'd felt. Tossing and turning, trying to find a balance where my mind can shut off, allowing my body the rest it needs. My subconscious wouldn't cooperate, the warnings I'd silently given myself to forget the idea, which has rattled around in my head since he dropped me off at my car. His kiss carried so much weight, such a simple act, but one I had written off as an impossibility. Yet this incredible man, with his staggering IQ, housed in a body, which would make a nun cuss, gave me the tenderness I craved. The touch I longed for, and the control I needed.

I tried again to remind myself this was completely crazy, the last thing I wanted to do was to give him the impression I was anything less than the woman I presented. Yet I still raised my hand to knock on Dylan's front door, knowing full well he was spending the weekend with Claire, celebrating her first three-day weekend in months. I was nervous. No matter how I presented myself, justified my actions or told myself a falsehood for why I was really here, as soon as he opened that door, everything would change between us.

Sleepy confusion greeted me, as he opened the wooden door. His hair was rumpled, giving him a sexy edge I had never seen. Not allowing him to question why I was here, or give me an ounce of room to back out, I pressed myself to him. As much as I enjoyed his tender kiss before, I needed more. I locked my lips against his, knowing he would take the hint of what I wanted, what I desperately needed.

I have never been confident enough to take the lead when it came to asking for sex. In the few relationships I'd been involved in, I had always let the guys come to me. Stepping out of that box, wavering from my comfort zone, I was about to take exactly what I wanted.

The hair at the base of his neck provided a small amount of leverage to hoist myself up, and onto his body. Austin clued in quickly, as my tongue passed his lips, tangling with his own. He tasted of fresh mint, and I chanced a swipe of my tongue across his smooth teeth, receiving a moan in return.

I hadn't bothered to change out of my sleep clothes before I decided to venture over here. Something Austin noticed when his hand found the lack of panties under the thin shorts I had on.

"Lainie, you sure?"

Many things in my life I wasn't sure of, wanting to be loved by Austin wasn't one of them. There were so many things I wanted from him, but even more I wanted to give him. I would start with my heart, which came with my body.

"I want you to love me." My words were my heart's fondest wish. A desire which ran deep within my soul, kept there out of fear of not being returned, crushed in the battle I fought every time I looked into his eyes. I wanted him to love me, not only in a physical sense, but in the way we've all read about. An all-consuming love, which is so strong, it makes forever take notice.

Blue eyes flicking between mine, labored breaths from rising chests, a realization passing over his glorious face. He needed no further confirmation as he pulled my feet off the ground, my legs wrapping around his hips, and my mouth once again crashed to his.

As he settles me into his bed, the sheets still relatively warm from his body heat, he followed me down, our lips never parting. I ran my fingers over his naked chest, traveling around to his back; I took his open shirt off in the process. As soon as the shirt left the top of his shoulders, he let go of the skin he caressed, long of enough to toss the shirt to the floor below.

His hands left a trail of fire, as he memorized every ounce of skin on my hip and sides. Every touch fanning the flames he had unknowingly started, by allowing me to have my fears validated.

"God, you're beautiful." His confession fell in waves of desire, hitting their intended target in the juncture of my thighs. It had been so long since I had wanted to be touched like this. Devoured by not only pretty words and thoughts, but by the skilled hands of a man such as Austin. I lost myself in his journey of discovery, searching for what lay underneath the thin material of my clothing.

"Touch me." Austin knew the significance of my request. Reassuring me over and over, he would wait for as long as it took for me to become comfortable with myself enough to let him in.

In that moment, two simple words changed everything between us. For me there would be no going back. No hiding behind excuses of why I couldn't accept the love I swear I saw in his eyes.

His touches were so gentle, soft, and patient. He kisses my shoulder, as his lips trail back and forth across my collar bone, and swell of my breast. A firm hand carefully approaches the edge of my other breast, his thumb testing the waters, as it flicks my nipple. So much time has passed since I have felt a hand, other than my own, stimulating the sensation, which seemed to be hooked to a cord connected to my clit. My back arched, pushing my breast into the palm of his hand. My shirt is tugged up and pulled away, giving him full access to my hardened peaks. Begging to be lavished by his tongue and mouth.

His touch is all consuming, so much I have to let go of his back, grabbing the headboard to keep myself in place. Austin nips at my left nipple, while his hands slide my shorts to my feet, and then off, throwing them to join the other clothes somewhere in the room. The way he moves, brings me close to the edge, only to shove me back. Making my breath come in pants, labored for no reason.

I can feel his kisses travel lower. My anticipation growing wilder, as he inches lower and lower, getting closer to where I need him most. However, he adjusts his position, his chest covering my slick core, shocking me, and sending me into an unexpected orgasm, as he plunges his tongue into my belly button.

"Austin!" His name falling from my lips like a grateful prayer, in appreciation for the euphoric feelings coursing through my body. I could feel the smirk on his face. It is without question an earned expression, one he can repeat anytime. It, partnered by the stinging of his prickly facial hair, the sexy stubble I love to see on him, are now heightening the anticipation.

"Look at me," he commanded. "Open those eyes and watch me love you." There was no fear, no shaky legs or flush of skin, as I released the headboard, and positioned myself on my elbows, obtaining a clear view of him hovering over my center. His eyes never close, never leave mine, as his tongue peeks out, licking from my entrance to the very tip of my clit. Everything in me wants to fall back to the mattress, close my eyes, and just feel. However, a large part of me, the one that is in control, refused to turn away, if even for a second.

He flattened his tongue, and felt myself growing wetter at the sight of him. The vine tattoo spread across his shoulder, reaching almost to his neck before diving back down his left peck, and then disappearing under his arm. I wanted to trace every line of it with my fingers and tongue, losing myself in his essence. His two fingers sliding inside of me, derailed my mapping of his ink, eliciting a cry of ecstasy, from deep within my belly.

"Oh, God." The feeling was intense, not from hitting that mythical spot buried deep inside me, but from the slow and wonderfully tortured pace he took getting there. His tongue joined his fingers, dancing together to bring me once again to the edge.

"A—Austin," I panted, aching for a release. Any residual fear found no room to grow and manifest in this moment. As slowly and carefully as he'd found his way to my apex, he took even longer to find his way back to eye level with me. I haven't looked at his cock, having been too lost in all he had given me to consider its size, until now as it pressed between us.

He reached down, running the head along my slick center. His eyes searched mine for the slightest warning. "It's been a while." I admitted, a waste of words since this conversation had already transpired over a game of chess. He'd confessed to trying to be like Dylan and failing miserably, and I had revealed I had only been with a few other men.

Just like every action Austin had taken with me this far, he carefully filled me with not only the incredible sensation of just being with him, but also the unmistakable look of love on his face. His strokes are even and measured, assessing my level of comfort before his own. He escorts me once again to the edge of that glorious cliff, and then holds my hand as we dive over together.

As we lay wrapped together in the dark, the whirl of the ceiling fan overhead is the only noise in the room. Austin pulls me tighter, kissing the top of my head. "I've thought about having you here many times. Although I admit, I fed you dinner before bringing you in here."

Something about hearing how he imagined me in the same way I'd imagined him, gave me the courage to lift myself from his side, straddle his pelvis, and begin climbing that cliff, over and over again.

Chapter Seventeen

Austin

Don't let labels define you.

S ome things in life you're prepared for, even anticipate. Like the first time you drive a car alone, or rent your first apartment. Being intimate with Lainie had most definitely been something I'd anticipated, yet could've never in a million years planned for the feelings which came after. I had prepared for a much longer wait. Dealing with the demons she was, cold showers had become a part of my daily routine.

Seeing her face as I brought her to release the first time, was something I will never forget. Watching as the skin between her breasts glistened with tiny beads of sweat, shiny droplets of assurance she was in utter bliss. I loved how her neck flushed red with her orgasm, extending to the tip of her rib cage, rising and falling with her need for air.

Even when the relationship with Keena was new and the sex was multiple times a day, the magnitude of what I felt could not compare. Lainie awoke something inside me, a locked door I never knew existed before she came along. Now that it was open, we could have a new adventure, exploring every hidden corner.

Having her sitting across the hall, I secretly watched as she worked on each project I handed her. I felt better having her there, not that she was in any danger, not anymore. I only wished freeing her from the fear of the attack was as easy as ridding the world of the man who gave it to her.

She was fidgety today, and for good reason, Heidi was going to court for her divorce hearing. Lainie had me check flight logs last night to be sure George had made it to Charleston. Heidi insisted she could handle it herself, telling Lainie she'd married the man on her own, and she could divorce him the same way.

I called Dylan while Lainie was in the shower, and he was sitting inside the courtroom, keeping an eye on the proceedings. Lainie had never come out and said George was violent. But I couldn't risk something happening, and being unable to do anything about it.

Right now I envied the relationship between the two sisters. Lainie standing up for Heidi, protecting her from a man she knew was wrong for her. Too bad my own brother couldn't be as rational as Heidi. Chase continued to ignore my calls and texts. According to Momma, he had himself holed up with that harlot, and hadn't been by their house since his welcome home party.

I felt as if I was failing the family, tearing it apart with speculations, and assumptions. The only evidence I had was a grainy photo, and the backside of a girl in a security video her own mother couldn't recognize. Maybe it was time I put it to rest, drive over to Chase's, and apologize to him and Harmony. Anything to bring the family back together, good and strong like we have always been.

"Well, look what the cat dragged in." Lainie walked in, her white skirt tight enough to give me reason to look a little longer. Dylan followed in behind her, his eyes looking past her, and on to me. Lainie continued closer, a wicked smile taking shape on her face. Gliding around my desk, she slid her slender thigh across my thighs, and then placed her luscious ass on my growing cock. My fingers found her hip, no directions needed, with the soft feel of her black, silk shirt under my fingertips.

"Heidi is officially divorced." Her bright and contented smile lit up my world, as she wrapped her tiny arms around my neck. "And that paper you wanted me to file, is on its way." Dylan planted his boots, one on top of the other, on the corner of my desk. Crossing his arms, and tucking his hands under each other. He gave me a quick nod, something Lainie was oblivious to.

Had Dylan not been in the room, I would have lifted her off my lap, and taken her across my desk. Showing her with my actions, what my lips failed to convey.

"What in the world is that?" Her index finger pointed backwards at the grainy photo, which had brought me no closer to the truth, and further from my brother.

"That, Miss Lainie, is a young lady who is more of a ghost than anything else." Dylan adjusted his pelvis to reach into his pocket, and retrieve his phone. Lainie's attention is unwavering, as she crossed the room, coming to stand a few feet from the screen.

"Austin, can you zoom in on her right hip?" Lainie's index finger tapped on the screen where she wanted me to concentrate the magnifier. Two clicks later, the screen was full of what appeared to be a clothing tag. Silver letters stood out against a black tag, a combination of Roman numerals and hash tags. Lainie moved closer, her eyes squinting to make out what the tag reads.

"Why are you looking for this girl?"

"She was in the car used to picked up Cash."

Her body flinched, and her finger dropped. As she turned toward me, her face was hard, with a fire in her eye starting to build. Resuming her place on my lap, this time she took control of the keyboard.

"Lainie, do you know who that is?" Dylan dropped his feet to the floor, moving around to the other side of my desk, his curiosity peaked.

"No, but I know those jeans." Her voice is hurried as if she couldn't move fast enough. I leaned back, not wanting to interrupt her, but also wanting to know what she was thinking. "Marcus Avery, he's a rather secretive designer out of Scotland, and very selective about who wears his product." Lainie's fingers were moving nearly as fast as mine tend to, her head bouncing back and forth between the keyboard, and the tag of the jeans. "You have to be someone, or have a stash of cash in order to even get an appointment with this guy. Lucky for us, I built his web page. It's more for bragging than selling, I can assure you." Pulling up to a firewall, the hot pink skull and crossbones caused me to smile slightly. "One good thing about Avery, he needs to keep detailed logs on every single pair he sells."

Lainie leaned back, finding my chest waiting for her, as the screen filled with columns of names and numbers. "I noticed someone recently wearing a pair, figured a certain Morgan brother was being particularly generous with his money."

Her words were cold, and for a moment I felt as if I had done something wrong. I knew it wasn't Claire. Dylan still had to fight tooth and nail to get her to let him spoil her most of the time.

"Harmony had a pair?"

"Yes, at the party at your parent's house." She turned to look at me over her shoulder, my need to kiss her overriding my sense of decorum. "Claire and I noticed them, but more importantly, your mother noticed them."

"Oh, she did. Wanna know what else the eagle eye noticed?" Dylan interrupted, a gleam in his eye. "How Audrey was mooning over Chase."

An alert tone sounded before we could quiz Dylan, the list of customers complete, and waiting for us to review. Several minutes of silence passed, as we each scanned the names. "Damn it, not a single Harmony listed." Lainie slapped the desk, as I started at the top of the list again.

"No," Dylan jumped to his feet, rounding the desk, and taking large steps toward the screen. "But look who is." Following his outstretched hand, his finger pointed at a name I had overlooked the first time. There, in black and white, was a name I hadn't uttered in what seemed like forever. Memories of the last time I saw her flashed in my mind.

The ringing of the phone was followed by the sweet sound of Lainie's voice filling the office, and pulling my attention back to her. We really needed to hire a receptionist. I had discussed this with Lainie, who didn't agree. I could tell she worried the cost was something a relatively new company couldn't support.

"Absolutely, I'll be here all day."

"Who was that?" I pulled her back into my chest, enjoying how good she felt so close to me. I craved the feelings she gave me, needing to be close to her as often as possible.

"A good woman will make you a better richer man." Granddaddy had been talking to our dad at the time. *"A bad one will fill you with regret, and empty your pockets."* When our Uncle Cecil was sneaking around with a lady from the wrong side of the tracks, Granddaddy had imparted those words of wisdom.

"That was Special Agent Greg Shaw. He is investigating the case against Jackie and Kennedy Fraser. He needs to ask me a few questions about what I saw while I worked at the company."

I anticipated tears, a shaking body or even hysterics; what I got instead was a shoulder shrug, and kiss on the cheek. A few minutes later, the man from the phone call presented himself at the front entry. Lainie led him to her office, closing the door, and increasing my anxiety in the process.

"We need to run a check on Virginia." Dylan allowed no room for my freak out, requesting my attention from the wooden door, which currently separated me from my entire world. "We need to see if there is a connection between her and Harmony."

Virginia Greyson was probably sitting on the porch of some trailer in the Midwest, smoking a cigarette, while screaming at her twenty kids. Not one time had she come to the hearings for Cash's trial, or did she attempt to post bail for him. Maybe she'd smartened up, and told him to fuck off.

I used every resource I had access to, but Virginia Greyson had no priors, not even a traffic ticket. She'd also disappeared the second she aged out of the system, with the exception of the designer jeans list. There was no driver's license for her in any state, no credit cards, and no property. Harmony Wells, until Dylan offered up her last name, I didn't even know she had one. After having hated the girl for so long, I really hadn't taken the time to learn anything about her.

Harmony Wells, grew up in Dallas Texas. The third child of Homer and Tammy Wells, she dropped out of high school to move to New York, to become a model. There was no record of her ever having worked in the state of New York, no driver's license, or state identification. Which would make perfect sense. As the last vital statistic was a death certificate filed in Rhode Island, after a traffic accident involving a Greyhound bus.

"Dylan, we have to show this to Chase."

"Show him what? That we have once again gone behind his back, and dug up more dirt on the girl he loves?"

Chase had not been too keen when I confronted him about moving in with Harmony. He'd accused me of being jealous of him having a girl who was ready for that particular step. He told me to keep my jaded views about women being spawns of Satan to myself.

He still wouldn't listen, even after we showed him the video we had of his girl dancing on a pole. *"Austin, you are a fucking computer genius, you could fake this shit with your eyes closed."* I wish I had, that way I could smack him upside the head and say, "gotcha". But I didn't fake anything, and if I didn't figure this shit out fast, Chase was liable to do something really stupid, like get her pregnant.

"So we just sit back, knowing she's lying through her teeth?"

Dylan shook his head, his smirk told me he had the perfect plan. I remained silent, giving him the floor to paint the perfect picture of what he had swimming through his head.

"Who is the one person, besides Harmony, Chase will listen to?"

Six months ago I would have said Granddaddy, but now, I wasn't certain.

"Seriously, Austin, besides Lainie who can still put the fear of God into you?" His eyes were wide, expecting me to know the answer from the way his arms waved around his body, or how his eyebrows shot into his hairline.

"Oh, for fucks sake…Austin, Momma!"

"You're a fucking idiot!" I pointed my index finger in his face, my frustration getting the better of me. "Chase stopped pissing his pants at the thought of upsetting Momma a long time ago. He's a fucking Marine or have you forgotten?"

Dylan had never been one to back away from a challenge, "He may be a Marine, with guns duct taped to his arms, and grenades for balls. But one look from that sweet woman, and he'll crack like a goddamn boiled egg."

There was no real point in arguing, he could call Momma if he wanted to. However, at the end of the day, Harmony held the one thing, which brought every warm blooded male to his knees, his constant supply of pussy.

Chapter Eighteen

Lainie

Truth is like the sun, you can shut it out for a time, but it ain't going away.
- Elvis Presley

"Weren't you scared to death?"

"With Austin and Dylan in the next room? Hardly." Claire called me just after I got home from work. Her conference turned out to be as dull as watching paint dry. Since she didn't want to sit in the hotel bar drinking her boredom away, she called me instead.

"You've got a point," she reasoned, chuckling under her breath. "Still, I would have been as nervous as a long tailed cat in a rocking chair store, if a federal agent flashed his badge, and wanted to have a word with me."

While Claire had a definite point, the reality was nowhere near the colorful image. Special Agent Shaw, turned out to be one of the nicest guys I'd ever met. Joking with me at first, making a comment on how he was slightly nervous to leave the building with my two bodyguards ready to pounce.

"What kind of things did he ask you?"

"Well, mostly about my time working for Jackie, and then a little about my interaction with Kennedy. Although that wasn't much, as I avoided him most of the time."

Agent Shaw knew about the specifics of several projects I had with Kennedy. "He did point out an area they had a few red flags on. Mostly, the fact I had worked for the company less than a year, and I had already been placed in a management position." I would keep the reason Agent Shaw gave me to myself, as it caused a shiver to run up my spine.

"Miss Perry we've interviewed Mr. Fraser, who has been all too willing to tell us everything he can in hopes his cooperation will help his case. He specifically included your name as a person he felt a certain…vendetta…against. When he was asked to elaborate, he said you had refused him, something women just don't do."

I had confessed everything else to Dylan and Austin, but those words would stay with me, locked inside a place I kept hidden from everyone

"So are you going to have to testify?" I could almost imagine Claire, sitting in the center of her hotel bed. White sheets like fluffy clouds surrounding her, and adjusting herself from a lying position to her knees. One of those fluffy pillows now in her lap.

"Actually, I didn't have much to add, since again, I hadn't been there long enough to really do anything."

"Did Austin go all cave man on you once the agent left?" Since being with Dylan, Claire had developed this Cinderella attitude. She now wanted a happily ever after for everyone walking the planet. I suspected she pictured white horses and gallant men coming to save fair maidens from evil dragons and wicked stepmothers.

"Not really. He and Dylan were in a deep discussion about Chase."

Speaking his name caused his face to flash in my mind, along with the photo of the girl's backside. "Hey, I nearly forgot. Do you know anyone by the name of Virginia Greyson?" Dylan had pointed at her name with a look I couldn't label. Austin looked as surprised, as if seeing an old friend at a class reunion.

"Well Greyson is the last name of Cash. Maybe it's his mother or sister? Why do you ask?"

I explained the list I uncovered to Claire. Still disbelieving someone like Harmony would wear such an expensive brand of jeans.

"Did you get a look at this Virginia?"

"Only a photo of her when she was being released from the custody of the county. Apparently, she and the guys were in the same state home. I kind of feel bad for her, she had an overbite so large, she could eat corn through a picket fence."

"Oh, my gosh! Lainie Faith Perry, that is so mean." Her words were chastising, but her tone was full of mirth.

"What? It's the truth. Hell, we should send her to Harmony and let her dentist take a whack at her."

"We could, they might even make friends. I mean they already wear the same designer jeans." We were both laughing like a couple of adolescent teenagers. Just as quick as the laughter started, it stopped and, like a cartoon light bulb above a character's head, silence captured us. Reality pinning us down, pondering over the revelation we just uncovered.

"You don't think?" Claire's words were drawn out in a questioning phrase, her mind working hard to rationalize the scene we had just given life to.

"It's certainly possible, right? I mean, anything is possible." How crazy did that sound? A young girl the guys shared a home with taking on the identity of someone else?"

"But didn't you say she had a massive overbite? That isn't something you can cover up with makeup. Besides, I didn't see anyone besides Cash's attorney on his side of the courtroom. Wouldn't you be there for your brother, if he was in trouble?" Claire had solid arguments against the possibility of Harmony and this Virginia being the same girl. Still, the edges seemed to touch, making the rate of possibility much higher.

"Speaking of siblings, my sister is officially divorced, and already moving on with her life." Deflection was my superpower, a skill I've perfected over the years. Claire and I could run back and forth all night with scenario after scenario, but words and theories would prove nothing.

"Something positive I hope?" Claire had a terrible poker face which reflected in her entire body, including her voice. She'd never get away with being dishonest.

"Well, if you consider being on a date with your legal representative something positive, then yes."

Heidi had come home all aflutter, running around the house like a kid after eating a bag of sugar. Preston had managed to hold off on his attraction to her. He'd taken her to a celebratory lunch under the pretense he did this will all of his clients. There he told Heidi she'd captured his soul the first moment he heard her voice, and how he had fallen in love with the remainder of her on their first meeting.

Before the hearing, Dean had pulled him into his office, offering him a scholarship to finish the last of his law studies, and then permanent position with his firm. Preston understood her studies will keep her here for a while, but would like to see where the relationship goes.

"And how did big sister take this news?" Claire knew me all too well. While I was happy for Heidi, I couldn't ignore the anger I felt in reaction to her choice. I thought she needed to be alone for a while, concentrate on her education, and find out who she really is.

"But, Lainie, you're not her mother and she is a grown adult. You can only love her, and be there for her. Besides, it could be worse."

Just as Claire knew me, I was well acquainted with her mannerisms. She had been stalling, waiting for right opportunity to slide in a piece of news, in hopes it would fade into the background.

"Claire?" I reassured I was here for her, just as she had been for me when I needed a friend.

"Cheyenne called today, leaving a message on my voicemail. When we broke for lunch, I called her back, only Shane answered the phone."

I'd heard the story behind how her sister and Shane had gotten together. I couldn't help wondering if it hadn't been Shane's plan all along, to wait until Claire left the state, and then go after Cheyenne. It didn't really matter though, since Claire spoke with conviction that her relationship with Shane had not been what dreams were made of.

"Cheyenne has gotten herself in trouble with the state of Kentucky. Apparently, she decided she didn't need to inform them she'd married Shane. Choosing instead to keep cashing the monthly checks they sent her to help with the kids."

"Is she at home, or did they arrest her?" I knew Cheyenne had several kids from different men. Claire and I had found this to be our common ground, a mother and sister with loose morals, and even looser panties.

"He said she was in jail, but they don't have the money to bond her out or to hire an attorney. Daddy told her to call me, figuring I would send a check from my hot shot boyfriend." Now I was the one sitting on my knees. I knew the conversation between Dylan and her dad was held away from her prying ears, and later Dylan had distracted her from asking what was exchanged.

"Daddy figured Dylan could pull a few strings, just as quickly as he could pull up a criminal arrest record."

"What?" I slapped my hand over my mouth, embarrassed by the volume of my voice.

"Yep. Dylan had showed Daddy just how much he knew about him. He gave him five minutes to leave and take his broke ass down the road, before he had him arrested on the three outstanding warrants he had on him."

So typical Morgan, holding all the cards, ready to use when he needed to. Scaring the piss out of people more effective, than actually placing them in the broken system.

"But Shane said to let her stay in jail. She had the use of a public defender, and if she went to prison, maybe it would wake her up." As much as I didn't agree with how he went from one sister to the other, I had to agree with him. Perhaps a little time to cool off, and think about her life would make things clearer for her.

"So, please, don't mention this to the guys. I was ready to call Dean to see if he could help, but I'm respecting Shane this time. It's time to let her see what her choices have brought her."

While I wanted to have a respectable relationship with Austin, giving my word to my best friend was more important. Besides this didn't impact the ties I had with Austin, or even the entire Morgan family. "Of course, it's your story to tell."

Claire shared some of the material they were covering in her lectures, trying to add as much animation into her story as possible, regardless of the fact I couldn't see her.

"Imagine for a second someone telling you how to do your job. Wait, that's a bad analogy, I'm sure Austin tries to hover over you all day." She couldn't have been further from the truth, if she'd stood across the ocean from it. Austin stayed in his office the majority of the time, giving his opinion only when I asked for it.

"Anyway, I had this speaker trying to explain to us the best approach for giving positive pregnancy test res—"Claire faded out, catching my attention with worry. "Oh, my God! I nearly forgot who else called me." Relieved, I shook my head in slight annoyance, adding in an eye roll to round it all off.

"You remember my coworker Shayla, the girl who fawned over Dylan?" How could I ever forget the infamous Shayla? Self-proclaimed, reformed slut-bag, something I silently doubted would last as long as a summer rain. Shayla enjoyed the thrill of the hunt too much. She knew of only one way to get what she wanted, and from the stories I'd heard, she hadn't left that life as far behind as she wanted people to believe.

"The girl with the playboy bunny necklace, right?"

"Yes!" Claire exclaimed, her voice taking on an excited tone. I wondered if she would still be excited if she knew where Shayla got that necklace from. One of her attempts to make it through the Morgan brothers. When I first went to work for Craven and Associates, I was handed Luxeum Brothers Jewelers to update their webpage. I had to stop in, see the layout, and take a few photos to get a feel for how the business ran. While I was there, Shayla came in, dressed in her standard whore apparel, saying hello to one particular girl behind the counter. As I took my photos and got a feel for the place, I overheard a conversation between the sales girl and Shayla. She didn't even try to keep her voice down when she told the story of how she and Dylan had gotten a little rough between the sheets the night before. During the activities, Dylan had pulled too hard on her hair, snapping the chain in half. I will never forget the turn the conversation took, or the way the dark haired girl sneered as she spoke. *"Imagine your luck, one brother gives it to you, while the other brother breaks it. What on earth could the third one have in store for you?"* Shayla had made her thoughts on that third abundantly clear, I hadn't thought about it until just now. *"Please! Austin isn't the type to know what to do with a woman like me.*"

"She is leaving the hospital, and moving to Ireland. After the whole fiasco with Dr. O'Leary and his cheating on his new bride, Shayla felt the need to comfort him. She invited him to stay in her apartment, since he had nowhere else to go. He, apparently, repaid her kindness by giving her a baby; she is due in four months."

"What? But he's married!"

"Apparently marriage is not a good form of birth control. You would think a nurse would know this, clearly not."

Well at least she knows who the father is, or maybe she is just picking the one who will give her the best life in the end. O'Leary can go back to his homeland, and practice medicine, giving her the finer things in life. She'd better hope he doesn't suspect the baby isn't his, and demand a DNA test.

"Did she mention if he was getting a divorce? I mean, if not that could make the holidays really interesting."

"She didn't mention it, but with her track record, she may not even care."

Claire began to yawn and since those things are contagious no matter if you're close or not, I told her to get into bed. "Besides Dylan should be calling you soon, and you can enjoy a little phone sex to help you forget the dullness of your day."

"Don't I wish." She scoffed. "Dylan is out doing some investigating for Ms. Priscilla."

"Huh?"

"Uh huh, she didn't like the way Audrey was acting the other day. She thinks there is something going on in her personal life that could be dangerous. So she has Dylan following her for a few days."

What in the world would be going on with Audrey? The girl was sweeter than homemade pecan pie, and twice as polite. I would have to remember to follow-up on that one.

Not a full minute had passed, as I ended the call with Claire that the bell on the front door sounded. I knew it wasn't Heidi since I'd asked her three times to show me she had her key with her. Looking out the peephole, a mass of scruffy chin waited for on the other side. Unlocking the door in a hurry, my need to be close to him increasing by the second.

As the lock disengaged, the door opened before I could turn the knob. Austin pushing passed the solid wood, lifting me to his chest, as his hungry mouth consumed mine. His hands cupped my face, as my calves find the corner of my coffee table. He doesn't stop as he moves us past the couch, down the hall, and onto my unmade bed. He hitched his hand under my left leg, grinding his very prominent erection against my heated core.

How does he do this to me? Takes me away from the shadows which plagued me, turning them into tiny prickles which carry me to a higher level of wanton. Rising up on his forearms, his eyes reflected the desire his body was conveying. I can't keep my fingers from reaching for his dark hair, diving up to my knuckles into his thick locks.

His eyes close as he tips his head back, a deep, guttural moan creating more heat in my core. Adding my fingernails, gently at first, then increasing until his pelvis once again grinds into me. His lips found the skin of my neck, teeth nibbling on the soft skin, eliciting my own moan.

"Lainie." Even his voice sends me into a new level, so masculine and fucking deep. Everything about him drives me crazy, making me willing to do things I have only read about. Anything to get me closer to him, beneath him, as he takes such care in pleasing me.

With his mouth busy sucking my nipple, his dark eyes locked on mine increasing somehow the effect of the pleasure. I have to watch him, take in every sensation he gives me. The point of his tongue as it circles around my hardened peak. How he flattens it as he licks his way around my tender flesh, flicking the nipple after every pass.

I have no clue how we are both naked, and honestly I don't fucking care. My breath is coming in pants, a side of effect of his fingers buried deep inside me. I'm already so close, always so damn close. Austin is skilled in leading me here, dangling me off the edge, and then just before I beg, he jumps with me.

He knows my favorite position, the one which allows me to control the pressure. I know he loves it too, as it brings my nipples directly in his line of vision. With his back against my headboard, and my legs straddling his hips, I crave the feeling of him buried deep inside me. Austin doesn't disappoint or make me wait. Tonight, he is letting me find my rhythm. I ride him without worrying how I look, or how embarrassing the halfcocked words are which race out of my mouth without my permission.

As I set across his pelvis, sweat covers the majority of our bodies. My forehead pressed to his, sharing our labored breathing, I love how his breath and body smell.

It happens naturally, we both pull back enough to look into each other eyes. There is so much I want to say to him, to tell him of the deep feelings I have. But it's too soon for me to have this passion, this need for him to stay right where he is.

His hands leave my hips, taking my face in his palms once again, there is something in his blue eyes, something deep and consuming.

"I love you, Lainie."

My breathing stops, heart skipping about thirty beats. He's said it, the words I've been keeping inside, afraid to prematurely release them. But he feels the same way, and the smile, which I can see reflected in his eyes, is just for him.

"I love you, too." I shake my head in quick repetition, the first happy tear journeying down my face, followed in a hurry by many more. Austin leaned forward and began kissing them away. This is bliss, happiness in its purest form. It's also rendering us both completely deaf. Neither one of us heard Heidi, as she called out my name when she entered the house, bounding into my bedroom where we are still connected in a lover's embrace.

"Oh, shit!" Heidi covers her eyes with her hand, her mouth still hanging wide open. "I'm so sorry." She mumbled as she backed out of the room, stumbling over the edge of her shoe, nearly falling in the process.

I'm too full of joy and Austin to even think of being embarrassed. Ignoring the sheet he tries to cover me with, I pull his mouth to mine, kissing him with everything I have.

Chapter Nineteen

Austin

Good women always think it is their fault when someone else is being offensive. Bad women never take the blame for anything.
- Anita Brookner.

Being interrupted last night, reminded me it was past time I found a place to live. While Dylan insisted he didn't mind having me, I needed a space of my own. Someplace where I was free to love on my girl, as often as I chose. It would solve the issue of Chase's refusal to have anything to do with me, including stopping by our parent's home if I was there. I wanted to shake him, ask him if the girl was really worth all this friction created by his attitude. Dylan believed in his plan to sit the boy down and have our parents talk with him. He wanted to present the facts we had, and the new evidence we'd uncovered. I had my doubts he would listen. Either way, I had my realtor looking for a place to rent for a year. I was hoping my home would be ready in that time frame, allowing all my plans to be set into motion.

Dylan and I had worked extra hard at the gym this morning, although he had almost fallen asleep several times. He was trying to wake up to face the day after being out most of the night. Momma had been known to have these uneasy feelings from time to time and both Granddaddy and Daddy warned us it was best to listen when those happened. Dylan had sat outside a single wide trailer in an older model Honda, sitting up on blocks, with the hood open and a tarp covering the exposed engine.

As we spotted for each other, he mentioned he saw Audrey park the car we had given her in the front parking lot where the manager's office was located. Then walk nearly five blocks to the trailer he watched her go into, yet not a single light had ever shone through the windows.

"Was there room in the driveway for more than one car?"

"Yep, even when the shiny new Chevy pulled up around three this mornin', there was still plenty of room." Dylan sat the weights he had just finished lifting back in the holder, and turned back in my direction. "Even when the tall guy went inside the door, the lights still didn't come on." He shook his head, a perplexed look on his face.

"Maybe the guy didn't want to wake Audrey?" I reasoned, trying to play devil's advocate.

"Oh, I highly doubt that." He picked up another set of weights, facing the mirror, as he began another repetition of curls. "He made enough noise to wake the dead when he tripped through the door, screaming her name like it was her fault."

Dylan was never one to hide his anger, he used different methods to control it, especially when a lady was involved. He also used it to intimidate people. I noticed how the veins on his neck were bulging; he was using the weights to release the anger he had toward the guy from Audrey's.

"Momma's right," he set the weights down again, using the bottom of his shirt to wipe the sweat from his face. "Something ain't right over at Audrey's."

As I picked up my phone, I suspected he wanted me to do a check on someone involved with Audrey.

"You know the drill, I need as much information as you can give me."

Lainie was as sweet as she could be, leaving a cup of coffee waiting for me on my desk. While the coffee was lukewarm, you'd never hear this old boy complaining. I'd drink cold coffee everyday if it kept her by my side.

I adjusted my keyboard closer so that I could work, but my ringing phone interrupted me. Seeing it was Dylan, I picked it up, but he spoke in a rush before I could respond with something crude.

"Listen, I need you to get in your car, and get over to Silver Dollar Pawn on Temple Street. I'll be waiting."

Dylan was still technically a detective, as his year of leave hadn't expired. He still carried his badge and his gun everywhere he went. So receiving a call where he gave such direct instructions, left no room for argument, and had me speeding down the road.

Silver Dollar Pawn, was located in what many of the locals referred to as pawn row. Being near the sheriff's office, the stores varied between pawn shops, and bail bonds offices. One could assume the two businesses went hand in hand. Dylan's car was parked right out front. Like a bait shop in the middle of Macy's, his Italian sports car looked out of place. I remembered the day he got the car, and the phone call he woke me with. He had gone with Carson and Miss Georgia to one of those auctions where they sell storage units when people forget to pay their bill. Dylan had gone, only to have Carson sign a report he needed to turn in. When nobody was bidding on this one particular unit, Dylan tossed out a bid for twenty five dollars. A few minutes later, the auctioneer pointed at him and hollered 'sold'. He'd paid the money, figuring it was going to be full of old clothes, and expired bills. Instead, there was a pinball machine, and the car currently parked, taking up two spaces.

Opening the aged metal and glass door, I was greeted by the dull sound of the alarm ringing off in the distance. Last time I was here, there was a copper cowbell hanging by a cord on the door. The owner must have sold it, and now had to make due with the vintage alarm.

Dylan stood against the glass display case, which doubled as the area to do all forms of business. His ankles crossed, and his belt buckle on display, reminding people who he was. Beside him stood a thick man, darker skinned, with initials cut into the hair on the side of his head. A thin line of hair followed the edge of his jawline, his skin wet with perspiration.

"Hey, Austin."

A conversation from not so far back flashed to the front of my mind. Dylan had spoken of a man who was a gangster wanna be. Seeing the letters carved in his already short hair, and as I grew closer, the tattoo of a crown on his exposed neck, I figured this was the man.

"Morgan." When Dylan first made detective, we all ganged up on him, as brothers often do, and gave him a landslide of nicknames. Since I wasn't certain the nature of the man beside him, I felt it best not to reveal our true relationship.

My eyes flashed briefly to the large, sweaty man beside him, and then moved to the side, revealing a shallow, flat box on the counter.

The box housed what appeared to be pieces of a chess set, one that looked familiar. Dylan picked up on of the pieces, the King to be specific, and then nodded to the space beside him, indicating for me to follow him.

As I approached the corner of the display case, I got a much better view of the remaining pieces. It became clear this was a set very similar to the one Granddaddy had given me. Pictures of me kissing the life out of Lainie last night, as I'd left her, and her embarrassed sister behind, flashed to the forefront of my mind. Endless kisses and assurance of new love had been exchanged countless times.

"Early this mornin', I got a call from Lainie." He placed a firm hand on my forearm, resting against the glass and cardboard. "Don't freak out, she is fine." He gripped my arm firmer, as I hadn't even realized my body had tightened. "She was leaving the house when she noticed your chess set was missing from the table. Heidi had already left for school, and the house was still locked. She didn't know if she should call the police or if—" Dylan's eyes took on a hard look, searching mine with a trace of disappointment behind his blue orbs. "—you had changed your mind about her."

My gut heaved from the weight of his words. Loving Lainie came so easy, made my world seamless, and complete.

"I knew better. Hell, a blind man could see how you feel about that girl. So I told her to stay home, take a hot bath and relax. I would find out where the chess set was. I assured her you were not the type of man to slide out the back door on a girl."

A huge lump was rising in my throat at the thought of my girl thinking I didn't want her. I would call her once this was all sorted out, but for now I needed to place her mind at ease.

Dylan told me everything. You can't get rid of me that easy, I'll call you later, I love you!

I looked up from my phone screen, as the swishing sound of the text headed toward its intended target sounded.

Dylan tapped his fist three times on the glass counter. "All right, Lardo. Tell me how this wound up in your sausage fingers, because we all know you are not a chess player."

The man he referred to as Lardo—a spin off on his actual name I assumed—adjusted his feet, the rubbing sound of cheap leather protesting from his movement. "How youse knows I don't play chess? I could be some champion or some shit."

"Sure, and I'm Mother fuckin Theresa. Show me which one of these is the Cycle." Dylan pointed to the box containing the set. I held my tongue, and my laughter anticipating him actually selecting a piece. The man huffed, and with as much confidence as I have when I play, pulled the Rook out, rocking it back and forth, just inches from Dylan's face.

"This is the Cycle. See I told youse I was a champion." Lardo presented it as if he truly believed what he was saying. If this was the same guy Dylan had spoken about, the gang member, he must have had a lot of practice.

Dylan snatched the piece from his fat fingers, disgust contorting his face. "Yeah, the champion of bullshit, even I know this is the Rook. A cycle is something you cut wheat with, not play chess."

Lardo didn't flinch or argue, only watched as Dylan laid the piece carefully back into the box. "Now, tell me how you got this." He moved to stand mere inches from Lardo's face, and I admit, without reserve, his tone caused me to take note.

He pulled his face back, smacking his teeth with his lips and tongue, resulting in an annoying sucking sound. "I told youse man, my girl goes to yard sales and shit. Some of it she puts online, other shit she has me sell."

Dylan moved his eyes to the man behind the counter, the same man who was here before. Everything in the store looked pretty much the same as it had before, with few exceptions. One being the new cameras I noticed now patrolled the front of the store. I was glad to see he had taken my suggestion.

"Give me a ballpark of how much this set is worth?"

I could have answered that question, as I had it appraised recently for my new insurance policy. With the pieces being genuine, the value reached the double digits. The pawn shop owner took a piece into his hand, and looked at it beneath his jeweler's loop, twisting and turning it in the lights above.

"It's a good clean set, very old. You're looking at around five grand." He removed his glasses from his nose, as he replaced the piece back into the box.

"The way I see it, Lardo, we can play this one of two ways. I can arrest your ass for possession of stolen property, and haul you down to the station, where I'll have them book you on felony charges since the value is more than five hundred dollars. You'll get a date with the judge, one that ends with you wearing a lot of orange, and your girlfriend getting a new man to sell her yard sale garbage to."

Lardo opened his mouth to protest, his finger pointed at the box.

"Did I give you the impression I was finished?' Leave it to my brother to add sarcasm to his interrogation. But Lardo bought it, shaking his head back and forth. "You can claim the set is your girls, but it won't matter because this set is in fact stolen, taken from the man beside you." He nodded in my direction. Lardo turned slightly in my direction, eyes wide with fear. "I know for fact he will want to press charges for you breaking into his girl's house, and taking his shit."

Lardo started backing up, hands raised and shaking his head. "Oh, hell no! I didn't break into no house. I ain't going down for that shit."

"Then I'd recommend you start talkin."

Lardo dropped his head, and placed both hands on the counter as if he were under arrest. "I swear, man, I didn't break into no house." Dylan waves his hand around encouraging him to get on with his story. "I know this chick, Gina, fine looking bitch. Big tits and tight ass, know what I'm sayin'?"

"Where do we find this big titted Gina? You have her tied in your momma's basement or something?"

"Nah, man. I was at this party like maybe two years ago, and there was this dude, he brought some blow, and was making friends with everyone. He and I gots to talkin', and I tell him about my gaming setup in my basement. With the grade of blow he is sharing, I tell him I can get him any game he wants for free. He seemed real interested in playin' online and shit. A few days later, I'm in the middle of kicking the shit out of some zombies, when he hits me with a request to join a party."

"And by party you mean—?" Dylan looked at me for an answer.

"A private room to play against each other. Some gamers wear headsets, and can talk back and forth, even play as a team against the computer." I added, not certain if this guy was really legit. Dylan nodded his head, and then turned back to Lardo.

"So, yeah, a few days later, I'm out with my boys when the dude texts me. Asks me if I'm interested in making a few bucks." Lardo is rather animated as he tells his story. Looking around at the three of us, as if this were just a typical conversation, and not a pseudo interrogation.

"I'm like, fuck yeah! I mean, who is gonna turn down money right? He tells me to meet him at this strip club where Gina works. He says she is looking to start a webpage, where motherfuckers can pay to watch her do X rated shit."

I catch Dylan's eyes, as his tale starts to get interesting.

"Gina is all kinds of fucking hot, dancing on the stage and shit. When she's finished, she takes me into a private room, where she tells me what she needs from me. I tell her what it's gonna cost her, and she asks if we can work something out."

The storeowner leaves when the phone begins to ring, turning his back to us as he answers the call.

"So, let me get this straight; you meet this dude at a party, snort some coke, and you trust him enough to do business?"

Lardo is shaking his head, hand raised about to correct Dylan. "Morgan, it ain't got nothing to do with trust. If the motherfucker has the cash, I'm gonna do what he needs. I mean," he does this weird thing with his shoulders, raising them several times, while simultaneously looking from side to side. "Last time I checked, starting a webpage ain't illegal."

I've often wondered, if the true criminals of this world were to all get together and use their brains for something good, what would they accomplish?

"I tell her I happen to have some extra parts I've been meaning to put to use, and I'm willing to help her, if she can meet my terms. Three days later, I have everything all set up, and she is fucking a vibrator on pay per view."

Dylan looked at me again. I can't argue with Lardo, what he just described happens multiple times a day. All perfectly legal, as long as the taxes are paid.

"So, if your business with her is done, why is she handing off stolen shit for you to pawn?" This is why Dylan is the detective. I've been listening so hard to his computer and gaming story, I've forgotten about the stolen chess set, the crux of why we were here.

"Bitches love me, man." He tapped his chest with the side of his left hand. I wondered if this is some gang signal, but dismissed it, as Dylan rolled his eyes.

"Come on, Lardo, you ain't had pussy, since pussy had you. Now cut the bullshit, and tell me what I want to hear. Unless you're fucking dying to take a trip over to county."

"Okay…okay, I'm gettin' there." The fat under his chin jiggled as he spoke, something I found slightly distracting.

"So Gina calls me up about a year ago, says she needs my help with some changes she wants to make. Only this time, she wanted me to show her how the shit runs. Teach her how to put the shit together and stuff. Only when I get there, she has these brand new computers already set up." The beeping of the bell from the door rings, as a new customer walks in, an older guy with a poodle under his arm. The shop owner finishes his call, and then proceeds to take care of the man on the opposite side of the room.

"So I'm like what the fuck? Why did you call me?" His hand goes out to his side. I doubt he could have a conversation if he was in handcuffs, by the way he is so animated.

"She's like, *'baby, I need you to set up a network for me'*." He raises his voice to mimic the sound of a female voice. My attention is peaked; setting up a network isn't child's play. If this Lardo is able to do this, we have bigger issues.

"And did you set it up for her?"

"Fuck yeah, I did. Gave her a stealth IP address, and shit, too."

Dylan looked to me, he may know gang-ise, but this is where I come in.

"IP addresses are like your fingerprints. They set you apart from all the other traffic online. By creating a stealth address, you essentially ping off legal addresses, but only for a short period of time. It's not long enough to track where the signal comes from."

Dylan nodded his head, "And you would use this for—?"

"Hiding illegal shit, and since porn isn't illegal as Lardo pointed out," I started.

"Hey, motherfucker." Lardo interrupted, his fat fingers smacking the center of my chest. "Morgan can get away with fucking up my name, but not you. You I don't know. It's Largo, not Lardo."

I want to laugh, but he's right, he doesn't know me, and I sure as fuck don't know him.

"Knock it off Kevin, or I'll let him kick your Crisco ass." Dylan knows us both, if he is confident how this would play out, then I won't back down.

"Like I said, *Largo*, porn ain't illegal. However, I suspect she had a different reason for wanting to ping off other addresses."

Largo nodded his head. "She never said. But once I set the server up, she thanked me, and said she would send me money. A week later, I got an envelope full of cash."

Dylan shook his head. "That still doesn't explain why she's having you front for her." He pointed at the box containing the chess set.

"I'd heard Gina was always hustling, turning tricks, or selling smack. Her brother is usually right behind her, following her like a fucking shadow. Right before you picked me up the last time, she'd sent a message to me. Said she had a business deal she wanted to team up with me on. Her brother, Cash, had been getting into a lot of heat and she was considering leaving him behind." He glanced between Dylan and myself, again using his hands to give his words a little push.

"Gina said she would be at the college downtown, something about taking some class, and I was to meet her at the coffee shop across the street. But when I got there, the block was full of cops, so we bounced and ended up back at the strip club."

My fists clenched at the mention of the very place where Lainie was hurt. Cash had been there not only to hurt my girl, but to set up some illegal shit, and Lainie was in the wrong place at the wrong time.

"She made a few calls, and then asked me if I knew of any programs to get around a firewall or piggyback on an existing break."

"And did you?"

"The fuck?" He tossed, annoyed with my questioning of his caliber. "Of course I did, you think just cause I have the Kings symbols, that I'm stupid or somethin'? I may have not gone to some fuckin' Ivy League, but I know how to fucking jump a pussy ass firewall."

"Slow up," Dylan stepped between us. "Austin what the fuck is he talking about?"

"You know what a firewall is, right?" He nodded. "Well piggy backing is just like it sounds. You attach on someone who already has access to a program, able to take the same information without being seen."

Dylan's cell began to ring; he checks the screen but ignored it. "How does this get you to having possession of stolen property?"

Largo started shaking his head. "After I set up the program, she asked if I had a car. I told her mine was busted, but I knew where to get one. She had me pick her up, take her to school, and shit like that. Every time I picked her up, she handed me money, said if the cops caught on I didn't know her."

"But I ain't going down for no bitch, especially not a crazy one like Gina. This morning she called me really early, saying she needed me to pick her up from the same place I always take her to; this fancy place over by the Battery. Only this morning she comes out with that box, telling me to take it, sell it, and keep the money for myself."

Dylan reacted quicker than I do, slamming Largo into the glass counter. "What fucking place, motherfucker?"

"The Bentley. She goes to class with this chick who lives there." Largo's face is beet red from Dylan's hands on his throat.

"You better not have fucking touched her." He shouts, as the man with the poodle leaves the store, the shop owner locks the front door.

"I didn't, I didn't! I waited in the car, never stepped foot inside." Dylan released him with a shove, and Largo slumped over coughing as he tried to get a breath.

"You stay the fuck away from the Bentley and the girl who lives there. If I catch you over there, I will personally make sure you never see the light of day again."

Chapter Twenty

Lainie

Fear is only temporary, regret last forever.

"Okay, baby, I'm going to go stand right over there." Austin had his arms wrapped around me, as the wind blew my hair across my face. I used my thumb to glide it to the side, reeling in the feeling of his love surrounding me. I've stood here dozens of times, giving myself an internal pep talk. Only to have it fall on deaf ears, as I failed time and time again.

This hold a dead man had on me, bewildered and frustrated the fuck out of me. It was out of character for me to quiver and quake over anything a man said or did. It was time to get back to myself, the ball busting, take no prisoners girl, I knew lived somewhere deep inside.

When I woke up the other morning and discovered Austin's chess set missing, I nearly fainted. I knew Heidi would never take something that didn't belong to her, and feared someone had broken in. I wanted to call Austin, but was too afraid to tell him, worrying he would blame me for being careless.

As I spoke with Dylan, he agreed to wait to tell Austin until he could investigate. He came over, checked the lock, and assured me the building was still safe. Two hours later, Austin sent me a text full of reassurance and his love. A few minutes after that, Heidi came home very upset. Her friend Ginger had experienced a death in the family, and had to leave town to help with the arrangements. Apparently this had happened as she waited for Heidi to use the bathroom this morning, leaving my sister to find her own way to school.

Austin and Dylan came over after they found the chess set, trying to be pawned by a street thug. While I didn't believe the line they were feeding me, I held my tongue as Dylan downplayed the story. I was certain I would never want to become a detective. I also knew the theory Claire and I had come to the other day was certain. Harmony and the girl from the home, Virginia, were the same person. The person who had befriended my sister as a way to get into my home, but why?

"You have Claire on the cell phone in your hand." He tapped the cell phone he had dialed into a video chat for the occasion. When I'd decided it was time to do this, to face this fear and kick it in the balls, I'd called Claire who suggested I surround myself with all my friends and family. "Everyone who loves you is here to help you conquer this." A final whisper of encouragement in my ear came from the voice I loved, but for the first time it didn't send a shiver down my spine.

With a kiss to my cheek, he jogged over to the line of trees, which bordered the back of the library. Even with everyone surrounding me, my legs still shook with a force I never knew they were capable of. I looked to my right, finding Dylan who was giving me a persuasive nod. He always stood tall; ready to take on the world if

I needed him. To my left was Carson, although older and certainly wiser than the guys, his youth and love for me shined in his kind face. Beside him stood Miss Georgia, the mother I never thought I ever wanted, with her polished looks and manners, which would make the queen blush.

"Lainie, don't let him live here anymore. Send him back to hell where he belongs." It was as if Claire wielded a magic wand, her words touched something inside. Setting my shoulders back and steading my legs, I took the first step.

"Come on, Lainie, I haven't kissed those beautiful lips in nearly three minutes. I'm dying here." Austin waited just under the cover of the trees, his feet wide apart, and arms crossed over his chest. Wearing dark pants with a grey t-shirt, my favorite look on him. When I had confessed this a few weeks ago, he'd started wearing the combination more often. It had certainly made working a rewarding experience.

One step became two, and then five, and soon I was within a few feet of the area where it all happened. Swallowing hard, I stopped on the very section of ground where my life changed that night. There was nothing really special about the spot. No stone marker to tell everyone who passed by that an attack had happened here. No battle stories to be share by a tour guide, or memorial to be celebrated every year.

Things would have been so different if I had chosen to walk five more feet to the traffic light. If I had taken the long way around the block, instead of cutting across an area thousands of college kids did every day. I would have never met Frances Greyson, and his horrible intentions. There would have been no suffering from nightmares, and anxiety of this place. But I also would never have met my best friend Claire, whose face was still smiling into the phone, cheering me on from the hallway of her conference. Dylan would never have rescued me, and would never have the opportunity to visit with her, never having a chance to fall in love with her. What are the chances I would have found Austin? The man who loved me to my core, protected me at every turn, and made me strive higher everyday, living life to its fullest.

"Frances Greyson, you were just a man of flesh and blood and while you hurt me beyond measure, I— I," swallowing back the tears, he didn't deserve them, he had taken enough. "I forgive you."

Priscilla Morgan stood beside Dean, close enough to reach out and touch if I needed her. She knew I needed closure, and swore to me on the day I was able to forgive Cash, she would be standing there with me.

"Lainie, hating someone gives them the upper hand. Forgiving them takes away the power they have over you."

While I'd never met her father, with as many of his slices of wisdom she shared, I felt as if I knew him. It was the combination of all the Morgan men, strong and handsome, with the heart of a gentleman. Born to love and protect the women around them, yet strong enough to let them grow.

I looked to Priscilla, her smile was tender, and her hand encased with her husbands, as she nodded her head.

"Rot in hell, you son of a bitch." I gathered up a wad of spit, and let it fly from my lips, landing in a cloud of dust on the dirt. While I forgave him, I still wished him an eternity of pain.

I took the last ten steps past the trees, to the area I never made it to that dreadful night. Austin arms were open wide, waiting for me to take my place. He lifted me up, as he truly loved to do. Twirling me around and around, as he chanted how proud he was of me, kissing every centimeter of skin he could get his lips on. "Now that rotten bastard won't steal a second more of your time, or cause one more tear to fall down your perfect face."

I had managed to drop my phone in all the celebration; Dylan picked it up, and was telling Claire how much he missed her. They've been apart for over a week, and while she was learning a lot, she also regretted she had to attend. If she had to do it all again, she would never have volunteered. But, getting her certification renewed was important to her. She loved helping people, especially victims of assault crimes. While the state required this refresher course, she would have declined it if given a do over.

Dean did insist on taking everyone to brunch. Carson waved off, saying he had to meet with a new client, before receiving the universal sign for 'call me' from Dylan.

As we drove, Austin had his hand wrapped tightly around mine. The sun seemed to shine brighter, and the air smelled cleaner as we drove back to the office. Perhaps Priscilla was right, forgiveness does give you back your power.

Brunch was a much lighter affair, as a small diner around the block from the hospital was chosen. I loved their French toast, and became quite the possessive person when Austin tried to steal a bite of the sticky, sweet goodness.

"Lainie, it's getting close to time for our family's low country boil. Everyone is invited, and I am counting on you and Claire to be there to level out the testosterone." I'd heard about this event, and as the months ticked closer to fall, I knew this announcement was coming.

"Of course, I wouldn't miss it for the world."

Austin had been checking his phone all morning. Looking at the screen, shaking his head or scowling, and then returning it to his pocket. I wanted to question him about it, see if it was something I could help with, but every time he looked at me, he smiled and pulled me close.

As we all stood in the parking lot, Priscilla pointing out the finer moments from previous country boils. Dean reminded her these were his employees who, when mixed with alcohol, became different people. It made me want to see this for myself.

"Let's go to my house and celebrate." Austin leaned over to my side of the truck, wiggling his eyebrows suggestively.

"No, Sir, we blew off work yesterday. I have webpages to build, and you have calls to return." After Austin convinced Heidi everything would be fine, and he didn't blame her for the actions of her friend, he insisted we have a lazy day of cuddling and the like.

"Lainie, this was an emotional day for you. I want to be able to just hold you, and be with only you for a while."

As we'd sat on my sofa, he received a call from his realtor. He had managed to locate a furnished apartment, which featured a short-term lease. We met him at the place, and I fell in love. After Austin signed the lease, he and I christened nearly every surface of his new house.

My inbox was full and running over, and our message line blinked with waiting clients. Still, Austin captured me against the wall in his office, devouring my lips until they were swollen, and red. He reminded me how much he loved me, and gave me one last chance to change my mind, go back to his house, and love one another again. Extricating myself from him, I reminded him my boss would not be happy if he knew I was slacking off to make out with a coworker. "I'd kick his skinny ass if he told on ya." With a wiggle of my hips, I exited the room, wishing I didn't have such a strong work ethic.

After eating so late in the morning, we worked through lunch, and well into the afternoon. As the sun began to drift along the horizon, I knew it was near time to call it quits. I finished the section I had been struggling with, a new design for a shipping company. I was unable to really figure out how to glamorize brown for anything except hot fudge. I shut off my computer and secured the passcodes, an extra measure Austin had insisted on. Given his profession, I shouldn't have been so surprised.

As I placed my purse on my shoulder, I could hear voices coming from Austin's office. Peering around the door, the back of a dark haired girl blocked my view. The conversation was heated as the volume of the voices began to rise. Fearing this was an unhappy client, I walked into the room.

"You're serious." Austin's face was ashen, as if he'd had just witnessed something horrible.

"Completely."

I walked around to make my presence known, revealing more of the dark haired girl as I progressed. I had to admit she was beautiful, definitely runway model material. From the back she was quite slender, but as I grew closer, her profile revealed a slight bulge on her lower belly.

"Mr. Morgan, is everything okay?" I glanced back and forth between the pair. Austin seemed to be in some sort of trance or perhaps shock. I had insisted from the beginning that we keep the office a professional arena, calling him Mr. Morgan when clients were visible.

Austin seemed frozen in time, and unresponsive to my question. Had he not been standing with his eyes open, I would have dialed 911.

"I'm sorry, we haven't been introduced." I attempted to get somewhere with the dark haired girl. She turned her green eyes in my direction, her pure, exotic beauty making me take notice. Slowly, a small smile took shape on her well-defined lips, revealing white teeth, which nearly glowed in the light against her tan skin.

"No, we haven't. I'm Keena Marshall, Austin's girlfriend." Her elegant fingers extended in my direction. Her voice sounding high pitched enough, I wondered if dogs barked when they were around her. "I've been trying to reach him all day." Her smile held a secret, one she couldn't wait to share. "We have reason to celebrate." She turned to me, since Austin was still in a holding pattern.

"Oh?" I quirked an eyebrow at her, hoping Austin would come

to the present soon.

"Austin is going to be a daddy." She said excitedly. Her voice going up an octave, her eyes bright, and her hand resting on that bump. This tiny, beautiful woman, who barely came to my chin, had just delivered the words, which knocked the breath out of my lungs.

"I was just telling him the good news, and as you can see, he is so happy he can't even speak." She closed the distance between them and placed her hand on his chest; on my chest, the place where my forehead rested as he'd finished his last orgasm last night. The chest he pulled me into when I finally walked across the area by the library. And the chest, which supplied the breath he used to tell me, he loved me.

"Wow, congratulations. I didn't r--realize he was seeing anybody."

When I was thirteen, I had found this little stream not far from the trailer park. With the summer so hot and no air-conditioning in the house, we had to find other ways to cool off. I'd spend hours sitting on the sandstones, letting the water rush by, taking the heat with it. My secret hiding place didn't stay secret for long, and neither did the lack of parental supervision. Tilly Eaton, Mark Eaton's momma, found out the stream was there. She came looking for him one afternoon, and found him about to slip out of his socks and shoes to wade out like the rest of us. *"Marcus Franklin Eaton, don't you dare step into that water, you will slip and cut your foot wide open!"*

Since my momma was nowhere to be found, I ignored her, and continued on placing one foot at a time into the cool water. She tried to tell me to stop, threatened to tell on me, but I was determined. Deciding the threat wasn't real, I took one more step onto the sandy stone, when my foot landed on the moss growing between the stones. My foot slipped causing me to lose my balance, but not before slamming my big toe into a jagged rock, slicing it clear to the center of my toenail. I knew Tilly was still behind me, but I wouldn't give her the satisfaction of being right about getting cut in the water.

"You comin', Lainie Faith?"

I swallowed hard, and bit back the scream, which wanted to see the light of day so bad. *"Yes, Ma'am, just watching this snake go to the other side."* I'd seen Tilly nearly climb a wall when a garden snake got in her flowerbed. She didn't disappoint me then either, as she snatched Mark by the back of his head, and ran out of the woods. I never cried as I wrapped my foot up. No one ever knew what happened that day. It was the most pain I have ever had in my entire life, until now.

"It's been hard, with me in New York, and him hidden away here in the sticks. But, we're together now, and with this little one coming." Her eyes locked on his, touching his face with her perfect, runway hand.

"New York? Wow, you're a long way from home." I torted, pain growing in my chest. I felt like I was being held underwater, restrained from rising to the surface.

"*Was* my home," she circled her arms around his neck, the place I found sanctuary. "I'm living here now, with Austin."

Keena's words ran on repeat for the next hour. I assumed Austin came back to the land of the living, since he'd called me about fifteen times, all of which I have ignored. I finally turned off my phone to silence the reminder.

I couldn't bring myself to drive. So I called for a taxi as I exited the elevator, not trusting mine, or anyone else's, safety. The thought of going home, to a place, which should have given me comfort, only reminded me of him, something I didn't want to think about.

Instead, I had the taxi drop me at the nearest bar. After I'd ordered a glass of wine, I took a seat in the corner. Suits of various shades of gray and black slowly migrated in, trying to rid themselves of the agony the day brought them. What I wouldn't give to trade them my pain for their obvious boredom.

"You know the alcohol only works if you drink it."

I slowly looked up from my glass of untouched crimson liquid to the overly made up face of the bartender. "Uh oh, I know that look. Child or husband?"

Holding on desperately to the last ounce of reserve I had. "Both," I whispered, my voice cracking with the escaping emotions. "Just not mine."

Chapter Twenty One

Austin

When everything goes to hell, the people who stand by you without flinching-- they are your family.
- Jim Butcher

"This is bullshit!"

Momma had grown sick of the rift between her children. When the first tear rolled down her cheek, Daddy called a meeting. Last time this happened, Chase and Dylan were chasing after the same girl. She didn't care for either one of them, and when they wouldn't take a hint, her daddy got involved.

"Did you do a background check on Claire and Lainie?"

"Yes." Dylan and I spoke unanimously.

Hearing her name made my soul hurt. I'd never experienced shock before, watching the world pass by you, and having no ability to join in. I didn't have to guess as to why she wasn't taking my calls, having had to watch Keena spread her lies like soft butter on warm bread. Momma told me to give her a minute to get over the sting of it all. I had called her as soon as my brain kicked back in, begging her to come and take Keena to a hotel for the night. Momma being well…Momma, refused to have her possible grandbaby anywhere except at home.

"Austin, I'll keep an eye on her, make sure this is all real." None of us boys had ever given her reason to worry about a baby coming. We'd known from the time our dicks got hard how to put a condom on.

"This is unbelievable!" Chase pulled at his still short hair, his body shaking with anger. "Dylan gets his first girlfriend, and she is welcomed into the family with open fucking arms. Austin changes jobs and now he thinks he can hunt down the fucking Taliban." Chase's face was red with fury, this however didn't faze our daddy, as he sat on the same bale of hay, as his son's voice rose in defense.

"And because I have a girlfriend, who is hot as fuck, everyone is jealous and trying to break us the fuck up!"

"Is that what you think? That I'm jealous?" Dylan was immediately on his feet, slamming into Chase with his chest, their fury filling the barn. "While your 'hot as fuck' girl is showing off her tits on a pole, my girlfriend is saving fucking lives." Chase attempted to shove him away, but Dylan wouldn't be swayed.

"I went there, Dylan." He shoved his finger in Dylan's face, pistoling his arm back and forth, as he spoke each word. "I asked her about it and I went there, nobody knew anyone named Harmony. She said she didn't work there, and I checked!" Something changed in Chase's voice. His pitch rose, as if he was still wading his way through puberty, but it was more than that. He knew we would never lie about something like this, not something as simple as a girl.

"Then where is she?"

When we left the pawnshop Dylan told me he knew Largo would run his mouth to her. *"He's going to call her and tell her we're looking for her. But you know what?"* He shook his head and wore the same smile he did after he won something. *"She planned for us to find this. She wanted to give us a new trail to follow."*

He had been right. Chase called later that evening, telling him Harmony had phoned in a panic, sayin' she had to leave town because her sister had to have an emergency C-section.

"I told you, she's with her sister, helpin' have her baby."

"Sure she is. And when that excuse expires, where will she be then, huh?" Chase hadn't spoken to me since I'd first confronted him about her. He had done everything he could to avoid talking with me, even choosing to work nights in the bike shop.

"Explain the photos and the videos. Are those all her sister, too?" Rage bubbled up like a volcano inside of me. Being away from Lainie, if only for a short time, was eating at me, killing me slowly. As was having the woman whom I'd placed in my past, currently fighting to get back into my bed.

"What? You think I'm going to believe a few grainy photos, and a video taken in a place where I know she has never been?"

"And what about the pawn shop? How do you explain that?" I was grasping at straws, anything to make him see this was all connected.

"Really, Austin? You want me to believe a story, told to you by a career criminal?" He laughed as he shook his head. "How many times have you arrested him, Dylan? And you honestly think this guy is credible?" His question rhetorical, considering he'd made perfect sense, his point was valid.

"Listen, I gave you guys my word, and no matter what I won't go back on that. But I draw the line on Harmony. I love her, and as soon as she gets back from her sisters, I plan to ask her to marry me."

"Are you serious?" I shouted, Dylan shoved me back as I advanced toward him.

"Absolutely, and she won't have to be pregnant in order for me to do it." Rage clouded my vision, as I pushed Dylan out of my way, and tackled Chase to the hardwood floor. He had no room to say anything about Lainie and I like that. Keena claimed she was carrying my child, but a DNA test would be performed before she saw a single dime. The timeline was slight, but it was still possible. Keena and I had sex the week before I found out she'd cheated on me.

Punches came automatically, and my knuckles cried out, as I hit his face and occasionally the floor, over and over. Chase got in a few good ones, before we were pulled apart.

Both of us stood there, bloody faced, chests heaving, and clothes torn. Historically, this is where the fight would end; we'd hug it out, and then go get a beer or watch a game. Not this time, more than age had passed between us. An invisible line had been drawn. While Chase would never back down from defending his girl, I would never stop trying to protect my brother.

"Tell me somethin', Austin," he started, as he wiped the blood from his swelling lip. "If Harmony is this thieving person, why hasn't she stolen anything from the bike shop?" He avoided looking back at me, as he examined the blood staining his white t-shirt. "Hell, I've taken her there a couple of times and never heard word one about something being stolen out of there. And let's face it, the shit we have there is a hell of a lot easier to pinch than your little toys."

In the end Chase agreed to come around the house to visit Momma. Daddy reminded him she hadn't chosen sides, and didn't deserve the avoidance she was receiving. We agreed to be civil when we were around her, and not have a repeat of today's battle.

After he left, the three of us set on hay bails, quiet as church mice, as we drank the cold beer Daddy had waiting. "I'm sorry I lost my cool there, but he hit the right button when he touched on Lainie."

Daddy reached over and squeezed my shoulder. "Have you heard from her son?"

I shook my head. My attention on the straws of hay, which littered the floor. My boots were covered in the dust that always seemed to fall from the large bails. "No, and I don't know how much longer I can stay away." Daddy nodded his head, and then did what he'd always done, he told us about a time when he was younger, just like Granddaddy did when he was alive.

"When I was about to head to Law School, I met this young lady who turned my world upside down. She had the reddest hair I'd ever seen, and legs which went on for days." His smile took shape, his eyes off in the distance, through the open barn door and past the rain, which had begun to fall. "I wanted to bring her home to meet your Nana and Papaw, but she was worried they wouldn't like her."

We never had the opportunity to meet Papaw, he'd died in his sleep the summer Daddy went to school. Nana lived about two years after that, dying from a routine surgery to check for colon cancer.

"Your Uncle Cecil and I argued over her. He said she was running around with a boy in the next county, and I told him he was a liar. Well, we fought just like you and Chase did, busted each other up real good." He was silent for a while, that smile growing incredibly larger.

"And?" Dylan demanded, smacking the back of his hand against Daddy's shoulder.

"Oh, sorry." He laughed, caught up in his memory. "Well, we were supposed to meet at this fair going on in Beaumont County. But your Papaw had to deliver a calf in Crescent Ridge, and needed my help. Now remember, this was back in the day when cell phones weren't as common as they are today. Anyway, I went with him to the delivery, and on the way back we stopped at this bar and grill for a bite to eat. We walked in, sat down at a table in the back, and when I looked up, imagine what I saw" He looked from Dylan, and then to me.

"My little redhead, sittin' on the lap of this other guy, his arms around her, while her tongue was clear down his throat. Years later, I recalled the story with your Granddaddy, he knew the girl straight off. The guy, the one whose lap she was sittin' on, was no regular guy, he was her husband. She was looking to trade up, exchange him for me, and the chance to live a little better. Now, when I asked Cecil about it, he tried to tell me he had told me about her being married, but I swear to God, I never heard that part." He shook his head, as he laughed at the end.

"So, what you're sayin' is, until Chase sees Harmony doing something wrong, he won't believe anything we have to say."

"That's exactly what I'm sayin.'"

"So what do we do? Just let her rob him blind?" Dylan worried, rising to his feet.

"Austin, can't you place any security blocks on his bank accounts? Cancel his cards or something?" Daddy was on to something. I could cancel all the cards issued to her, making it near impossible for her to get any money.

"Of course, and since he said she has been to the shop, you better change the security code. We don't need her breaking in now that she has an alibi." Both Dylan and Daddy stopped in their tracks; a sinister grin taking hold of Dylan's face.

"No, I don't think I will." He held out his clenched fist, his smile multiplying, as I met his fist bump. A silent agreement to let her think her plan was working.

"Honestly, I don't think you have to worry about her using the credit cards or visiting an ATM."

"Good point," I agreed, though I would still create a safety net, as soon as I got to the office.

"Purchases can be tracked and, if what we suspect is about to go down, the last thing Virginia Greyson wants is to be located." I was sick of calling her by her alias, this twisted bitch can call herself whatever she wants, but I'm calling her out.

"If you freeze the accounts, and she attempts to use them, can it be tracked?" Daddy presented an interesting question, one that would work to our advantage.

"I can set up an alert, and a limit. Let her think she can access the account, like those identity theft people who charge a dollar to see if the account is active. When she does try to use any of the cards, I'll have her location, and more importantly her walls down."

"Sounds like a good plan," he hesitated long enough to look at me with concern. I suspected what was coming, questions I wasn't ready to face. "Is it true, about this baby Keena is carrying?"

I could see the disappointment in his eyes. The plans of a proper courtship, a momentous proposal, and wedding to mark the ages, disappearing with that one word…baby. Then after a respectful passage of time, children to carry on the Morgan name. In his mind, I had stepped out of turn. Regardless of what society held as the norm, Morgan men were raised different.

"If you're asking me if we had sex during the time when she could have conceived this baby, then the answer is yes. If you are asking if I think this baby is mine, then the answer is, I don't know."

"You *will* do right by her." Dean Morgan was a powerful man with ties in many circles, both above and below the law. Growing up, he was the man I based nearly everything off of; how I walked, spoke, and even the kind of girl I went after. I could count on one hand the number of times he'd had to seriously discipline me, setting me back on the straight and narrow. He used actions, not just words, to show us the way men carried themselves. But in those few times, the handful of events when I crossed a line, which was clearly drawn in the sand, I paid the consequences for, and learned what was expected of me.

"I understand what you're saying, and I will take care of any child which is proven to be mine. But—"

Granddaddy's words, spoken to me in this very barn, right before I was about to tell Momma I was moving off to New York, came back to me. *"Being a man is more than an age you reach. It's not only doing what's right and just, it's also standing up for what's in your gut, even if it isn't the popular vote."*

"—But I won't marry a girl who has no moral compass, or isn't about to be a shareholder in a relationship which would benefit us both." I had shared with Dylan the state in which I'd discovered Keena, before I tossed her out of my house. I suspected he'd given that information to our parents, but it was never really discussed. "Just as you don't want to see Chase end up with a whore as a wife, I don't want one clouding the mind of my family by pretending to be something she isn't. Keena Marshall will never be Keena Morgan, unless she manages to marry Uncle Cecil."

Our only uncle on daddy's side was too much of a bachelor to marry anybody. He worked hard at his job, following in Papaw's shoes of being a veterinarian. He loved what he did, but he loved his freedom even more. He never bothered to keep a girl for very long, using the excuse there were far too many pretty ones to enjoy, than picking just one.

"Dylan, what did you find out about Audrey?" With Daddy, saying nothing about something was the same as accepting it. I had stood my ground, offering no apologies about how I felt.

"Well, she's still living in the trailer park on James Island. The manager tells me the rent is paid up, which is a new thing since she started working for me. For the last week, a man I believe is the boyfriend, Lucas Campbell, has been coming over every few days. Always raising hell, and then storming out madder than a wet hen."

Dylan had been burning the candle at both ends. During the day, he's elbow deep in motorcycles and chrome, but by night, he was following the trail Momma was certain existed.

"I followed Mr. Campbell to a house which is rented to who I assume is his daddy. A Clifford Campbell, currently on house arrest for burglary and possession."

"What about the wife? Amy Campbell?"

Dylan glanced away from Daddy, taking a pull from his long neck bottle. "Currently a guest down in Georgia. She got pulled over by the highway patrol with a little too much weed in her purse."

"Anything else?"

"Yeah," Dylan said regretfully. A look I couldn't place taking residence on his face. He may present himself as a hard ass, but being with Claire had softened his resolve, a little.

"Every time Lucas stops by, he trips over something when he first walks in. At first I gave credit to him for just being a dumb ass, but then it made me think. So, I made a visit to the power company, flashed the lady behind the desk my smile, and then my badge. According to their records, the trailer had its power shut off for nonpayment nearly a month ago. Miss Audrey is behind almost six hundred bucks."

"Did you take care of it?" Daddy questioned in a tone, which needed no definition. We were all taught to take care of the women in our lives, keeping them safe and happy. Something I was failing to do in my own wheelhouse.

"No sir, I didn't." Dylan held up on hand, a warning he wasn't finished. "Not because I didn't want to, 'cause I did. But because if I had, she would know I knew about her financial issues, and I'm not done looking into her. I want to know why she's hanging around known felons, having a relationship with a married man, but yet doesn't have a record herself. Until I'm satisfied with a solid answer to those questions, I'll keep watchin' and waitin.'"

Sitting at my desk, having Lainie's empty office only a short walk away, was a torture I wouldn't wish on anyone. She had left a text message on my phone while I met with my brothers. She needed the day off to handle some things. I had texted her back to see if anything was wrong, she denied it, and wished me a good day.

Lainie and I had spoken about what had happened. I'd tried to reassure her nothing had changed, but she reminded me something really big was about to happen.

"Austin, I grew up with only an old photograph of my dad. He went to prison three days after I was born. My momma stopped going to visit him after she got pregnant with my sister. I hated being the little girl with no Daddy."

I'd sworn to her, that if this child turned out to be mine, that I would fight Keena for custody.

"Austin, this is a child you're talking about, one that needs both parents. Don't rip him or her away from a mother who seems to care enough to find you."

She was right, and I fucking hated it. I hated the fact that in a matter of hours I'd watched her go from top of the world, to broken and scared. She had been the bigger person, and stepped back, allowing me to deal with all of this. Lainie was one in a million, and I was going to prove to her that I was the guy for her. I just had to figure out how.

Momma had called me last night, told me she had been able to pull some strings with the help of her own gynecologist.

"Dr. Perkins doesn't deliver babies anymore, but he was able to get me the name of one of the best in the country. A, Dr. Sabrina Olsen, fellowship trained and a leader in her field."

I didn't even try to hide my distaste for Keena from Momma.

"Austin, I'm not certain how you stood her for so long."

A very good question, with answers growing from being a horny man in his twenties.

"In the time she has been here, I've had to tear her away from the television to eat, and take a shower. She watches the same shows over and over, not a care in the world for anything else."

Somehow her interest in the lives of others made dealing with her a lot simpler. When she was enamored with the goings on of the Hollywood elite, she didn't complain about the hours I kept, or the lack of devotion I gave to the relationship.

"She has an appointment tomorrow, not that I'm asking you to go, but—"

I knew what she was going to say, until science proved one way or another; I had to assume the baby was mine. Including attending doctor appointments, and all that entailed.

Chapter Twenty Two

Lainie

*Never let the fear of falling, keep you
from learning how to fly.*
- Cayce Poponea

Rain pelted down around me, blending in with the tears, which seemed to never end. People ran around me, scurrying for the safety of dry cover. I welcomed the rain. Its downward motion taking with it the sadness that had taken over my body. The icy temperature, the only thing reminding me I was alive, and awake in this living nightmare.

Was it a dream when I'd stood on this same sidewalk, wrapped in the arms of a man I imagined only existed in fairy tales? Stories made from the hopes and dreams of lonely women who searched for the impossible. Had I become so desperate for love that I too had created the perfect man? One who cherished me to the ends of the earth, bathing me in his love and passion for me, promising me the world only he could give?

I had worked so hard to send one demon back to hell, removing him from my slumber where he had worn out any welcome long ago. I never expected he would be replaced by a man who smiled the perfect smile, said the words I longed to hear, and chased the darkness away with a proclamation of love so fierce, the heavens themselves admitted defeat.

My celebration seemed premature. The battle I'd waged against Greyson was really just a skirmish, one I couldn't make happen by myself. Today was different. Today I was bent, bruised, and in need of healing, but far from broken and defeated. This time the battle would be won. Not out of sheer numbers or surrounded by a multitude of people who could defend me against the ghosts which lay in shadows, waiting for the moment they could attack. This time, I would win because the fire, which had nearly gone out inside of me, thanks to fear acting like drips of water and slowly extinguishing the flames, was now raging once again. My will and determination rising inside.

Today, there was nothing except the shadows, and no multitude of people rallying around me. The rain had clouded the sun, making everything bleak and dull. Anything I could have feared from this place has been replaced with a sorrow I never imagined existed.

My first step landed in mud, not surprisingly since the rain had been coming down since yesterday. I was grateful Austin had a meeting with his family, a pow-wow on what to do about Keena, and the blessed event. I took the time to get some real work done. The sadness giving me the edge I needed for a client who ran a tattoo shop not far from here.

Today, I knew he would be in the office, only feet from the desk I loved. He had tried to convince me things wouldn't change between us. But by that statement, it was clear he already saw the change happening without our permission.

My second step sealed the fate of the shoes I'd loved from the moment I first saw them. Austin and I had been headed to a restaurant down town when we passed a high-end shoes store. I hadn't meant to gasp and cry out like I had. But the shoes, with their feminine heel and strap, which would wrap around the wearer's ankle, spoke to the inner shoe whore I refused to claim. Later that evening, as Austin and I shared a desert, a man dressed in a suit presented me with a box, the shoes from the store nestled inside.

Now they were ruined from the rain, being exposed to forces they were never meant to face. Leather may work well for cows grazing in a field, but when it is processed and manipulated into a work of art, water and mud can be a death sentence. Much like the reappearance a pregnant girlfriend does to a relationship you thought was crafted with love.

The lights from the library cast a warm glow on the soggy area at the bottom of the tree. I'd chosen this spot to take a rest, and have a real conversation with the evil, which happened here. My clothes would be joining my shoes in the garbage container, as the dark mud and grass stains will never come out of my white skirt. Another gift from Austin, after he'd accidently left a stain from a highlighter, on the one I had for years.

"So, Cash, tell me. Do you have an army of people you left behind, all intent on ruining anything good that ever crosses my path?" Warm tears joined in the lake which had formed around me. Maybe if I stayed long enough it would wash away the pain. Stitch up the gash left behind in my heart.

"Was your time here on Earth so fucked up you had to dish out as much misery and hate as you possibly could?" I grew tired of the irritation of my hair clinging to my skin, and wiped it back with the palm of both of my hands.

"I forgave you the other day, spit in your face, and then told you to go to hell. I still mean all of those things, but I want you to listen to me and listen good. I'm going to stand up on my own two feet and walk away from this place. I am going to wake up every morning, and try like hell to make at least one person smile. So you remember this," I stood up and away from the edge of the tree, dead leaves clinging to my wet exterior. "You remember as you're sitting in hell, paying for every second of every moment of forever for the shit you inflicted while you were here, that I will get past this. I will be happy again. It might not be with Austin, but I will be happy in my own skin. You think about that as you sit in your prison. One you will never escape."

Crimson Door Tattoo parlor turned out to be on the block I would have come out on, had I not been stopped by Cash. The black building looked odd nestled in the historic sections of Charleston, surrounded by various businesses.

I knew from their web page, since I had created the damn thing; they specialized in creative alternatives for tattoo enthusiasts. The owner, Slash Dorsey, a self-proclaimed lover of nineties heavy metal, insisted if I was ever in the market for ink, to call him up.

He had me design an interactive page where the visitor could create a tattoo using clip art, uploaded photos, or even one of the thousands Slash had available in his gallery. The artist in me couldn't help but take a stroll through the work he had done. One particular tattoo he had created for a woman, who had survived breast cancer, triggered an idea inside of me. Before I left the office yesterday, I composed a sample, which would have meaning just for me. Selecting a passage I had read in a romance novel awhile back.

I had convinced him to make a feature where the creator of a tattoo could have it saved to the webpage for a short amount of time, that way they would have to come to his shop, as printing wasn't an option. We also added a feature I created as a school project, someone could just snap a photo of the item. The only thing that would appear on the photo was a picture of a scary clown, blood dripping from his teeth.

As I opened the door to the shop, the sound of an aged hinge creaked in protest at having to work after all these years. Music filled the space, welcoming me with the fact that I had evidently walked into the jungle, instead of a shop. "Mornin' darlin' be right with ya." Having spoken with Slash a number of times in the last few days, I recognized his gravely voice from the back room. He sounded like he smoked ten packs a day, and had to be about forty years old.

On the walls were the planks of colorful tattoos I expected to find. Hundreds of butterflies and dragons, all waiting to catch someone's eye. All of the walls were painted dark. A mix between a deep red, with an undertone of black. Light cast down from panels in the ceiling, giving a spotlight to every single piece of art in the place. On the far back wall, the area I heard Slash's voice resonate from, was a large poster of what looked like a band.

Curiosity getting the better of me, I sloshed my way over to inspect the poster more closely. What I had assumed was a photo of the band who could be heard over the speakers, was actually a photo of a very well presented cover band. Someone had taken a great deal of time, and effort to make them look extremely close to the originals.

"That was taken in nineteen ninety nine, the year the world was doomed to financially implode due to a possible computer error. I worked in the corporate world back then, until I couldn't take it anymore."

Slash looked nothing like I imagined. I pictured a buff, completely tattoo covered, human wall. What stood before me was a tiny guy, with studious glasses and thin greying dark hair, which was pulled into a low ponytail.

"Several of my coworkers walked away from the banking industry, and into the fields we loved as a result. For a while, I played with this group of misfits. Driving around the country playing cover songs for whoever would let us in the door. One night, we were playing at this hole in the wall bar. It had maybe six people inside, which was the family who owned the bar I think, when a group of guys came in and ordered drinks. We didn't pay them much mind, until they started shouting for us to play this song and that song. Before they left for the night, they had us come over to their table, where we instantly recognized them as the band we had just butchered. They were really cool about it, even gave me this hat as a thank you." Pointing to a display case I hadn't noticed. There under plexi-glass was the top hat, ever so familiar, with the guitarist who played for the real band.

"Now, that is my story of how I wound up here. What's yours?" He held out a hand for me to shake, his candor surprising me.

"I'm Lainie Perry, I designed your web page."

"Okay, that tells me who you are, but not why you're here."

He had a valid question, one I hadn't expected from a tattoo artist. More like what can I do for you, followed by it will cost this much.

"Come on, beautiful, you look like I did the day John Lennon died. Let's get you warm, and a little drier before we discuss any tattoos."

Two cups of spiked coffee and a seat near the heater later, my clothes had stopped dripping, and my teeth were no longer chattering. Slash wrapped me in several blankets, as he took care of another client. My pocket had vibrated several times, text messages from Austin, telling me how much he loved and missed me. When Slash returned after finishing his ten thirty, he deemed me human enough to discuss a tattoo.

While I didn't have the urge to tell a complete stranger the entire story of what had happened, I did fill him in on the reason behind the design of tattoo I chose.

"Now, Lainie, I'm not one to judge, but are you upset because the man has a past?"

"No, of course not. I'm upset because—" I paused, unsure of what to say. "Well, you see, um—"

"Lainie, you can't be born into this world and not have a past. But by the story you tell, he seems to have chosen you over the mother of this child." His gray eyes were filled with truth and wisdom, something I needed to hold on to.

"But I want him to be a good father. To have the same relationship with his child that he has with his dad."

Slash took my hand, still so cold, his warm skin felt almost like fire. "Being a good father is more than being married to the mother. It's teaching and nurturing, loving and discipline, finding the perfect balance between them. Let me ask you this; would you rather have a happy, healthy child who thrives in school, sports and social aspects, yet lives with only one of his parents, while the second lives in another house and has another family there? Or would you rather have a child who covers their ears at night to block out the shouting, learning from his father how to hit the woman he is married to, instead of love her in his own way?"

It's funny how we buy into the commercial advertisement of how a family should be, parents sharing a last name, and living under the same roof. All the while secretly wishing to be rescued by the guy on the movie screen.

"One last thing, and then I will place that tattoo where we discussed. The woman may be carrying his baby, but she is an ex for a reason."

Slash was just finishing up, when the door hinge announced a new customer. I didn't bother to look up, as I was too focused on the mirror he had strategically placed so I could watch him work.

"Afternoon, Ladies. I'll be with you in a moment." Slash continued with the last few lines of the phrase I wanted to use, without removing his eyes from the gun, which buzzed as he worked. The pain at first had been intense, but as the skin numbed, it changed to something less harsh, and more of an annoyance.

"That's all right, Sir. We're here for her anyway."

A smile slowly made its home on my face, so much better than the marathon crying I had been doing. "How did you guys know I was here?" I hadn't told a single soul I was coming. Intentionally wanting to be alone as I took this step.

Claire held up her cell phone, shifting it back and forth in her hand. "Really, Lainie? You know your boyfriend, do I really have to answer that question?" Of course he would have been able to use the location finder my phone used for webpages. I wanted to be mad, but it wasn't worth the effort. Austin had done this for good reason, not to check on me or to catch any dishonesty he feared I was up to.

"No, I guess you don't."

Claire and Priscilla moved around Slash, both admiring the work he was doing.

"'Never let the fear of falling, keep you from learning how to fly.' I love it. Did you write it?" Priscilla was asking Slash, who shook his head, but kept on working.

"I read it in a book. The story behind it was very similar to what I'm dealing with, and it just fit."

"All finished." Slash said, as he rolled his seat away from me.

I stood from my chair, my clothes were now dry, but still looking like a homeless person. Turning my back, I used the hand mirror hanging on the wall. Taking a good look at the angel wings which surrounded the phrase Priscilla had just read. It was exactly what I had pictured, both when I designed it, and when I imagined it on my shoulder.

"It's perfect."

Slash came around with a big fancy camera, taking shots from every angle he could. This was his condition for placing the tattoo on my front shoulder, hidden from eyes, unless I wore something really revealing, something I had never done in the past. He gave me detailed instructions on how to take care of it, and said he would see me the next time I was ready for new ink.

"Once you get a taste, you always want more."

Priscilla wanted to have lunch with her girls, but first we would stop by the salon where I would get 'presentable' as she called it. As we climbed into her car, I looked around the block, what a mess I had been when I first walked in, ignorant to the beauty which surrounded me. Charleston was full of old world charm, houses lined the streets on both sides, each one prettier than the last.

Priscilla pulled her car into the valet parking area, handing her key to the young attendant who knew her by name. Once inside the revolving door, the sounds of piano music filled the air. I felt like a crazy person dressed in ruined shoes and filthy clothing. While the area around me was lush with cloth covered sofas and chandeliers hanging from sky high ceilings. I wanted to climb into a hole and die.

"Constance, do you have my bags?"

Priscilla called to a woman who stood ramrod straight by the bubbling fountain in the center of the foyer. Her navy blue suit matched that of the valet attendant with a gold plated nametag, sitting perfectly straight above her heart.

"Yes, Ma'am. It has been placed in the Morally Suite just as you instructed."

I got the feeling Priscilla didn't care for Constance, but since I looked like an extra from a Zombie movie, I wasn't about to pass judgment. One quick elevator ride later, I was shown to a room with the largest shower I had ever seen. The damn thing felt so good, I took a video of the inside, just so I could remember it.

After I dressed in the clothing Priscilla had procured for me, a nice pair of slacks and a complimenting top, which was thick enough to keep me warm, yet not cook me. As I went to stand, I noticed a shoebox sitting on one of the tables in the room. A note card with my name scrolled across the front was taped to it. Pulling the card open, noticing Austin's manly penmanship scrolled inside.

It's my fault you ruined your favorite pair of shoes. Here's a new pair to make up for it. Well, it's at least a start of how I'm going to make this up to you. I love you, Lainie.

Nestled inside the shoebox were my heels, well, a replacement of the ones I'd had to throw away. Even with everything going on in his world, he took the time to care about me. Holding the card to my chest, I closed my eyes as I mouthed the words, *I love you, too.*

When I walked out to join them, Claire and Priscilla were enjoying a drink by the window that overlooked the street below. While the building wasn't a skyscraper, you could see the hospital, and office buildings, which surrounded it. The rain had stopped, finally, leaving just a hint of a cool breeze in its path. The waiter, who stood against the entrance door, pulled out my chair so I could join them.

Conversation was kept to a minimum, as we all seemed to be extremely hungry. I had lost my appetite over the last few days, but in the light of today, it seems to have returned.

"Okay, my bestie. I have allowed you to marinate your feelings long enough. I want to know your side of the story and don't hold back."

I watched the traffic move along the bridge as I told her everything; the way Keena had presented herself as his current girlfriend, and how she'd wrapped herself around Austin like he belonged to her.

"So you stopped talking to him, because of what an ex said? That's doesn't sound like you."

"It's not that I'm not talking with him. I just feel like he needs to have an open mind about his child, without me complicating things."

"Oh, and removing yourself from his arms is your way of *not* complicating things."

Claire Stuart was me with brown hair. She held nothing back, just as I wouldn't with her. Cutting past the layers of bullshit, and getting to the core of the problem.

"I'm jealous, okay."

"Of?"

I wanted to take the admission back, ignore I had just ripped a scab off the hole in my heart.

"Claire, what would you do if Portia came over, and announced she was pregnant with Dylan's child?' My eyes moved from the midday traffic to the face of the girl who had saved me from so much. "Would you dance around, and then throw her a shower? Hell no you wouldn't, you'd curl up inside just like I am."

"And you would come in and kick my ass, just like I'm doing for you." Claire's hazel eyes flashed between mine, no ill feelings, just simple truth in her words. "Lainie, you don't give up on something just because it's hard. Hell, you and I have battled far worse than anything Keena and Portia could dish out. Now is the time to show your strength, not how fast you can run and hide. You didn't fall in love with the man the first time you met; it developed as you got to know him. Don't think for one second it's going to go away any faster. You need to be there for him, show him you are in this for the long haul, no matter what happens."

She was right, and the reason she was my friend.

"Claire is correct, Lainie. Besides, Keena would never fit into the family the way you two do." Priscilla moved her body so that she could hug me. "Don't give up, I know this will work out."

Claire had spent the time I was showering filling Priscilla in on our suspicions of Harmony. She agreed we were on to something, but made us swear not to do anything on our own.

"Did she ever confirm which dentist she worked for?" Months ago, Claire shared with me the conversation Harmony had during dinner, telling Priscilla she needed to have her teeth whitened.

"No, but how many dentists are there in Mount Pleasant?"

"Six," Priscilla responded. "Three of them have wives I've known my entire life, the other three have ex-wives I've known just as long."

Priscilla Morgan may be a socialite and the good wife of a prominent attorney, but behind all those masks she wore, she had the cunning of a southern girl on a mission.

"It just so happens, I've had lunch with all six of them recently." She commented, while applying her lipstick, as if she was discussing the weather. "According to one of the ex-wives, a dental procedure was performed free of charge, by one Howard Stevens. Which was the reason for their divorce."

My eyes opened wide at the scene playing out before me. Priscilla Morgan was as good a detective as her eldest son was.

"See, something went wrong with the aftercare, and Howard got a call in the middle of the night. He apparently got out of bed to meet the patient at his office and forgot to remove the backpack one of his children left behind in the car. When Cynthia got the kids up for school, her son announced his project was in said backpack. So Cynthia did what any good mother would do, she drove over at the early hour to get the backpack. Since the car was locked, and she didn't have the keys, she had to go into his office to get them. Imagine her surprise when she finds good old Howard with his assistant slash patient, naked as the day they were born, having sex in one of his dental chairs."

I could almost picture an older gentleman with a young woman, bouncing up and down on him, in a reclined dental chair.

"She took him to court, and got half of everything he owned, including current ownership of the dental office. She'd never suspected the assistant would do such a thing, as she had the worst overbite she had ever seen. She also knew Howard was too cheap to help the girl. Cynthia took great pleasure in firing the assistant with everyone watching, calling her every name in the book. A few weeks later she found out the girl was working at one of the strip clubs, and wasn't surprised in the least."

Priscilla thanked the waiter as she signed a slip of paper, never showing a credit card, or handing over any cash.

"Did she tell you her name?"

"Oh, she did better than that. She emailed me the file with her before and after photos included."

Priscilla extended her cell phone presenting side-by-side photos, Virginia Greyson on one side, and a plain faced Harmony on the other. Under the photo, in black and white block lettering were two words, Ginger Greyson.

Claire and I sat at that table, mesmerized by the change between the two photos. I'd always been a fan of those makeover shows, where the girl who'd been picked on for not being the prettiest, was made into this super hot girl. Virginia must have found one of the makeup artists they used, because she looked so much different.

"I would never pair the two photos as the same girl."

"According to Dean and the boys, neither will Chase. They all agreed, until he witnesses her in the act, he won't believe anything we have."

Part of me felt incredibly bad for Chase, loving someone so much you ignored the evil everyone else saw. When he finally did see it, come to grips with the truth, I hoped he had the strength to love again.

"Enough about that harlot. Tell me what you think about Audrey?" A tiny woman had delivered refills on our sweet tea. It was nice to sit back and enjoy this time with these two ladies. I was discovering different sides to Priscilla, sides I wanted to be friends with.

"Well, I think she is sweeter than this tea. But, she has some dark secret she's hiding, something she is trying to protect." Claire could read people like a seasoned psychic. It made her an excellent nurse, and a perfect friend.

"I have to agree with you, Claire. Something just isn't adding up with the girl."

I gazed once again out the massive window, watching the wind blowing the branches of the palm trees. I watched as an expensive car pulled up to the building across the street, and a large man pulled himself out of the tiny space, locked the car, and then ran into the building. Three stoops over, a door opened, and a man and woman walked out. I did a double take, as I would recognize that body anywhere, even in the dark of night. Keena stepped heavily down the steps, a file wrapped tightly in her arms. She looked angry, as if he'd upset her, or something. For the first time, and I hoped Priscilla didn't see him do it, Austin Morgan didn't open a door for a lady before he got into his truck and drove down the street.

Chapter Twenty Three

Austin

Hold a door open for your girl, not because it's expected of you, but because it gives you a moment to appreciate her as she walks ahead of you.
- Granddaddy VanBuren

"In today's top story...

"Police are investigating the body of a man found during an investigation after a tip was called in to crime stoppers. Investigators were called to a residence in the eight hundred block of North Calvin Street. Several allegations of suspected drug manufacturing have been reported to the crime stopperss number in the last few days. Police officials reported the body was found in the home's attic. Preliminary toxicology reports show no drugs were found in the body, which has been identified as former Bank of Charleston CEO,

Franklin Benson. You may recall a story earlier this year where Mr. Benson resigned his position when allegations of spousal abuse were reported by members of the community. He pled not guilty, but later recanted his plea when his then girlfriend, and mother of his youngest child, called police to her residence after an altercation had occurred. The unidentified woman, placed a cell phone in the room after she said he'd struck her the first time. Police found Mr. Benson locked in a storage area after the woman had escaped his imprisonment."

I tossed the remote to the table after lowering the volume on the television. "You having fun without me, Bro?"

Dylan looked over his shoulder, his hands covered in gear oil. I stepped back out of his range, as I wouldn't put it past him to smack his dirty hand on my shirt.

"Fuck no, I haven't seen that motherfucker since we all went hog boiling." Dylan continued working on the bike, a custom order from some celebrity in California. Dylan never got excited by the dropping of a name, he gave them a target date, built the bike, and then made them pay to ship it. If they chose to come see the bike, Dylan made sure he was around to talk with them. "I'm too goddamn busy with all the shit around here."

While Carson had screened several people who came to him seeking our help, we hadn't found anything, which panned out. Either the claimant didn't show up, or the situation fixed itself.

"Austin, let me ask you something?" He had his red towel in his hands, wiping the residual grease from his skin. "Do you think if I asked Claire to marry me, she would say yes?"

When we were younger, Chase thought Daddy had forgotten it was Valentine's Day. He knew how much Momma loved to be spoiled every year with the flowers, and such that went along with the holiday. So Chase took all the money he'd saved from hauling hay the summer before, and went into town to buy her all the flowers he could. What he didn't know was Daddy had booked a vacation to Italy for them to celebrate. When Chase got home with his truck full of flowers, he'd gone inside, changed his clothes, and then covered the living room with the flowers. Momma had been out in her greenhouse planting seeds for her new garden in the spring. When she came in, Chase stood proud as a peacock, and asked her to be his Valentine. When Daddy came home, bags already packed in the car, he'd watched as his youngest took his wife to dinner in the city. Dean Morgan called the airlines, and delayed his vacation by two hours, so his son could make his Momma smile.

Dylan had slipped his own money back into Chase's stash, since everyone agreed Daddy's secret would be kept. Chase left for sports camp the next day and never knew of the trip our parents shared. He'd prided himself for years that he was the reason Daddy stayed out of the doghouse for not remembering Valentine's Day.

"You remember the time Chase bought Momma all those flowers for Valentine's day?"

"Yeah, the year Daddy took her to Italy."

I nodded my head, "And what did Momma say when Chase asked her to go to dinner with him?"

"She told him she would be honored." He smiled the smile of a boy remembering the joy found on the face of his beloved mother. Dylan really was a good guy at heart.

"And so will Claire when you ask her."

Dylan cleared his throat, as the security camera showed three beautiful women walking up the drive, each with a pan in their hands. I turned as fast as I could, heading in their direction to help with the load. Lainie looked so beautiful with her hair flowing down her back, wearing an Absolute Power t-shirt, and well-worn jeans. I'd missed her smile, something I wanted to bring to her face everyday.

"Mr. Morgan, the girls made me keep quiet when they asked to bring supper over." Audrey worked far too many hours for my, or

Dylan's, liking. But he knew she was drowning in debt, and needed the money. Momma came over most afternoons with a pan or sack of something homemade that would have gone to waste if Audrey didn't use it. Dylan said he would find the clean containers inside a bag in the back, as if she hadn't bothered to take them home, and eaten them here at her desk.

"Hey, Baby." The term of endearment warmed my heart, as I took the large pan of what looked liked shrimp and grits. My Lainie was a hell of a cook; fighting me most nights to enjoy a home cooked meal, instead of a restaurant. I couldn't resist as I leaned in, kissing her soundly on her soft lips. "Let me put this down, so I can welcome you proper."

Dylan did the same to the pan of fried chicken Claire carried. Shooting Audrey a furrowed brow when she raced past him carrying a bowl of biscuits, and a gallon of sweet tea. "Next time, wait for help." He chastised, his way of trying to be a gentleman.

"Ignore him, Audrey. He hasn't had enough of his girl lately." I pulled Lainie into my arms, inhaling her unique smell, its effect giving me a calm I hadn't felt in days.

"Can I talk to you in private?" She mumbled into my chest.

I dreaded the conversation that I knew needed to happen. "Dylan, I'm going to get something from my truck. Don't eat all of that chicken." I warned, knowing my brother and his appetite for our Momma's secret recipe.

"I make no such promises, first come first serve!" He hollered as I shut the door, not letting go of Lainie for a single second. I had backed my truck in to unload some parts Dylan had ordered from a local supplier. It gave us the privacy we needed to have this conversation, and the kiss I planned to give her in about ten seconds.

"Austin, I wanted to tell you I'm sorry for running out like I did. I was scared and jealous of Keena." If the sun had still been out I bet her face would show a blush, the same one she wore when she orgasmed.

"Why would you ever be jealous of Keena?" The question popped into my head, and out of my mouth before I could stop it. Lainie lowered her head, focusing on the buttons of my shirt. "Because there's a chance she is gonna give you a baby."

I raised her chin to face me, not understanding why this would bother her. "And?"

"And—" Her bottom lips began to quiver, a sure sign I had to shut this shit down.

"Hey, hey. No tears."

"I'm sorry. I'm just so angry because she gets to give you a baby, and I won't."

The honesty in her admission broke something in me. I knew I wanted so much more with this beautiful girl, but never dreamed she shared the same desire. "Who says you won't give me a baby? I could take you in the back of this truck, and get the plan in motion." I was completely serious, if Lainie wanted a baby, then by God she was gonna have my baby.

"No, not like that. I want it all. I know it is the craziest thing in the world to tell you all of this, considering all the shit you're dealing with, but I can't help it. I love you, and I want everything with you. The crazy fights over dirty towels, the game of rock paper scissors over who changes the poopy diaper, everything, and I want it with you." Her eyes were full of tears, happy ones I hoped.

"You know my granddaddy always said that if you make your girl happy, she will be inclined to return the favor." I leaned over, pulling her face into mine. "Lainie Perry, I've been without your taste for far too many days. Rest assured, one day I will lower myself down on one knee, and beg you to marry my poor soul. But until that day, I'm going to give you the fairy tale prince of your dreams."

Kissing her had always come naturally, like breathing or blinking. Not having her around to kiss when I wanted, told me I hadn't worked hard enough to show her how much I felt for her. I pulled her impossibly close, wrapping her tightly in my arms. My lips taking command of hers and sliding my fingers into her hair. My hand guiding her head where I wanted her to go. I wanted to take away any doubt she'd ever had, any thought Keena held any importance to me. My tongue parted her lips, tasting the sweetness, which was distinctively Lainie Faith Perry.

When I learned her middle name, I said a silent prayer of thanks to Granddaddy for telling me to find faith, keep it close, and go as far to find a Faith. I had one, and I was going to fight like hell to keep her.

I hoisted her up on the hood of my truck, finding my place beside her. "I had lunch today with your Momma." I looked up to the stars, I knew she would bring this up. "You sent me a text to find me, didn't you?"

"Partially, but I meant the words I said."

"I got a tattoo today." She announced joyfully.

I knew this too, having seen it on her bankcard, as I followed her around the city. "Can I see it?"

"Later." She winked and I knew we were headed on the right track. "I had a discussion with your momma. She reminded me of some things I had either forgotten or chose to ignore. First, she said your daddy never faulted her for not giving him the experience of helping her along with a pregnancy. That when she saw the three of you, she knew you needed them as much as they needed you. They didn't care where you had come from or what you had done, only that you needed love, and they had so much of it to give."

Momma had told us many times how much of a treasure she found in each of us and if someone came in, taking every dime they had, she would still be happy because she had us.

"I've always been a believer in happily ever after, and I wanted this to be the one I got to experience." She motioned back and forth between us. "You know I never knew my dad, never sent him a birthday present, or made him a ham sandwich. I wouldn't wish that on anyone, no matter how mean of a person they were." She took my face in her tiny hands, the smell of the shrimp still lingering. "If this baby turns out to be your son or daughter, I swear to love it, and help you raise it the best way I know how. Because at the end of the day, he or she will be a mini version of you."

Lainie showed me, with her words how pure of heart she was. Accepting a child she didn't give life to as one she would help raise, spoke volumes to me.

"I won't lie to you, Austin. When I saw you today, coming out of the building with Keena, something in me changed. While I've always wanted the fairy tale story, right now I feel as if I'm the antagonist in my own tale. With Keena carrying your baby, I feel as if this is my sequel, and I didn't get to enjoy the original story."

If only Lainie could have been with us at the appointment I'd taken Keena to. How she huffed and puffed when her cell phone had no service, making it impossible for her to watch the YouTube version of her favorite show. Or how rude she was when the receptionist asked her politely not to use her phone, since it would interfere with the band strength they used for their ultrasound machine. Or even how she'd refused to say anything if I remained in the room with her, forcing me to wait in the lobby for her to finish.

"Lainie, you know I have found the second half of any story is the best part."

"Really, why?"

"Because that's where the happy ending is found. Where the prince makes his beautiful girl's wishes come true."

"I love you, Austin."

"I love you, too, princess." I kissed her forehead, something I knew she loved for me to do.

"Oh, and just so you know. I didn't tell your Momma you forgot to open that door for Keena. You and I both know she would have skinned you alive if she knew."

While Lainie was correct, no matter the manners of the lady, my job was to open and close doors, walk with my body between the traffic and them, and to always hold their hand when we are together. But I'll also admit, considering who it was I disrespected, even Granddaddy would let it slide.

Chapter Twenty Four

Lainie

Every girl deserves a guy who looks at her everyday like it's the first time he saw her.
- Anonymous

Living with regret had never been something I planned to do. This afternoon I'd come home to an excited Heidi, who had received a promise ring from Preston.

"Lainie, I know what you're gonna say and believe me, I don't want to jump into another marriage anytime soon. But he cares for me and I care for him. He has two years living in New Jersey, and he swears to me he is coming back. He's going to work for Mr. Morgan, and make me completely happy."

After the day I had, I wouldn't begrudge anyone finding their great white buffalo. "I'm happy if you're happy." Simple enough words, which gave her reason to smile.

After I laid down for a few hours, Claire burst into my apartment, a bag of groceries in her hand. She had a little helper, that tiny speck of a girl by the name of Audrey. As I struggled to wake up, Claire tried every way imaginable to get any information out of her, but she wouldn't budge. I was more convinced than ever there was something serious going on in Audrey's life, and it wasn't good.

Dean and Priscilla had called Dylan, letting him know they were on their way over to the garage to spend the evening with us. But, they were having a hard time trying to drag Keena out of her room and into the car. Austin said she'd confessed to having an ultrasound, but wouldn't show him. How sad was it to have a baby growing, and being unable see the images of him or her.

"It's always been this way with her, never wanting to leave the television for a single moment." Austin admitted, as he scooped up a large helping of grits.

"Come on, bro, she had to have left the boob tube long enough for you to get her pregnant." Dylan always the crass one, had obviously left his filter in the dishwasher tonight.

"Ever heard of doggie style, Dylan?"

I could see the regret on Austin's face, watching as he cringed from his slip of the tongue. I placed my plate of food down, and crossed the space between us, ignoring the silence his words have created.

"Lucky for me, I've never felt the need for a distraction while having sex with you." I kissed his parted lips, sending him a mischievous wink. "I've always had too much trouble remembering my name, to worry about what's on television."

I loved him enough to accept his past, regardless if that past included a responsibility, which would last a lifetime.

"Sorry we're late everyone." Priscilla slipped in, hugging and kissing each person she passed. "You look well rested." She soothed as she hugged me tight. "Make sure she stays that way, Austin."

"Yes, Ma'am."

Dean came in carrying a pan I hoped contained the infamous banana pudding I've heard so much about. She had made some for Chase's welcome home dinner, but with my quick departure, I'd missed out.

"Keena, get over here, and eat something." Priscilla sound irritated, and rightfully so. The last time I had contact with Keena, she was all confidence and persuasion. Now she resembled a petulant child who needed a good scolding. Keena shuffled her feet, as if being led to the dungeon, turning her nose up at the smorgasbord of southern goodness that had been laid out.

"Is there salad or anything cooked without butter?"

Priscilla rolled her eyes, and Dean stifled a laugh. Austin mumbled something under his breath, before taking his plate over to the couch against the far wall.

While Keena picked at the plate Priscilla had filled, everyone else dug in, savoring the flavors of the comfort food we all loved.

"Okay, I'm going to just go ahead and poke the elephant in the room." Claire stood up, her glass of tea in the air as if giving a toast. "Keena Marshall, I hear you had an ultrasound today, and we want to see if we are having a niece or nephew."

Keena's eyes grew to size of a saucer. "Um, I didn't bring the picture with me." She shoved a spoonful of grits in her mouth, her face taking on a disgusted look, as the flavor hit her pallet.

"Oh, honey, I knew you would forget, so I ran back in the house and got them out of your room." Dean announced proudly, holding the same file I'd seen earlier in the day.

Keena stood slowly, placed her heaving plate on the table beside her, and took the envelope from Dean's outstretched hand. Opening the lip, she pulled out a white sheet of paper, stared at it for several minutes, and then shoved it back in the envelope. "I don't know how to read it."

"Well, you're in luck as we have a nurse among us." Dean said with a glint in his eye. "Claire, will you take a look at this please? I'm dying to know what Austin is having."

Claire set her empty plate into the trash beside her. Dylan let her go long enough to open the envelope, pull out the paper, and then rake her eyes over the photo, going from top to bottom several times.

"Keena, you had this done today, with Dr. Olsen, correct?"

"Um yes, this morning in her office." Her response was filled with attitude.

"And, Austin, you took her to Dr. Sabrina Olsen?" Claire's eyes never left the paper before her.

"Yes, that was what she introduced herself as."

Claire lowered the photograph slowly, a smile creeping across her face. "You know, I've always wondered how this would feel. Being the heroine in a tough situation, the one who rides in and saves the day." Dylan gave her hip a squeeze, as he joined her smile. "I just need a minute to savor in this moment. I want to remember how this feels for a while, being the superhero and all." She placed the photo flat against her chest, her closed mouth smiling just for herself.

"You see, while I was out of town, I spent the good part of a day listening to a lecture given by the incredibly intelligent Dr. Sabrina Olsen. She is so passionate about what she does, and more importantly the product she has been a consultant on during the invention process. Now, where she may be excited about helping mothers bring new life into the world, she also stands to make a shit load of money from the research she'd done with this particular machine she swears an undying dedication for." As Claire speaks, she had this animation to her words, almost like she was making fun of this physician.

"The one thing I came out of that lecture knowing is the signature she insisted the company include on all the ultrasounds this machine produces. A digital signature which is encrypted in the serial and lot number of the paper, and machine used to document the progression of the babies development." She slapped her index finger repeatedly on an area at the top of the photograph.

"Now can anyone explain to me why the woman who invented the fucking machine, would even consider using the machine which is branded with the name of her largest competitor?"

Dylan snatched the photo from her, looking at the numbers in question.

"Keena, either you are lying about being pregnant or Austin is lying about taking you to Dr. Olsen. Since I know the lie would never come from a Morgan man, lift your fucking shirt, and show me that bump."

Kennas face raged with anger, "Fuck you! I don't have to show you anything. I had that picture done today, and I don't have to prove anything. This is Austin's baby, and that is the end of it!"

"Oh, honey, that is where you are wrong. Your shitty attitude may have influenced a room full of your New York friends, but here in the south, we have our own way of handling shit. Now, raise your shirt or I'm gonna raise it for you."

I didn't give Keena time to argue, and raced across the room in her direction. I had almost pulled the hem up to her pant level, before she slapped at my ascending hand. But it was just enough to give Priscilla a bird's eye view of what was beneath.

"Raise your shirt, Keena." Priscilla had raised three rambunctious boys, she had perfected the stern mom voice. "I won't say it again, raise the hem of your blouse." She enunciated each word slowly.

Keena reached down with a shaky hand and raised the shirt. As if it was sealing her fate, which in this case, it would. Where a swollen belly should be, a pillow was in its place. The kind women used when they were shopping for maternity clothes.

Voices began to raise, words were tossed around about legal ramifications, and lying bitch. I'd never seen Priscilla this angry or Dean make a phone call as fast as he did. But the real surprise, the one which silenced the entire room, was Chase walking through the door, just as Audrey turned to clean up Keena's spilled plate.

Just like in the movies, the world slowed down into slow motion. Audrey froze with the wet towel in mid air, as Chase devoured her face like a man seeing water for the first time in days.

Austin pulled me close, playfully nipping the shell of my ear. "All I can say is Harmony who?"

I held my laugh, wanting this moment to last for them as long as possible. Chase would need a girl like Audrey when the truth came out. I knew she had a secret, one she worked overtime to keep. I just prayed it would be something Chase could handle when she was ready to share.

"I'm sorry, we haven't been introduced. I'm Chase Morgan."

I'd spent enough time with Chase to know this wasn't a tone he had used before. He was gentle and reserved as his hand took Audrey's, an almost electric glow could be seen.

Audrey stood wide-eyed in surprise, a rare smile finding a place to rest on her delicate face. "I'm Audrey Helms, I work for Mr. Morgan."

In the best love stories, the players finally realize they are not the only people in the room. Usually this is discovered on their own, but this time the blaring of a truck horn was responsible.

Audrey is jolted back to the present. Although Chase keeps hold of her hand, and while she doesn't protest, she also doesn't pull it away.

"Who the fuck is this ass clown?" Austin questions, as he looked into the monitor. The security cameras showing a truck in the driveway, flashing its high beams, and repeatedly sounding its horn.

"I'm sorry, it's for me. I'll be right back." Audrey dropped Chase's hand, and jogged to the front door. Chase followed her, but stood just inside the door, watching as she handed something to the man behind the wheel.

We can all see what is happening on the large monitor on the wall. Dylan has called one of his buddies to come and take Keena to jail. Austin isn't questioned if he wants to press charges, he doesn't have to say a word.

"You fucking bitch, I said five hundred!" The shout is heard clear as day inside the shop. One minute Audrey is backing away from the truck, and the next she's on the ground, with the driver out of the cab and standing over her, his fist pulled back ready to strike her again.

Chase is out the door before Dylan or Austin can blink. Tackling the driver to the ground and slamming his fist into his face so fast, I can't count how many times he connected.

"Austin, you have to stop him," I pleaded; worried he was going to get hurt if they didn't do something.

Austin grabbed me around the waist, holding me tight to him. "No, Ma'am. This is how southern boys become men, or women, as it looks from here."

Both Dylan and Austin watch, as Chase beats the living shit out of this guy. Stopping only when the cops pull up to take Keena away. Dylan is the first to speak with the officers, and then they walk around to the guy who is bloody on the ground, shooting him a look of pity, but continuing on.

"You keep your fucking hands to your goddamn self, you hear me motherfucker!?" Chase shouted, as he pulled the guy to his feet. "You stay away from her, or I'll fucking end you."

The guy stumbled to his truck and jumped in, revving the engine to life. He points his finger at Chase and says something, which is drowned by the rumble of his engine. As he pulled out of the drive, screeching his tires on the pavement, Chase gets in one last shot by tossing a beer bottle clean through his back window, shattering the glass in the process. The words *Yankee Stomper,* crumbling into the bed of the truck

We all watched as the truck screeched around the corner. Chase turned to Audrey, who was still sitting on the ground, a line of blood trickling from her nose. Chase reached back and pulled his t-shirt from his back, placing the cloth to her bleeding nose.

"I'm so sorry, Sweetness. Are you okay?" Chase questions Audrey, her expression, like most women who first meet a Morgan man, is stuck on stupid, and I just know, this has changed everything.

Afterword

I cannot thank you enough for reading, *Absolute Corruption*. *Book Two* in the *Southern Justice Trilogy*. If you would be so kind as to leave a review so others can enjoy and appreciate the world of the Morgan Brothers.

Follow me on my webpage, Twitter, Goodreads, and Facebook for information on future works of fiction.

Cayce Poponea

Caycepoponea.com

www.facebook.com/cpoponea/?fref=ts

www.goodreads.com/author/show/9015457.Cayce_Poponea

Twitter @Cpoponea

Other work by Cayce Poponea

Shamrocks and Secrets

Event planning, dealing with demanding clients and defusing situations before they get out of hand are all in a days work for Christi O'Rourke. But when a mystery man seems to appear at every turn will she have the ability to handle him as well?

Power and wealth are staples in the world of Patrick Malloy. But when family obligations dictate his future, a future involving a certain spirited young woman, will Patrick have what it takes to win her heart or will his lifestyle place her in more danger than he ever dreamed of?

Claddagh and Chaos

Shamrocks left us with Patrick posing an intriguing question. What exactly happened during those twenty five years? We know that they got their happily ever after, but how did Patrick and Christi get there? Could love have a shelf life?

Crain's Landing

When life threw her a curveball, Natalie Reid adjusted her stance and hit a home run. With her life packed neatly into the back of her SUV, she bids goodbye to her college life and steers toward adulthood. With the help of her father, she has been given the opportunity of a lifetime. Will she be able to win the hearts of the sleepy southern town. Or will it's hidden secrets be more than what she bargained for? How long will she be able to resist the persistent Grant Crain?

Grant Crain is well acquainted with the joys of living in the south. All his life he's known that when Ms. Connie makes her famous pecan pie, you better hurry and get a slice. That when the fireflies dance in the dusk, it seems to make the heat of the summer day a little more bearable. He had decided long ago this town would always be home to him. He never expected that a tiny, Yankee girl would turn his comfortable and carefree world upside down. Or that a ghost from his past will do more than come back to haunt him.

Absolute Power

Dylan Morgan has it all; a prestigious career as a Detective for the city of Charleston, devilish good looks and a selection of girls whenever he chooses. Southern born and raised, he lives by the pearls his Granddaddy imparted to him. But when he questions his worth to the citizens of Charleston, his fears are realized when someone close to him is in danger. Does he follow the letter of the law as his position dictates, or does he follow his conscience, which will cause him to straddle a fine line? Can Dylan overcome the demons he creates for himself? Or will he toss everything away in a moment of reckoning?

Claire Stuart has fought hard her whole life not to fall into the same trap as her mother. She refuses to allow men to use her and toss her away. Needing to escape the hardship her family creates, she seeks education over acceptance and uproots herself from the backwoods of Kentucky to the charm of Charleston. She knows all about Dylan Morgan and his choice to bed every woman he comes across, yet she finds herself unable to listen to the warnings her mind and friends give her. Can Claire ignore Dylan's past and allow herself to let someone in? Someone who could shatter her very soul

Coming Soon

Absolute Valor Summer 2016
Stolen Secrets 2016
Make Me Believe 2016

Made in the USA
Columbia, SC
09 May 2018